LOST GIRL

FAÎTE FALLING
BOOK TWO

MARY E. TWOMEY

Lost Girl

Book Two in the Faîte Falling Series

By

Mary E. Twomey

COPYRIGHT

DEDICATION

For Madeline Freeman,
Who finds me when I'm lost.

And when we're both lost,
I'm not so scared if we're
wandering together.

1

THE LOST VILLAGE

"Not to be a downer, but I've been through the ringer, and I'm playing my Commoner card. I have to sleep, guys. It's a lousy habit of mine, and I can't shake it." My joke fell flat when the identical looks of doom were displayed on Bayard's and Rousseau's hairy Chewbacca-like faces. Every mile of distance we put between us and our enemy was another exhale we all desperately clung to. We'd been riding for hours into the night, moving in the opposite direction of the Queen's Army.

My mom's army. Morgan le Fae, the most hated, feared and revered queen Avalon had ever seen was my birth mother – a woman whom I'd thought died while bringing me into the world. Apparently, she took the wicked queen thing to a whole new level, poisoning my dad so he couldn't overthrow her. King Urien remained sickly and weak, tucked away in her castle like Sleeping Beauty. I'd always pictured having a dad, but he'd been more the Superman variety than the damsel in distress kind of dude.

Whatever. I now had a dad who hadn't abandoned me. He may not be Superman, but he wasn't a deadbeat, either. Bonus, for sure. I kept having these fantasies of me walking into the castle I'd been born into and calling out his name. Somehow, just the sound of my voice would be enough to break the evil queen's spell, and he'd sit up with new life. My father would know my voice, though he hadn't heard it since I was a year old, and he'd instructed his sister-in-law, Lane, to take me away from Avalon into a world where Morgan le Fae couldn't find me. In the words of the immortal Will Smith in *Independence Day*, "'Welcome to Earth.'"

Morgan had been given an enchanted gemstone from the illusive Master Kerdik, just like her eight sisters. Unlike them, she wanted more. She stole enough of their Jewels of Good Fortune to make her province the most bountiful one in Avalon. I guess she wanted like, vats of fruit instead of mere buckets of the stuff. I dunno. All I knew was that some crazy shiz was tied to those gems. The women in the provinces without the gems had a harder time getting pregnant, and the land wasn't as plentiful. Not cool.

While I was horrified and ashamed that this was my mother, the little girl part of me still kind of wanted to meet her, to see her face. I'd never even seen pictures. I wondered if we might have the same heart shape to our faces, the same skin that tanned easily, and if we have the same uphill battle brushing out the tangles from our brown, wavy hair. I wondered if she was dyslexic, or if that struggle was my blight to contribute to the family tree.

Remy's unspoken voice wafted into my tired mind. *"I wish I had something that could rouse you. I've been trying to keep quiet so I don't exhaust your magic further. I'm so sorry, Princess."*

"It's fine, Remy," I answered him aloud, cluing the others into our psychic conversation. "Not your fault. I like our conversations. It's normal for me to be tired."

Bastien sighed heavily – a sign of his attitude not taking a much-needed vacation. "There's nowhere to stop, Rosie. Just sleep on me."

I was already leaning my back to his chest as he steered the horse we shared. I wasn't totally stellar at riding horses, only talking with them. It was part of my birth blessing, I guess. I can speak hidden languages (though I got a D+ in Spanish by the skin of my teeth. Go figure). I can also find things easily enough to be called the Compass. The horse I was riding on was named Pierre, though he hated his name. He wanted to be called Fleur-de-lis, which was his favorite flower. Having a flower name myself, I couldn't begrudge the guy a little happiness. I let my hand rest on Bastien's thigh as we galloped through the starlit prairie, a smile teasing my lips at his barely audible intake of breath. Though we'd been connected for hours, each brush of a touch painted a crackle of something new and exciting between us. "As great a pillow as you are, I don't really think I can fall asleep upright on a horse."

"I'll catch you if you fall."

I ran my fingers along his left arm that held the reins, loving how the muscle in his scarred forearm popped out when he tensed up. "That's only like, the greatest pickup line ever."

"Is that so? Is it working on you?"

"I almost just invited you back to my bed. To keep me cozy while I sleep, of course, but still. It's a step up from the stables," I teased him. It was a flirt I couldn't help but indulge in. We hadn't even kissed, though I wanted to a thousand times over. "But seriously, folks. I do need to sleep at some point." Apparently the only reason I required sleep as a Fae was because I used a crap ton of magic when I spoke to animals, or people who had a hidden language. I contemplated cutting back on that, but it really wasn't an option. I was a foreigner here, and the animals had my back. With Remy having his tongue cut out, as Morgan had done to all the healers long ago, he was overjoyed to be able to speak with anyone. I didn't have the heart to tell him I was falling asleep.

"I can help with the sleeping problem," Damond volunteered, guiding his horse to our side with his hand raised, like the proper young lad he was. I mean, he was probably a year or two younger than me, but he seemed so much older and controlled. "You might not like the place, but it's safe. Safer than anywhere else, but that's only if we can get you in without announcing you. No one will bother us. The Queen's Army is clear across Avalon into a new province by now, so they've already swept this area looking for Reyn. We need to feed and water the horses. Refuel a little. The princess can rest then." He cleared his throat. "Duke Henri doesn't know I come here, though, so this stop needs to be kept secret." It would be strange to an outsider to hear a son call his own father by his regal title, but it made a little more sense after meeting the pompous and nasty Duke Henri. That my cousin had grown up into such a well-mannered and kind young man was a wonder.

Bayard nodded curiously that the obedient son had secrets from his old man. "Yep. Fine. Lead the way, kid."

Damond bristled at Bayard referring to him as a kid, but he was too polite to correct him. I knew the feeling. In a group of rulers and warriors, we were the young-uns. "When we get to the village, let me do the talking."

Bayard caught Damond's eye and nodded his approval, his horse's tail swishing back and forth in time with the horse he was riding. Chewbacca never looked so cool. "Look at you, taking charge now that Daddy's gone. Good for you, kid." Bayard was slightly less hairy than the shaggy horse he rode.

"Yes, well. Follow me. The princess looks like she's barely alive anymore."

Rousseau turned his hairy red head to me and winced, letting me know I looked exactly as terrible as I felt. "Oof, you're right. If sleeping cures that, then let's get the princess a bed. I'll take her there myself." He winked at me, earning my middle finger and a blown kiss. I'd quickly learned that Wildmen were kind of pervy, if Bayard and Rousseau were any indication.

When no eyes were on us anymore, Bastien placed a kiss to the space between my shoulder and my neck, making me shiver through the chill of the night that nipped at my damp jeans and t-shirt. Lane had Abraham Lincoln (my brown bear cub) tucked closely on her lap, but every now and then he whined that he needed me to hold him. Hamish (my squirrel) was happy to be in the lead with Damond, always seeking out new nuts and adventures. Seven flew overhead, but not too high, staying close to make sure her black, leathered wings weren't spotted above the trees. She was a fantastic lookout bird, turning traitor from the Queen's Army to come hang with me.

We rode for two hours more before the sparse trees lining the prairie started giving way to a hint of civilization in the form of a city's wall. It had hooks with hanging lanterns shedding light on the perimeter. When we trotted up to the wooden wall made of trees that had been cut in half and stretched several feet higher than our tallest horse, Damond dismounted, motioning for us to do the same and hand him our horses.

Lane moved to me, gripping my hand that wasn't in Bastien's. She had a sixth sense about things sometimes, and I could feel the tension in her grip. "Stay close," she insisted.

Reyn held her other hand, looking gaunt and sickly. His dark features were harder to see against the night, but the circles under his eyes were visible even under the flickering lantern's light. The shadows that danced on his face made him look like he was coming down with the flu – only he wasn't. This was one of the things I wasn't allowed to ask Bastien about, because he'd flip his shiz and turn into a sullen brat. He was protective of his bestie, not wanting anyone to know what was obvious – Reyn was a very sick man. He might even be the kind of sick that didn't get better. It had something to do with his low supply of magic, but if I sniffed any closer to the problem, Bastien's bark turned painful.

Damond looked over his shoulder, pausing as he raised his fist to knock on one of the trunks of the great wall. "Um, Lot? You might want to keep your head down. You won't want to be seen here. Aunt Lane? Rosie? Um, you might want to cover... all of that up." He motioned to our whole bodies, and like a dummy I looked down.

Right. I had boobs now. Lane had changed my appearance with some magical object, making me go through life on earth with a hump, a wonky eye and a fair amount of acne. When Bastien ganked my concealment necklace, my skin cleared up, my eye and my posture straightened, and my chest... grew. I looked like Lane more than I ever had before, and wasn't sure how to gracefully handle going from being the ugly girl no guy wanted to ask out, to attracting attention without meaning to. It was a steep learning curve.

Lane pulled a sweater out of her backpack and put it on to iron out her obvious curves. Bastien took his flannel off so I could thread my arms through it. It fit me like a dress, but it was the coolest I'd felt in a while. I was finally the cheerleader who got to wear the jock's letterman jacket. I was the girl the hot guy was looking at. "Thank you. Is this my invisibility cloak? Am I totally incognito now?"

The corner of Bastien's mouth tugged upward. "Keep your head down. I wish we had a hat for you or something."

"Here," Lot offered, taking his gray riding cloak from his shoulders.

Bastien frowned. "You need to keep your presence here hidden, too. Dukes don't come to places like this." He looked over me to Damond. He took out another flannel out of his pack and slid it on himself, flipping the collar up to obscure his neck tattoo. "The Lost Village? Really? I don't want Rosie here, and I can't imagine Duchess Elaine should be seen in here, either."

Seven made her home in my arms, tucking her body inside the cloak Lot fashioned around me. Lot took his time tying the lace at my neck. The hood flipped over my head, and just like that, I was the grim reaper. Or like, a super-fly Hobbit or something. Lot studied Lane, and then tugged the hood of her sweater over her hair. "It's the best we can do. I'll sacrifice my reputation for the safety of Avalon."

"Thank you for looking out for Rosie," Lane said, touching his wrist.

"Of course," Lot replied with a modest smile. His perfect blond hair wasn't even windswept from our long ride – dude was just that smooth.

Damond held his ground against the wariness in the others. "If she doesn't announce herself, I highly doubt anyone will know it's her. Keep your heads down, and don't make eye contact."

"Why are we hiding in here?" Lot asked, his brows furrowed. "Only scamps end up in the Lost Village."

"Exactly. No one's going to look for us in here." Damond moved a stray black hair back to join the others that were slicked back in a wave. He had naturally paler skin than mine, but he looked white as a sheet at what we were about to do. *Awesome.*

I whispered comfort and affectionate reassurances to Seven, who remained in my arms under my cloak. Abraham Lincoln let go of Lane's leg and reached up for me like a toddler, but I was too weak to support myself on my bum leg for too long. Blame it on the in-home surgery I'd had that removed a million snake babies from my calf muscle.

Bastien took Abraham Lincoln from me, hitching him on his hip like a baby. "There you go, little buddy," he said quietly, revealing his soft side to me. I couldn't help but swoon at the cuteness. Bastien looped his arm around me, holding us together. "I know you want your mama, but you'll have to settle for your dad until we get settled."

My heart did a happy little skip that Bastien was playing house with me and our cuddly love child. He leaned down to kiss my cheek when the others were distracted, warming my whole body to his touch. "Stop seducing me," I admonished him with a blush. "It's working too well."

Bastien leaned his head down with an impish grin. "Never."

Damond knocked on the wooden wall, and a single stump opened halfway up the twelve-foot expanse to reveal a sort of window. A scared man's round face looked out from it. "Who goes there?" He looked out from his window that was about the same height as Damond's head. "Oh. Hey, kid. You here to see your brother?"

I heard Lane's intake of breath and saw her lift onto her toes. Her eyes were wide with excitement, and something that looked like nervous regret.

Damond stood on his toes to be better seen. "Yeah. I brought him a healer, some new girls, a couple clients and a few horses. He said he needed them. I hired these Wildmen to help me bring them in." He jerked his thumb to Rousseau, Remy and Bayard, who were right behind Damond, holding the reins of their horses after dismounting.

The man in the window was only a pudgy head who leaned back to take notes with a quill and parchment before leaning forward again. "Alright. You picked quite a night to visit. The Queen's Army was just in here yesterday, searching through the place for the Judge's son from Province 2. Boy, do they make a mess when they come through. Draper's probably still recovering. But go on in. You know I won't turn you away."

The window shut, and something that sounded like a lever turned from the inside, opening up a door that was seven trees wide. Bayard and Remy went in guiding their horses with careful steps, while Damond led the way.

Reyn and Bastien sandwiched Lane and I between them, with Lot taking up the rear. I ran my tongue along the roof of my mouth, worried that we were going somewhere I didn't understand, and might be doing something that might be more dangerous than we could handle. I wished we weren't downwind of Rousseau. His nervous stomach kept letting noxious gas out with a blast after every third step.

Damond shuffled ahead, leading the way through the cobblestone village that was decidedly shady. There were loud fistfights coming from a street to our left, and angry bickering over who broke whose window to our right. The sound of the quarrel was broken by a woman's scream that pierced my ears with the passion of a good horror movie howl. I shrank into Bastien and brought Lane tighter to my side.

The night was lit by intermittent lanterns that high-lighted trash in the street. The city wreaked of piss and neglect. The shops we passed by reflected the crime city factor, missing the cheery push to bring in newcomers. Instead we were greeted with filthy storefronts and clientele that milled about with surly scowls that concealed none of their shady intent. Several toppled carts were left half on the street, and hay was strewn about in the middle of the main road we were headed down. There were no houses, only businesses with stucco roofs and barred windows. Though Damond was a couple inches taller than me, he looked small leading the way. I worried for him having made this trip before without us to back him up.

A woman in her mid-sixties with thick ankles and a torn and stained housecoat flew out from one of the buildings. She didn't give any care to who could see up her tattered brown outfit, nor did she care that I could smell her armpits even from the distance Bastien kept me as his arm tightened around me. I winced when I caught a peek of her panty-less, pudgy butt through an ill-placed slit up the back. "Damond! Good to see you, sugar pie. Tell me you've got an hour to spare for me. I see good things in your future, boy. I've got a special price on fortunes tonight. Only one silver coin for an hour. I'll never charge so little again!" She gripped onto his collar with fingers that should know better. She had green eyes, like Reyn, so I knew she was a Rétif. They were supposed to be good at trickery. While Reyn used his deceit to try and appear healthy when he was clearly not, and Lane had used hers to hide me from Avalon, this woman apparently used hers to predict the future.

Damond shook her off as politely as he could. "Not now, Gerta. I've got to see Draper. Then maybe tomorrow, if I catch you."

She cackled through the night, truly sounding like a witch. "If only your father knew you came here. He'd tear the whole place down rather than let his precious boy ruin his good name in our village." She winked at him, leering without apology. "Come ruin your name with me, boy. You've never had so much fun."

She was missing one of her front teeth and breathed heavy when she spoke in his face. I could only guess by Damond's reactive jerk backwards that her breath wasn't all that appealing. "Not this time, Gerta. Try your luck with one of the Wildmen after they help me with my delivery."

Bayard gave her a clear "I'll pass," but Rousseau looked her up and down appraisingly. As if on cue, Rousseau let out a loud, spluttery fart that exploded out his back end. Match made in Heaven.

"Let's keep moving. These horses need to be watered." Damond led the way, pulling the horses forward down the darkened street. He turned right at the end, introducing us to what could commonly be known as crime central in any world. There were men out on their front porches, shaking hands with scowls as they traded coins for pouches. There were two dudes brawling in the middle of the street, getting in punches over someone named Celine.

"Damond! Not so fast. You know you don't get to pass through without a stop at my place." A man with a beer belly and no shirt on held open his front door. I didn't want to guess what kind of toll Damond paid to get through to see his brother. "In here, boy."

Damond's voice shook, but he stood his ground. "Not today, Norris. I've got to see Draper."

"You brought my payment, didn't you?" He slammed his door shut and waddled toward Damond, who stepped back on instinct.

Bastien gripped my hand, and I could tell he was debating between keeping a low profile and beating the snot out of Norris. Bayard handed his horse to Lot and stood next to Damond, his hand heavy on my cousin's shoulder. "What sort of payment?"

"A silver coin. Don't care whose pocket it comes from. Your money's just as good here, Wildman. But if you want to pass, you pay to walk down my street." He touched Damond's chin, and I flinched when Damond jerked away guiltily. "I take other payments, too. Isn't that right, boy? One way or another, I get my hand in your pocket."

Lane was shaking with grief, but I was trembling with rage. My voice came out quiet, but each word was punctuated with a rage that was bubbling up inside of me. "At what point am I allowed to kick that guy's butt? I mean, I'm supposed to be discreet, but I don't think that's as important as ending this dude." Seven burrowed against my abdomen, her wings stiffening at my tension. My sweet bird begged me to stay quiet, not wanting to risk me getting hurt in a fight. I could hear Hamish's angry chittering from Reyn's pocket. My squirrel didn't understand all the politics of the situation, but he knew when I was pissed, and took my causes on as his own, like a true friend.

Bastien held tight to my hand, anchoring me to the spot. "Your identity stays secret. Let us handle it. Keep your head down."

Bayard reached his beefy, hairy fingers out and gripped Norris' face, squeezing his cheeks until Norris squealed. "I tell you what. I'm going to go make sure Damond makes it to where we're headed, and then I'm coming back for you. See how you like getting your payment from me."

Bastien moved me closer, securing me to his side protectively. I held onto Lane's hand, ensuring she didn't leave my sight. Her head was bowed beneath her hoodie, but I could see her jaw was set in deep planning mode. I didn't want to be on the business end of whatever she had in store for Norris.

Norris let us pass by after Bayard released him with a knee to his groin and a punch across his face. "L-let's go," Damond said, and I desperately wanted to hug him, to tell him it was going to be alright.

Damond led us down several more streets, fending off aggressive street urchins and a few jags who tried to steal the horses. Bastien set Abraham Lincoln down, and the two of them defended the horses while Lot and Remy guarded Lane and I, who were unarmed. Abraham Lincoln bit one of the attackers, and raked his claw across the leg of one of the others.

"That's right, buddy!" Bastien called to his fur baby. Bastien landed a few punches on the robbers, knocking two of them clean out with a force Mike Tyson would envy. The entire fight was over in a minute, but Damond admonished all of us to try harder to keep a low profile. Bastien offered up a "What do you expect?" kind of shrug I adored him for.

The streets themselves grew filthier as we neared the three-story building with a stucco roof at the end of the street. It appeared to be the grand finale of the city, with the cobblestone ending at its imposing doublewide entrance. There had been mud on the road and some spilled food, sure, but soon we were stepping over glass and out and out garbage.

My nerves were shot when we arrived at the noisy bar with too many drunk middle-aged and older men inside for me to be chill. We peered through the scummy window, making sure to keep a healthy distance from the drunken brawling that was happening inside.

"This is no place for us to stay!" Lot scolded Damond in a whisper that could barely be heard. There was a piano that played off-key, but no one seemed to mind. The men's attentions were all glued to the scantily clad women who danced for them all around the large common area. There were women dancing on the bar, women sashaying from table to table, women wearing sheer swaths of fabric that left nothing to the imagination, and a few women wearing absolutely nothing.

Damond was firm. "Do you really think Morgan will search for her here? This is the best we've got. Rosie has to rest, and her leg is only going to get more injured if she keeps on like she is. This is the best I can do, so keep quiet for a little longer until I can get us a room. Wait here. I'll be right out."

Damond disappeared inside, and none of us spoke of the strippers earning their keep, but remained in stunned silence until he came back. Damond's smile broke the uncertainty, spreading wide across his face. "We can take the horses to my brother's stables around back. Draper's meeting us there! Hurry!"

I hadn't known Damond had a brother, but that was on the long list of things I didn't know about my own family.

We scurried around back, looking over our shoulders and making sure we weren't followed. Everyone exhaled in unison when Remy shut the stable doors behind us, though Bastien and Reyn kept tight to Lane and me.

"I don't know about this," Remy warned me. *"The Lost Village is no place for a lady, or men who want to go about a life unscathed. You'll stay near Bastien, Princess."*

I glanced up at Bastien, and the sight of him holding my bear again warmed me down to my toes. "If you insist."

2

DRAPER THE DISAPPOINTMENT

When the barn door opened again, Bastien and Reyn quickly ushered Lane and me into one of the horse's stalls to hide us. I was worried to meet another member of my family. I hadn't done so well with Uncle Duke Henri, and hadn't been able to coax more than a greeting from my cousin Gwen. Still, I couldn't help but peek at the scene, nervous as I watched with too much trepidation.

A man around Reyn's age came in, a cigar in his hand and his white shirt unbuttoned and untucked. He had the build of a tall soccer player – lean but muscular. His suspenders hung from his waist and swooshed at his sides as he walked with slightly bowed legs. He had messy black hair that looked like a comb might give up hope if it tried to tackle the artful mess. Abraham Lincoln tugged on my pant leg, whining to draw me further back into the stall, but I needed to know what was happening. I stroked the feathers of my bird, hoping the motion soothed at least one of us.

I felt Lane stumble back from her peeking place beside me, gasping at the man she knew. She pressed her back to the stall's wall, tears sparkling in her eyes that she didn't bother to dab away with the sleeve of her navy hoodie. Reyn didn't speak, but reached out and held her hand, steadying her as something big hit her in the feels. Hamish wanted to know what was going on out there, but followed Reyn's lead, and ran from Reyn's pocket down his arm, and up Lane's arm, so he could wrap his bushy tail around her neck like a hug.

The man wore a wide grin that split his angular features, looking on Damond like the boy was a breath of fresh air. "Damond! Brother, what're you doing here? And with horses? What'd I do to earn these?" He wrapped Damond in a hug I could tell they both needed.

Damond gripped his older brother hard, wiping the smile off his face and letting down his brave front in a gust. "I'm so glad to see you."

"What's wrong? Is it Gwen? Has she decided to finally break Duke Henri's wishes and speak to me?"

"No, she still says she has only the one brother. Gwen is still under Duke Henri's thumb. I had to see you. I did something," Damond admitted. "Something big, and I need your help hiding it, Draper."

Draper looked at the two Wildmen and nodded to

Remy. His eyes fell on Duke Lot with confusion. "I see. Don't you worry. I'll take care of it. What's the problem? Money? Women?"

Damond shook his head. "I need a room for the night."

Draper postured. "No. You're not taking one of my girls for your first time. With my luck, I'll send you home to the great Duke Henri with the groin's disease and really disgrace the throne. No, you'll go straight home if that's what you're after. You're the good son. Duke Henri needs you to be the good one, and I'll not wreck that for you. You've got the throne to think about when he passes his crown to you."

That was news to me. I would've thought the older son would inherit the crown, or the daughter, if this was the matriarchal society I'd been told. Then I recalled that Gwen was adopted, and Morgan ruled that legal parentage didn't count as much as birthright did.

"The room's not for me. It's for my friends. And we don't need any of your whores." Damond didn't say the word like it was a slam, but merely a profession he was too familiar with. "We need a place to hide for a few days."

Draper's words came slow from his wide lips that matched his sibling's. "That's fine. I've got a room you can crash in. That's it? That's all you need? How bad are things with Duke Henri that you're coming to me? What are you hiding?"

Lane flew out of the stall, causing Hamish to spook, and scurry off her shoulder. She lunged at Draper, smacking him on his tall shoulder over and over. "How could you do this?" she shouted, angry tears rolling down her cheeks. "You were supposed to be more! I wanted more for you! How dare you let your baby brother into a place like this! How dare you let me find you in a place like this!"

Draper ducked, guarding his head as he tried to make heads or tails of the woman who appeared out of nowhere just to smack the sense back into him. "Whoa! Who are you?"

Lane gasped, scandalized. She stepped back for a minute, tearing off her hood. Her hands covered her mouth as she got a good look at the man she knew well enough to be disappointed in. "Who am I? Who am *I*? You've forgotten the most important question, Draper. Who are *you*? Know who you are! This place isn't you! It can't be!"

Draper stumbled backwards, paling as if he'd seen a ghost. "Laney?" He'd looked tall and strong when he'd come into the stables, if not a bit disheveled. But cowering under the gaze of Lane, he looked impossibly smaller, his shoulders hunched inward to hide his shame. His arms raised to shield himself from her disapproval.

"I didn't raise you like this! How could you do this? Do you work here? Are you a prostitute?"

"No, ma'am. I own the place."

It was the wrong thing to say, and he flinched like he knew it the second the words escaped him. "That's so much worse!" She resumed smacking him, taking out her hurt on him as tears poured down her face. "What would your mother say if she saw you here?"

"Laney, stop! Wait! Would you just... Let me look at you!"

Lane paused, her hand raised to strike him again. I'd never seen her so angry. She'd never hit me before. I'm guessing if I took out a loan and opened a brothel, I'd be in for the same treatment. I made a mental note to cross "Shady Madam" off my list of jobs to apply for after I graduated college.

Draper's chest heaved, and I saw tears dotting his black lashes. In the next second, Lane was scooped in his arms, clutched tight to his chest as he wept openly into her hair. "I thought you were dead! I thought there was no way you'd leave us for that long. You had to have died, and that's why you didn't come back. Why didn't you come back?"

"You know why," she worked out through her sobs. "I told you why. I had to take care of the baby. Morgan was abusing her. You know I took her to Common so I could raise her apart from all this."

Abusing me? I didn't know about that part, and made a mental note to ask about it later. Bastien stiffened, his hand coiling around my arm in the privacy of our stall, as if readying to jerk me away from the mere mention of Morgan.

"Why didn't you take me with you?" he demanded in a shout, not caring that Rousseau, Reyn, Remy, Bayard, Lot and his brother were watching with wide eyes. "I would've come! I was good with the baby! I helped you with Rosalie every day!"

"I know, sweetheart. I know. But I couldn't take you away from your home."

"*You* were my home! It's only in the last two years that Damond's been able to sneak away to see me." He motioned to the building that held the strippers and drunken men. "This is what I have without you!"

Lane clung to his rumpled shirt, crying into it and wiping her eyes on the white material that was dotted with a few stains. "As much as I wished you were my son, you weren't. Not legally, anyway. I couldn't steal a child, Draper. Urien gave me Rosie."

"I had you and Rosie, and you left with her! You took my family and ran!"

"I had no choice!"

I drank in every word like it was a key to understanding who I was. Learning that I had another cousin who had known me as a baby blew my mind. I tried not to blink, lest I miss out on a millisecond of this new dimension of a past I didn't remember.

"Duke Henri sent me to live with you because I was a disappointment to him. Did you really think that would change? Just because I wasn't officially banished back then didn't mean he would suddenly take me back in once you were gone." He gripped her tight, shaking her with his passion that poured tears down the sharp edges of his cheeks. "How could you do that to me?" he roared. "When Damond was born, Duke Henri had a new chance to start over with a son who'd never disappoint him!"

Damond looked down at his boots, taking no joy in the fact that his father loved him more than his older brother. I could tell he looked up to Draper, trusted him, even idolized him to some degree.

"I'm sorry, honey. I'm so sorry. I was wrong. I should've found a way to take you with me. I didn't think it would end up like this for you."

Draper dropped down to his knees, hugging Lane around the middle like a child holding onto his mother's apron. He cried into her dirty jeans, holding her legs tight as he could. He had no shame in the open emotion – he only saw Lane. "You're here? You're really back for me?"

Lane brushed her fingers through his haphazard black hair that matched Damond's in color and in cut, though Draper's didn't need product, and stayed spiked and pleasantly messy. "Of course I came back. The old team, together again. You feel like getting into trouble? I'm sure we could find some around here."

He laughed through his tears into her thighs. "I thought I'd never hear you say that again. You have no idea what it's been like without you, how hard it's been. You shouldn't have left me."

"No, I shouldn't have. I should've taken you with me when I ran out with Rosie. Maybe I should've stolen you away. It would've been hard, but... Oh, Draper! How'd you end up here? How'd it all get so broken?"

Draper stiffened, standing up with fear that pulled at his blue eyes, pushing his eyebrows together in worry. "But if you're here, what happened to the baby? Is my Rosie still alive?"

Lane turned in my direction, motioning me forward. I darted backward into the stall like a child, wanting to see everything, but scared to be part of it. I wanted to go to her, to meet my new cousin, but hiding seemed like a good option, too. I wasn't ready to face the man who would no doubt hate me for taking his mother figure away from him. I'd been in a creek, in the mud, on a horse and without sleep, a proper meal or a shower for far too long. On my best day, I wouldn't be ready for this, and I was certainly not having my best day. His dad hated me. Like, actual hate. If Draper took one look at me and decided the same? A girl can only take so much.

Bastien studied me with a look of confusion that told me I was being a baby. "Let's go on out."

I shook my head with fear plain in my eyes. "What if he hates me, like Uncle Duke Henri?"

Bastien held my gaze, and didn't blow off my concern. His arm moved slowly as he extended it to me, silently beckoning me to face my life, even the scary parts. He didn't take my hand, but waited for me to give it to him. When I finally moved forward, Bastien held my hand to his stomach, leading me forward slowly with the top of my head buried in his back as I clutched Seven to my chest under my cloak. "Come on, Daisy. It's alright."

Draper gasped when we rounded the corner, pointing at Bastien with dread. "The Untouchable! Lane, you have to know the Queen's Army is looking for him and the judge's son. They came through here not too long ago. You shouldn't be traveling with them. It's like painting a target on your back!"

"Well, that's the thing," Lane began. She motioned toward Bastien and me. "We're in a bit of a jam."

3

THE NOBLE WE WERE BORN TO BE

"Oh, Lane. No, no. Damond, is this your doing? What's going on here?" Draper pointed at Abraham Lincoln in accusation, who ambled out behind me. He shoved his cigar between his teeth and whipped a dagger from his belt. "That's a bear! Get behind me, Lane."

Lane waved off his concern. "That's just Rosie's new baby. First things first, we need a place to stay. Rosie sleeps, and she's long overdue. We need to wash up and eat. Can I buy a room off you? It would have to be secret that we're staying here. No one can know I'm here. Or Bastien. Or Reyn. And of course not Rosie. And really Lot shouldn't be seen here, either."

Draper looked around at the guys, taking in the scope of the damage before seeing how he could be helpful. "Alright. I can take care of that if you can sneak upstairs. I can have food sent up, new clothes, whatever you need. Under one condition, though."

"Anything, kid."

Draper's smile shone through the tears he started to wipe away. "You take me with you. Whatever it is you're doing here, I want in. I just got you back. Promise you won't leave without me this time."

"Oh, honey. You might change your mind when you hear what we're up to, but sure. If you still want in, you can come along. It'll be dangerous, though."

"The fun stuff always is." Draper turned toward Bastien. "Are you actually hiding my cousin from me? Is this her?"

"No. She's nervous, is all." Bastien turned his head over his shoulder to stage-whisper to me. "You know you look ridiculous, right? Come on out and say hello to the poor guy."

Seven hopped out of my arms and clawed her way up Bastien's back. She peered at Draper over Bastien's shoulder, startling him and adding only more confusion and chaos to Draper's shaken world.

Draper brought his hands over Lane's ears, clamping them down in case Seven unleashed her deadly squawk. Though I didn't know Draper from Adam, I loved him a little bit for protecting Lane without question. Uncle Henri had smacked her, but Draper shielded her. It was too much to hope that he would like me, too, but before I could stop it, the emotion bloomed in my chest, making me wish more than anything that Draper would be okay with me being around.

Lane patted his hands before removing them. "It's all fine, hun. You remember that Rosie can talk to animals. She did it around you all the time when you helped me take care of her back when she was a baby. She was always babbling to the birds."

"I guess I didn't expect her to find such dangerous animals." His voice turned soft and careful when he spoke in my direction. "Rosie? I'm your cousin, Draper." When my reply stuck in my throat, and I couldn't bring myself to take off my hood, he pushed on. "You wouldn't remember me, but the three of us used to live together back in Province 9. I was only ten when you were born. Yeah, you couldn't remember me." He sounded sad on that last note.

"Hi," I said lamely from behind Bastien. "Um, yeah. I mean, no. I don't remember Avalon at all. I know that's not what you want to hear."

"Can I get a look at you? The last time I saw you, you were just learning to walk. I imagine you've grown since then. It's been twenty-one years." He said it like a joke, but I could tell he was nervous. He let out a noise of distress. "Twenty-one years!"

"It's fine, Ro. Come on out." Lane held out her hand to me, and I knew I couldn't not go to her. I released my hold on Bastien unlaced the cape, sliding the gray, coarse material off my shoulders. My ponytail fell forward over my shoulder, and I shoved my hands in my jeans pockets, staring at my soggy shoes as I limped to Lane. "Rosie, this is Prince Draper of Province 2. He's Damond and Gwen's older brother. Your cousin."

"Actually, it's Draper of the Lost Village now. I was cast out of the royal family."

Fire rose in Lane's eyes as her fingernails dug into Draper's forearm. "You are *not* lost. You're a prince, Draper. Just because your father's a fool doesn't make you less than the noble you were born to be." Her words took on passion I'd heard a thousand times in my childhood. "I know who you are."

Draper closed his eyes and touched his heart. "I love you, Laney." Though they were only six years apart, Draper spoke to Lane with the reverence reserved for a mother. He tore his gaze from her to meet my hesitant eyes. "Rosie." My name sounded like honey on his tongue.

I ducked my head, trying not to mess it all up. "Hey. Good to meet you. Or re-meet you."

Draper's rapid movements drew my eyes upward as he hurriedly tucked in his shirt, buttoning it and pulling on his suspenders. He stuck out his hand, hiding his cigar behind his back. "It's a pleasure to meet you, Rosie." He shook my hand, and I knew he was holding back for my sake. I was punking out, and he was being cool about it. "You really don't remember me?" He was hopeful, sincere. I wanted to give him good news, but I didn't have any for him.

I kept my head down and slowly shook my head. "I'm

sorry. I wish I did. You seem like a nice guy."

I felt Draper's eyes on me, studying every hair that was out of place (all of them) and every detail that made me the girl he'd known as a baby. I was riddled with guilt, thinking that I'd taken his mother figure away. Yet he didn't look at me as though he hated me. When I picked up my head to peek at him, I saw nothing but pure, unadulterated and earnest love beaming out from his clear blue eyes.

Draper slapped his hands together and rubbed them, addressing the group. "Well, let's get you all cleaned up and warmed up. Your horses will be taken care of. I'll call everyone in the bar over to the piano, and then you'll have the space to go upstairs if you're quick about it. Go up to the third floor to my room. It's the one all the way down at the end of the hall. You can rest there, and in the room to the left of it. That one's vacant tonight." He reached out and held Lane's hand, speaking quietly to her while the others picked up their packs and I hobbled back to Bastien. "I don't want to let you out of my sight. I'm afraid you'll disappear again. Promise you won't leave without me."

Lane leaned up and pressed a kiss to the grown man's forehead when he stooped to accommodate her. He softened like a little boy under his mother's affection. "I promise to take you with me wherever I go, if you still want to come with me after you hear what we're up to."

He squeezed her hand. "I'll be up after one song."

"I'll be waiting," she promised.

4

KISSING AND COUGHING

Draper's room was exactly what one might expect of a man left unchecked. Clothes were everywhere, old dishes, and women's underwear of various shades and sizes were strewn on the floor. The stink of thick cigar smoke permeated the bed, chair, thick rug and walls. The Wildmen, Lot and Remy opted for the room to the left, which was smaller, but far better maintained. Bastien sighed and started cleaning the mess basically by throwing all the clothes in the corner and stacking the dishes outside the door, making himself useful while Lane and I took turns bathing in the tub behind the partition. I felt amazing when I got out, finally clean as I wrapped the cigar-scented towel around me. I peeked around the edge when I heard the guys talking.

"This place is filthy," Bastien complained, and I could see his military training coming into play. His house had been empty, but immaculate. "Reyn, don't lie down on that bed yet. We need clean sheets."

"It's fine, Bastien. I just need to sit."

"I want you sleeping tonight. I mean it. Your magic's nearly broken, and I won't have that happen on my watch. Just wait until I can get some clean sheets up here."

"Don't boss me around like I'm some patient! I'm not sick!" I was shocked to hear Reyn raise his voice. He had a line of sweat dotting his sallow forehead, and his breathing was labored.

"You're barely upright!" Bastien pointed his finger in Reyn's face. "You need a transfusion. Don't even bother fighting me on this. I need you at least functional for the journey. I won't have you passing out on the job. And no more magic. I mean it, Reyn! I'll do the protection charms. I'll do whatever concealment we need."

Reyn's usually cool demeanor was marred by a snarl. "Don't older brother me. We're the same age. We're equals in the Council. Don't talk down to me like you know best!"

Bastien pinched the bridge of his nose, for once thinking his words through before speaking. "You're right. I was out of line. It's just... I already lost Roland. I can't lose you, too. Not over this. Not when we're so close."

Seeing Bastien expose his underbelly softened the fight in Reyn. His shoulders relaxed as he stood, placing a feeble hand on Bastien's shoulder. The two hugged in that fierce brotherly way that pushed emotion up inside of me. I'd seen them embrace before, but Bastien's arms usually remained at his side. It seemed Reyn being sick pushed Bastien to a more desperate edge, which forced his air of distance out of the way.

Reyn hadn't looked well on and off since we left Remy's place. He had bags under his eyes, and was constantly either sweating or breathing too heavy for what we were doing. I could hear the smack of doom in Reyn's voice. "Yeah, fine. But don't tell the others. I don't want them treating me like I'm sick or something. It's bad enough Lot knows."

"I can't imagine they don't already know, but sure. So long as you sleep tonight and stop using your magic, I'll keep whatever secret you want."

"Thanks." He gripped Bastien harder before pulling away. "I'll go see if Remy's got the supplies for a transfusion." He left, and I felt Bastien's tension going down a notch, now that Reyn would be safer.

I moved out from behind the partition in my towel to grab clothes for Lane and I while she bathed. Bastien hissed at the sight of me, coming near to offer his hand for me to lean on. I could tell he wasn't sure if that was appropriate, given the state of my partial nudity.

"You're killing me," Bastien whispered, taking in my dripping form.

"Oh, you love the danger." I took a bold step toward him, leaned up on my toes and touched my lips to his cheek. His arm slung low around my waist, pressing my body to his. We tried to stay quiet, so we could prolong the moment as much as possible.

He pulled on the knot I'd done to hold the towel in place. "One tug is all it would take. Just one little tug." His hand drifted up and thumbed my lower lip, taking in the swell with clear intention burning in his caramel eyes. "Rosie," he whispered, swallowing hard. "I want to be with you so badly."

My skin was alight with too many nerve endings dancing and taunting me to come out and play. Oh, did I wish I could play. I wanted to throw so many rules out the window and throw Bastien down on Draper's bed. I wanted to kiss him, despite the warnings I shouldn't. I slowly leaned up in time with Bastien's advance toward my lips, ignoring the alarms and the many reasons I should stay away.

"Babe, could you grab me some clothes?" Lane called from the other side of the partition.

Bastien dropped his hands and stepped back, blowing out a breath of longing so he could look at me like a dude friend, and not the girl he'd just almost kissed.

My face fell. The crash was unavoidable. "Sure, Lane. Be right there."

I hadn't packed properly because I hadn't packed at all. I didn't have any pajamas, and I didn't look forward to sleeping in jeans again. I fished through for yoga pants for Lane, underwear and a sports bra tank top, bringing them to her and setting them on the floor next to the tub. Her eyes were a million miles away as she hugged herself in the water. I kissed her forehead, and left her to her many troubled thoughts.

I came back out, and Bastien had his flannel shirt removed, offering it to me as if it was a bouquet of roses. For all the romance to the gesture, to me it smelled just as sweet. He didn't say a word, but opened his shirt to slide it onto my arms. I turned to face him, and he kept his eyes locked in on mine as he worked his way down the line of buttons until my body was closed inside. I uncinched the towel and let it fall to the rug at my feet. My mouth went dry and my palms moistened when his sharp intake of breath and unconcealed look of desire told me he knew exactly how naked I was under his shirt. The flannel brushed my knees, but I felt the scandal of near-nudity all the same. "Told you I'd get that towel off you," he whispered low in my ear, giving me goosebumps and all kinds of ideas. His shirt on me was actually completely modest, but my skin felt alive, tingling with the daring of youth I'd never had the opportunity to indulge in.

He was half a step away, and when he reached out to hold my hand, he drew even closer. His thumb grazed my chin, gripping it and directing my face upwards so he could get a good look at my lips and gauge my willingness to finally cross this milestone. "Please?" he whispered, wrapping his other arm low around my hips and pulling me flush to him.

I was so entranced by the lantern's dim light reflecting

off his earnest eyes; I would've given him anything if he asked like that. "Please," I begged, reaching up and tugging on the collar of his t-shirt. I could feel his breath on my lips, and my lashes fluttered with wanton desire for all the things that were Bastien. I adored his Christmas tree scent that, thanks to his shirt, engulfed me. I'd fantasied too many times about his velvety lower lip, his broad shoulders and hard muscles. I drank down the insecurity in his eyes that told me that, as big of a deal as this was for me, it was as much of a game-changer for him, too. He was nervous, which made me feel a boost of boldness I wouldn't have otherwise possessed.

Bastien's lips were even softer than I'd imagined. They pressed gently to mine and then parted slightly to taste more of me, to melt me beyond recognition.

Oh, now I melted in his arms. My body felt spineless and weightless as I floated in his embrace. My leg didn't hurt anymore, and neither did the exhaustion feel like it might overtake me. I was alive with something I'd never experienced before, and it tasted deliciously addictive.

When Bastien's tongue teased mine, I let out a quiet and unrefined noise of desire, my arms trembling as I reached for his neck to pull him closer, to get just a little more of the thing I'd been pretending I didn't need, didn't want. I wanted Bastien, so I didn't hold back when the kiss picked up speed, gaining momentum and mingling that with the passion we'd been denying for far too long.

It was as if our bodies had been waiting on the edge of

their desires for our minds to get with the program. Though this was my very first kiss, it built with the momentum of a far more experienced collision. I didn't hesitate to wrap my good leg around his waist when he lifted me off the ground and turned us to press my back to the wall. The ankle from my good leg wrapped around his hips as the music filtered through from the floors below, drowning out his zealous moans so I could swallow them without Lane overhearing us from behind her partition. Each impassioned noise was just for me. The loud and bawdy piano from downstairs served as the backdrop for our scattered hunger, which was finally coming into focus. "I love you in my clothes," he breathed between kisses. "I love you in my arms."

I tugged his lower lip between my teeth, bringing out a guttural growl that started in his chest. I arched my back when the thrill of the sound worked its way through me, vibrating too many things and leaving me ravenous for more of him, and still more. I couldn't believe that this was what I'd been missing out on all these years.

Bastien smeared his lips across my cheek so he could bite my earlobe like a savage who couldn't get enough. "I love you against the wall like this. This'll be what I think about all day long. You, exactly like this."

Bastien felt right to me, and it wasn't because my world felt all wrong. He had the similar twist in his humor that matched mine, and a prickly way about him that I also got when the bandage was ripped off too soon or too publicly.

I wanted him on an animal level, but I also liked the warrior in him, and wanted to be near him. I wanted to take care of him, and for the first time, I wanted to let a man take care of me. Each kiss felt like a stamp of permanence I had not expected, but there it was, pressing itself on my lips and daring me to deny we had some pretty explosive chemistry. Each gasp from his mouth settled into a permanent place in my heart. It was my first kiss, but dang if we weren't knocking it out of the park.

Something warm started forming low in my belly. It collected into a ball of taffy-like heat that was easy to hold onto as it rose to the surface. I felt it rise up in me, almost like Bastien was coaxing it out of me. The heat tickled my insides, making me cough when it reached my throat and stuck there. I turned my head to the side, casting Bastien an apologetic look as I coughed into my fist. He kissed my neck and lowered me back to the floor, though I felt like I was still floating on a sea of deliciously heated jelly. The warm ball of taffy in my throat stayed there, though, making me cough more and more to dislodge it or swallow it down.

Of course this would happen. Of course the hottest moment of my life would be interrupted by a coughing fit. Why wouldn't that happen?

I held up a finger to Bastien, who was still coming down from the high of our kiss.

"Honey? You alright?" Lane called from behind the partition.

"No!" I choked out as my breathing passage narrowed. "Something's wrong!" My throat felt hot from the inside and the outside now, radiating an uncomfortable degree of warmth through my body. It burned my throat, scaring me with its sudden insistence that it be dealt with. I heard the splash of water from the tub and slipped through Bastien's fingers, coughing on the rug on all fours. "Help!" I tried to catch my breath, but it was harder to come by as my chest spasmed. The ball of heat was trying to decide if it was going to move up and out of me, or down and back into me. It kept going up an inch, and then scorching me afresh as it regressed.

Bastien came to himself and knelt in front of me. Lane was at my side in the next instant, wrapped in a stained beige towel. Her hand was on my back, trying to see if I was choking or not. I picked up my head as I coughed uncontrollably, and Lane and Bastien both cried out, their eyes on my throat. "The *lueur*! Her body's giving up her *lueur*!" Lane cried, whirling on Bastien. "You! You did this to her! You did this to my daughter!"

"What? No! No, I didn't! I never promised her anything! She did this on her own!" Bastien backed up, looking like he'd been caught touching the girl with two pink lines on the pregnancy test.

Lane's voice was a feigned calm that only made me more afraid. "It's alright, Ro. Your throat's glowing with something called a *lueur*. Just push it back down, and it'll go back where it came from. Trust me, you're not ready to choose who you give that to yet."

The door opened and shut quietly, and I heard Draper voice his confusion until he saw my glowing throat. "Oh! Sorry, I didn't mean to walk in on a ritual. I didn't know. You're her *Guardien*?" he asked of Bastien, holding out his hand in congratulations.

"No! No! I barely know her! I'm no one's *Guardien*! Stop it, Rosie! Put it back!" Bastien's voice was higher pitched and cracked with the stress.

Tears pooled in my eyes from the coughing and the cruel words. We'd been through so much, and he was acting like I was some lovesick teenager with a crush on a guy who had no idea she was alive. I'd been that girl, so I knew that wasn't what we had. I wasn't imagining our connection.

Lane clamped my mouth shut and shouted in my face. "Swallow it down, Rosie!"

I couldn't swallow. I could only cough. My face felt red from the strain of trying to obey. I was simultaneously freaking out and heartbroken, all while trying to pull in a breath.

"I can't do this! Lane, I'm sorry, I've got to get out of here." Bastien ran – literally ran away from me, charging out the door, and leaving me to choke on the floor.

5

DRAPER'S PUMPKIN

"Here, this'll help." Draper knelt to my left on the other side of Lane, tipping a cup to my lips and pouring water down my throat. "Drink it down," he urged, unperturbed when I coughed a portion of the water back up onto the filthy rug. He closed my mouth and covered it with his larger hand that stank of cigars and sex, and then pinched my nose with the other. He tilted my head back so my body would have no choice but to swallow. I stared up at the dark wood slats that lined the ceiling, hoping this wasn't as bad as it looked and felt. Draper's voice was soothing, like a lullaby as he sang, "There you go. Just swallow it down." He ignored my struggles for breath and Lane's panic that it wouldn't go back down. Draper held my face in that awkward way you wouldn't even let your best friend do without a good five-minute explanation first.

But I didn't have five minutes. The heat burned me as it migrated slowly back down my throat, feeling like a log jammed into a pencil sharpener. I swallowed harder, coughing with my mouth closed until the heat finally went back into my belly and began to dissipate. I slumped, and Draper scooped me into his arms, leaning my temple to his chest that moved in and out unevenly with the adrenaline we all shared. I was small in the long arms I found myself curled up in, blinking in confusion while I tried to figure out how I got there.

"What was that?" I croaked. Tears squeezed out of me, and I prayed I could dismiss them as condensation from coughing too much.

Draper stroked my cheek, holding me tight to him. "The Untouchable. He's not your *Guardien*?"

"I don't even know what that means!" I wailed, the tears no longer concealed. "I don't know what any of this is! I don't live here!"

Lane held my hand, moving in front of me so I didn't have to turn my head from Draper's embrace. "Your *lueur* is a portion of your magic – a portion of you. When you give it to the Brownie who swears to protect you and your household, it links you to him. He keeps that portion of your *lueur* inside of him. It gives him access to your magic without it wearing you down. It's like an energizer battery. Makes him a stellar protector for you." She shook her head. "You can't give your *lueur* to Bastien. He's not ready for a commitment like that. I know you like him, but that's way too serious a decision to make after knowing him less than a month."

"What decision? I didn't mean to give him anything! It just started burning in my belly and climbed up in me when we were..." My voice trailed off guiltily, though I knew I'd done nothing wrong.

Lane clamped her hand over her mouth, her hard gaze softening. "Oh, Ro. Honey, did you kiss him just now? Was that your first kiss?" Her heart visibly broke for me all over her face as she took in my nod of confirmation. My tears multiplied at the mess it had all devolved to.

Draper grimaced like he'd never heard of such a ridiculous thing as a woman out of her teen years never having been properly kissed. He kept his mouth shut, though, tightening his arm around my back as he rubbed the stress from my tricep. "So you didn't mean to give the Untouchable your *lueur*?"

"No! We were kissing, and then smack in the middle of it, I couldn't stop coughing and choking." My cheeks were pink at having to talk about the intimate things I would only ever want to tell Lane or Judah over a couple beers, days after the fact.

"This is a problem." Lane rubbed her forehead. "Let me get some clothes on, and we can talk about it." She stood, going behind the partition to exchange her damp towel for the clothes I laid out for her.

"Do you want some more water?" Draper offered. I could tell there were a million things he wanted to say, but he was holding himself back so as not to make me too uncomfortable.

I nodded, expecting him to hand the glass to me. Instead he pressed the edge of the cup to my lips, tipping it slowly so I could get used to swallowing without the log obstructing my esophagus. "Thanks. Sorry you had to see all this. Total mess."

He ran his fingers through my wet hair, loosening the tangles that curly hair always managed to find. "I'm glad I walked in when I did. You shouldn't give your *lueur* to some guy who runs out of the room to get away from it. I'll help you. We'll figure out why it came up so easily. Has that ever happened before?"

"Never. And it won't happen again." I knew I wouldn't be kissing Bastien again anytime soon. I doubted I would see the guy before we had to leave, if he came back at all. He didn't owe us anything. He left me while I was choking on the floor. He ran out, not knowing if I'd be alright.

He left, which was bad enough.

Then something awful dawned on me. "Oh, but wait! Is that going to happen every time I kiss a guy? I'll have to choke down my *lueur* or whatever so I'm not saddled with each new guy for life?"

Draper was hesitant. "I'm sure it won't be that bad. We'll find a way around this."

My childish panic was quiet, but no less urgent. "What if we can't? What if I die having only kissed a guy one time before he ran away from me? Is that my life? Is that all I get?"

"No. No, that's not for you. You're special, meant for grander things than this. Only a Brownie can take your *lueur*, so perhaps just avoid kissing Brownies until we can get a hold of this." His eyes closed and he gripped my hair. "Oh, your first kiss was in a whorehouse? I'm sorry, Rosie. That one's on me."

The tears fell all over again when it was boiled down like that. "My first kiss was in a whorehouse!" I wailed, wiping my face on Bastien's sleeve. "Can I borrow some pajamas or a big shirt or something? This is his shirt, and I don't want it on me." My heart was stony against Bastien, stung too deep to be understanding of his side of the panic.

"Of course. Anything you need. Lane said you still sleep. Is that right?"

"Yeah, and I really need to now. I can't keep going like this. I don't even remember the last time I ate. My leg's busted up. I kissed the biggest d-bag in Avalon, and I just want to go home!" I hated myself for whining, but you try being awake as long as I'd been and see if you've got the smile of a cheerleader on the top of a pyramid.

Draper held me close, kissing the top of my head, as if he knew that's what I needed to center myself. "Alright,

alright. I can take care of the food well enough. And I've got a healer on staff to take care of my girls. Do you want me to call him to look at your leg?"

"No. Thanks. I've got my own healer. I was just complaining. I'm sorry. I'm usually not such a sopping mess." I wiped away my tears. "Thanks for letting me freak out, and for not freaking out yourself. I know I'll get over it. It's just a little much right now. Can I lie down?"

"Sure, pumpkin." The affectionate term came naturally from him, and landed on me with the grace of a delicate dove. He smiled softly at me. "That's what I used to call you when you were a baby." Draper took to me so easily; I didn't understand how he could be so sweet without knowing the adult me for more than an hour.

Lane came out from behind the partition in her sports tank and yoga pants. "Here, let's get you to the bed."

"No!" Draper's protest was unexpected. I looked up and saw embarrassment coloring his cheeks. "I mean, give me a minute. That's my bed, and I don't use it for sleeping. You shouldn't lay down yet. Let me change the sheets." He looked around the room, as if taking in the mess for the first time. "And let me straighten up while you get changed. Here, I'll get you a fresh shirt."

Lane's teeth ground together. "You and I are going to talk about your bed and this whole place after she goes to sleep, young man."

Draper ducked his head down, but a small smile

brushed across the right side of his face. He was easily half a foot taller than Lane and me, but he submitted to her easily, as I always did. "Yes, ma'am." I could tell he'd missed having any sort of accountability, or having anyone looking after him, telling him to brush his teeth, and making sure he had a lunch packed for school. It was kind of cute.

Draper moved me from his lap, and went to his wooden dresser in the corner. He pulled out a thermal long-sleeved gray shirt and handed it to me, giving me a light push to go change behind the partition after he helped me to stand.

I heard Lane mumbling things like, "filthy whorehouse" and "no boy of mine could" while she helped Draper straighten up.

The fit of the gray shirt was only slightly baggy, and actually hugged my hips a little. The hem fell to the middle of my thigh and made it look like I was wearing a low-budget party dress. Jill would've been proud at my display of legs. Then she would've winced at my stitches, handed me a pair of knee-high boots and told me politely to cover that nonsense up. I hobbled over to the bed, my face red and splotchy as I clutched Bastien's shirt in my fist. Lane was tucking the edges of the fresh black sheet under the mattress. For not using it to sleep in, the bed was impressive. It had a carved blond wood bedframe, and four tall posts. It looked positively brimming with good dreams and cozy naps.

Lane was still muttering under her breath at the state Draper's life had devolved to. She started making a collection of women's underwear that she tossed into a large bowl with aggressive hisses and unintelligible mutterings of disapproval.

I looked up at Draper, deciding I couldn't be shy around him anymore if he'd seen me at my worst. He had a tray he was filling with dirty dishes, all of which had old food that looked dried on for days. "Draper?"

He stopped what he was doing and turned to me, surprised I was making conversation that wasn't angsty crying and wasn't forced by Lane. "Yeah, baby Rosie?" He shook his head. "Yeah, Rosie? Sorry. Old habits. I look at you, and I get that you're twenty-two, but you're still that little chubby-faced baby I sang to sleep every night."

"Really? You sang to me?"

"Every night, for like half an hour. You screamed your head off if I didn't. Lane delegated bedtime to me when we first got you."

"That's... That's really cool of you. I wish I remembered that. I always wanted a brother. I mean, I have Judah, so that counts, but other than him."

Draper set down the tray of dishes to implore me with his eyes and splayed hands. "I *am* your brother!" he said, too earnest for a casual conversation. "Lane raised us like that. I know we're truly cousins, but I was supposed to be your brother. You were my responsibility. When you cried, I ran and got you. Even though we had the whole palace to pick from, your crib was in my room! I did everything with you because you would scream whenever I left your sight. Lane did my lessons with you in my lap. I ate one-handed. All of it. Every day, every night, not an hour of space between us." His face fell. "And then one day?" He snapped his fingers with a sorrow to his eyes that moved me to emotion. He had that way about him that made me empathize with whatever he was feeling. "You were gone, and I was being shipped back to Province 2. I stayed there for a month before the great Duke Henri decided I was unworthy of the throne, and unwelcome in his home. 'Draper the Disappointment' was my nickname. Old Duke Henri said I didn't have the iron grip needed to rule, so he sent me to live with Aunt Avril." He shuddered. "She was terrible. Worst was that I knew you were screaming some-where without me to sing you to sleep, and I couldn't find you! I searched everywhere. I ran away from Aunt Avril so many times, eventually she stopped looking for me. That's how I ended up here."

"King of the gutter," Lane muttered. Her eyebrows were knit together in concern for his plight, but her mouth was still frozen in a tight line of disapproval.

Draper was distraught, so he took a half-smoked cigar out of his pocket, and unrolled it from the wrapper. He took a match from his dresser and lit the end apologeti-cally. The first puff seemed to center him. The second relaxed his shoulders. "Sorry. It's all just a little much." He leaned against the wall, his eyes far off as the cigar took him back to places I could tell he didn't want to visit without a lifeline. "I tried to go back to Duke Henri on one of my escapes from Aunt Avril, but he kicked me out. Disowned me after putting a stash of gold in my backpack and sending me on my way. He had Damond at that point, and didn't want the people in Province 2 worrying that I would inherit the throne."

Lane had her arms around him in a hot second, holding him together, in case he wanted to fall apart after giving a voice to his wounds. "Oh, sweetie. I had no idea it would be like that for you. I wanted to take you with me so badly! I wanted to steal you away, but that would've actually been kidnapping! Urien begged me to take Rosie up to Common to escape Morgan. I was scared, and I was wrong. I should've taken you, or at least stayed and explained things until you understood. It wasn't just Rosie who cried for you every night that first year; I did, too. That's how we got through it. I held her, sobbing my eyes out with Rosie until she exhausted her little lungs. You're worth more than that sack full of gold. You're the whole treasury! Please forgive me, Draper. Please."

Draper swiped at his face, looking down with adoration at Lane. "It never even occurred to me to be mad at you. I get it. But don't leave me this time. I really... I can't go through that again."

"Never," she promised, jerking him with her squeeze. When Lane turned, she motioned me forward, bringing me into the hug that almost hurt, she was gripping us so hard. "My kids. My sweet kids."

Though it was new to me, the love was there, ripe and beautiful.

When the hug broke, Lane helped me to the bed, digging a thick red comforter out of the chest at the foot of the bed. I held up Bastien's shirt to Draper. "You're sort of like my brother now, right?"

Draper nodded, his face beaming with adoration that I accepted this new branch in our stapled-together family tree so easily. "Yes. I'm a great brother. Ask Damond."

"I'll take your word for it. This shirt is Bastien's. Can you make sure something totally disgusting happens to it before he gets it back?"

Draper grinned at the first job in his resumed post as my big brother. "How disgusting are we talking?"

I shrugged, laying down on the clean sheet and letting Lane tuck me in. I knew she missed me being little, so I indulged her every now and then. "We're in a whorehouse, Drape. I'll let you get creative with it."

He laughed, nodding as the wheels began turning. "Oh, this'll be fun. You just rest. I'll take care of the big brother stuff. Bastien will wish he never broke your heart."

"Thanks, dude." I held out my fist for a bump, but I could tell he had no idea what to do with the salute. I tugged his fist to mine, knocking our knuckles together. "Like that. It's called a fist bump. It means we're on the same team, and we're both awesome."

"I like it." He held up the flannel with an evil grin. "Don't hug him after he gets it back." His gaze sharpened. "And with how fast he ran out of here? Maybe don't hug him for a while, or ever again."

"I have a good feeling about you, Draper. An even better one if you turn out the lamp and let me get a good six hours of shuteye." I tried to be casual to shake off the pain of Bastien running out on me.

Instead of making a quick exit, Draper sat down on the edge of the bed and fished for my hand. He played with my fingers as he debated something in his head. "I can't imagine you'd remember the song I used to sing you."

My face fell into a frown. "I wish. Could you sing it for me? Maybe it'll jog something loose."

I didn't think Draper would do it, but after a few quiet beats, his low voice caressed my ears. "Climb all the mountains, run off when you're grown, but for now, little girl, my song is your home."

I tried not to get too emotional, but it was hard not to. "That was my bedtime song?"

"I made it up myself for you."

I pursed my lips, wishing so many things in my life could be different. "I think I would've liked to hear that every night for five or ten years. It's pretty. I like when you sing."

He indulged me in the simple lullaby again, and then kissed my knuckles before he stood. "Come on, Lane. Let's go catch up in one of the other rooms. Tell me what I missed in the last twenty-one years."

"Only the last twenty-one? Well, that shouldn't take too long."

The two left with armloads of dirty dishes, disgusting sheets and clothes, encasing me in total darkness so I could be alone with my regret.

6

DAMOND'S DESPERATE DEEDS

"*Y*ou did not," Damond chuckled, his spoon of porridge raised to his mouth.

"We did so. Never looked back, either. See how he liked walking around in a corset." Lane was in full swing with Draper, reliving the good old days. I'd contented myself with my porridge at the breakfast table. I knew I needed to eat, but my appetite waned when I pictured Bastien walking back in through the door. We were all sitting or standing around in Draper's bedroom, all of us but Bastien, eating porridge and apples while trading war tales and play stories.

Abraham Lincoln sat in my lap, while Hamish went from person to person, inspecting their pockets for nuts he suspected we were hiding from him. *I want to go outside and play,* Abraham Lincoln said to me, his schnozzle rubbing up under my chin. *Come play with me.*

"Go ask Bayard or Rousseau to take you out, baby. I'm not finished with my breakfast."

"*No!*" Abraham Lincoln was scared, wrapping his arm over my shoulder to hold me closer. "*I don't like them. They killed the fat one. And the juicy one. And the ripe one.*"

"Huh? They eat people food, just like me. Actually, more like you. You eat plump and juicy things, too."

"*But they didn't eat. They killed and laughed. I didn't like it.*"

The others were joking and chatting animatedly, glad to have the mission on hold until my leg healed. I felt bad bringing a serious note to the conversation. "Bayard? Abraham Lincoln's trying to tell me something, but it doesn't make much sense. He said you killed and laughed? What's he talking about?"

Bayard set his porridge down, his smile falling to a tight sneer directed at my bear. "Your bear's a dirty snitch. Fine. Rousseau and I went out last night on an innocent little stroll around town. You know, to see the sights. We happened to run into Damond's pal Norris, and things got heated. He said he wanted to keep messing up kids, and I said I didn't think that was such a good idea. So I killed him." Bayard put the cap on the sentence with a horrible matter-of-fact that sent a chill through me.

Rousseau got riled up, bursting into the conversation with a loud, "That's a bold-faced lie! No one ever gives credit to the one who holds down the pig who needs gutting. I killed him just as much as you did!"

"Hey!" I clapped my hands twice. "Besides the fact that we're traveling incognito, did you ever think of just calling the cops on him? Making him pay his debt to society? Why is your first reaction to kill?"

"Cops? You mean the judge?" Bayard resumed his grin and picked up his bowl again to eat. "You're funny. I thought you were serious for a minute there."

"I am serious. You can't murder everyone who's terrible."

"Actually, that's exactly what I had to do. What a sweet world Common must be. Maybe you didn't catch that Norris was making Damond do... How do I put this delicately? Sexual favors to pass down the street to see his brother."

"What was your *in*delicate way of saying that?" I blanched, turning toward Damond, who hung his head in shame. I'd gotten that vibe from Damond's brief exchange with Norris, but to have it confirmed felt like a punch in the gut.

Lot glowered at Bayard. "Yes, what exactly was the indelicate way of saying that? There are ladies present, Bayard. A maiden, in fact."

Draper's teeth ground together. "Damond, is that true?"

Damond looked at his porridge as if it was a bowl of worms – fascinating but unappetizing. "It's none of your business how I get through the village. When I found out that was what I had to do to see you, I learned to bring enough silver instead." He scowled at Bayard. "Thanks for spilling that to everyone."

Draper looked down, steadying himself while he started and stopped a sentence several times. Lane put her hand on Draper's and looked Damond in the eye. "It's done then. Good for you, Bayard. Let the bastard burn." She turned toward my intake of breath at her swift judgment (that I actually pretty much agreed with), and said to me, "Baby, it's a different world here. Especially in a place like this. The Lost Village is where people come to avoid the law. There's so much dirty money in here, rulers who can actually do something don't bother with the place."

Draper was livid. "Yeah? Well, *I* bother with it. Why didn't you tell me, Damond? I would've taken care of it for you."

Damond's wide lips were gathered in the center, pursed as he wrestled with his desire for privacy and also the need to speak. "I know what you would've done. You would've told me to go on home. That it was too dangerous for me. That no prince of Province 2 should be caught dead in a place like this. You'd send me away." Damond blinked several times. "But you're my brother. Without you, I have no one."

Draper stood from the floor where he sat with Lane, Abraham Lincoln and me, and pulled Damond up. "You're going to go into the other room with me and write down the name of everyone who harassed you. Then I'll take care of it. You should know you can lean on me when you're scared." Draper was taller than Damond, so he kissed the top of his head, grimacing as he wiped the too much product off his lips.

Rousseau spoke up before they left the room. "You don't need to write down Gerta's name or Hank's. Or Giacomo." With his hairy thumb, he mimed slitting his own throat.

Bayard didn't look up from his porridge when he spoke. "Saw another Untouchable, but not ours. Didn't know Link the Terrifying frequented these parts."

Draper quirked an interested eyebrow. "An Untouchable, eh? Not bad for business."

"Hank never harassed me," Damond protested, confused.

Bayard shrugged. "They tried to mess with Remy." Bayard stabbed his fist to his chest, mimicking the punch of a knife. "Our healer was just trying to buy some herbs at a reasonable price." He reached down to where Remy was seated and slapped him on the back in camaraderie.

Remy cast me a what-can-you-do? kind of look. *I really did get taken down by two men after buying some herbs to replenish my medicine bag. They must've seen my silver and followed me. The whole thing seemed rather rehearsed.*

"You poor thing! Are you alright? Did they hurt you?"

"Only my pride. Truthfully, it's been a while since I drew my sword. I was grateful Bayard and Rousseau were there. Some knight I would've been," he muttered dejectedly.

"Scouring the Lost Village to find medicine for the

princess? A brave knight if I ever saw one," I said kindly to Remy, who managed a smile for me.

Lane's arms were around Damond, kissing his hair and making a fuss over all he'd been through. "Draper, we leave in a few days. See what else you've been missing, and tie up any loose ends. And get this poor boy some pie. Growing boys need pie!"

"Yes, ma'am," Draper said, ducking his head and exchanging a sheepish smile with his brother. I could tell Damond had also been starved for motherly affection. Any regular teen would've pulled away after a second or two of a hug from their mother, but Damond leaned into the embrace, letting Lane start to fill the hole that his mother's death had left.

7

ROOMMATES AND KINDRED SPIRITS

We stayed in Draper's room for three days, eating, laughing, planning and getting to know each other's quirks. Bastien was gone, and it didn't look like Reyn expected him to come back anytime soon. Reyn kept kissing my forehead with these pitying looks. It was sweet, but super annoying. I wouldn't pine for a jack-wagon who didn't want to be with me, but I think Reyn was expecting me to.

We started packing after my nine-hour night of sleep on the third day. My leg was finally well enough to put pressure on it. I couldn't wait until we were in the open fields, so I could run again and test out the lasting damage I'd have to muscle through. Remy assured me it would heal good as new, but I remembered how deep the cut had been, and had my doubts.

Draper and I were starting to become friends. He stuck by my side or Lane's almost the entire time, except when he had business to attend to. Then he'd come back fumbling and embarrassed, needing his cigar to calm his nerves. I could tell he was worried we'd be so mad at him that we'd leave, but I'd never had a brother before, and wouldn't give him up without a fight.

I educated him all about modern cars, and he taught me a new card game I'd never heard of called *Barbu*. I completely sucked at it, but neither of us cared. We were just happy to play together. He treated me like I was five, which, after being yanked from my life with little say in anything after that, didn't feel patronizing. It felt like we were both trying to be extra kind to each other to make up for lost time, and to pay respect to the long roads that somehow led us to playing cards together, like it was the most natural thing in the world. Plus, I could tell he needed someone to baby; poor guy was so turned around.

One night while the others were eating downstairs and entertaining themselves with the women, or eating in the second bedroom, Lane, Draper and I decided to spend a little family time together, just the three of us in Draper's room. Draper lit a fire while we ate and traded stories about what life had been like for us in Common.

We'd settled on lighter stories about Lane's job and day-to-day schedule, so I was surprised when Lane dipped into her emotional pocket and pulled out something deeper. "I've been thinking of taking a roommate."

My head jerked toward her. "Wait, what? A roommate? Who?"

She shrugged, avoiding my gaze. "No one in particular. A female roommate looking to pay half the rent. It would make things easier. I could come to see you more often. I could get that rattling sound in my car fixed. I could eat name brand food." She stopped herself. "Well, I don't want to get too crazy. But yeah, a little break in the bills would be nice."

"Where would she sleep?"

"Your room. Honey, it's not like you'll be using it. You live two hours away."

"I come home for the summers!"

"Not forever. You'll be taking a summer internship next year. I'm talking about doing this after what's left of this summer. We'll have one last hoorah when we get back. Then I'll get a roommate when you start up fall classes."

She talked like we were headed home tomorrow or something, and had the whole of summer ahead of us. I had a feeling it would be a bit more complicated than that. If I learned anything from playing Dungeons and Dragons with Judah, the bottom always dropped out just when you thought you had your hands on the jewels.

"I'll do my internship back home and get a job to help with the rent, then. You don't need to take a roommate."

"Honey, an internship *is* a job. It's an unpaid job, and you'll need to be available for that."

Draper held up his hands as we went back and forth,

confused. "Wait, I thought we already established I was coming to your world with you when this was all over. I'll get a job and pay half the rent. I'll take Rosie's room and keep it exactly how it is."

I grinned at him, loving how permanent it all felt. "That'll work. You won't mind my poster of Andre that I keep on the ceiling over my bed, right?" It was the one image Judah hadn't vetoed when we'd put the treasured space to a vote.

Draper blanched. "Um, I don't know who that is, but I don't want to come eyes to eyes with a man when I lay down."

"Seriously? You might change your mind when you see him. Andre's pretty handsome."

Draper snorted, the firelight dancing off his angular features, erasing the years of loneliness and abandonment. He looked younger, his shoulders rolled back as he leaned on his side, shuffling cards for the game I still didn't totally understand the rules of. It was a good thing I wasn't expected to be good at this new game; dyslexia made reading cards more of a chore than a relaxing pastime. I was pretty much just picking up a card and throwing it down at random.

Lane was contemplative, her eyebrows furrowed as she reasoned through everything. "I thought you were just saying things. Being impulsive. Draper, you don't want to leave Avalon for our world. You'd have to start all over."

He gave her a look like he'd been sucking on a lemon.

"Um, what life do you imagine I have here? I'll pack up everything I need and leave in a heartbeat to start over with you and Rosie. This isn't just for this adventure, me staying with you. I wasn't kidding. We're a family again, and I won't let us get separated."

Lane leaned over the pile of discarded hearts and squeezed Draper around the neck. "Oh, kid. You have no idea how much I love you. If you're sure, you can come live with us, no problem. I just want you to be absolutely sure. Our life... We don't have a castle. It's a big choice, so give it another few days to let it settle."

"No. I'm coming with you. That's not going to settle into any other decision. I love you. You're my mother. You took care of me when I was a boy, and now it's my turn to look after you."

I knew the fire that burned in Draper, to claim Lane and pretend that any life without her didn't exist. Draper and I were kindred spirits in that respect. My general rule of thumb was that the more a person loved Lane, the more I took a shine to them.

Lane quirked her eyebrow to me. "What do you say, babe? You up for having your old brother back?"

"Only if he can kill the more daring spiders," I ruled with a grin.

Draper leaned over and kissed my forehead, gripping the back of my head as if vowing something significant. "Anything you say, pumpkin."

Lane looked on the both of us as if she couldn't fit

another inch of love into her heart without it bursting with fruit flavor. From that moment on, the three of us were a family.

8

POSH SPICE

*I*n the morning, Draper had filled Lane's bag and mine with new dresses and even a couple of his shirts for me to sleep in. There was a rhythmic thumping coming from the floor below us, which happened often. I mean, it was a whorehouse. This time, two other rhythms started pounding themselves out, banging bedposts against the wall. The noises were accompanied by grunts and operatic screams of embellished delight.

Lot brought in a bowl of apples left over from breakfast to share with us. He'd had something to say when he first walked in, but he closed his mouth at the obvious sounds and smells of sex wafting in. He handed Lane an apple, and then started helping me shove the rest into the pack Draper had bought me.

Lane's teeth were set on edge. After the initial shock,

she'd been quiet about the whole whorehouse thing. I could tell Draper thought he'd gotten off easy, but I knew Lane. She was planning something.

"Draper, dear? Could you get me one of those sheer skirts your girls wear?" she asked as if she was requesting a tube of toothpaste. She shoved a few apples into her blue backpack, shooting me a look that told me to be cool and go with whatever she had in mind.

"Um, I guess. Why?"

"Rosie doesn't really have many skirts. I was thinking she could wear one, like your girls do."

Lot dropped an apple, letting it roll across the wood. His mouth fell open, and his gentlemanly demeanor was temporarily marred. "What did you just say?" he asked, his throat suddenly hoarse.

I tried to picture myself in the completely transparent gauzy skirts I'd seen on Draper's girls. They had tiny jingle bells at the hips so they made a Santa Claus sound when they walked by. It had been four days of Santa bells and heads banging on headboards. The thing about the skirts was they weren't really skirts. It was basically a matching pair of foot-wide pieces of see-through material that hung to the floor: one for in front and one for in back. They didn't wear any underwear or anything on top. It had been quite a culture shock. Maybe Lane meant for me to wear the skirt over jeans and a t-shirt or something? Maybe she was going to use the material to sew something awesome; she was pretty crafty. I looked down at my comfy freshly washed jeans and my purple Andre the Giant t-shirt, trying to picture how the skirt would look over the jeans.

I was confused, but Draper was horrified. "No. And why would you even ask me for that? She's your daughter!"

"Go get me one of those skirts, or I'll have to blow my cover and get one myself."

Draper stared hard at Lane. "What's your game here? Turn Rosie into a stripper? That's not her."

"Why shouldn't it be her? Is there something wrong with what you're doing here?" She jerked her thumb toward the door, her tone sharpening in that way I knew better than to argue. "Boy, go get me one of those skirts!"

Draper's eyes narrowed, and his wide, charming smile was a distant memory. He turned on his heel and left, coming back with a pink gauzy non-skirt. He clutched it in his hand and looked at me with dread, as if *he'd* rather be wearing it than see it on me.

I couldn't have agreed more.

"Draper!" a guy called from down the stairs. Draper had made a firm rule to his staff that they weren't to set foot on the top floor. The staff knew he had guests, but they'd only seen Remy, Bayard and Rousseau, who made themselves at home with the women downstairs.

Draper ignored the person calling his name. "This life isn't for either of you."

Lane snatched the skirt and shoved it into my arms. "Rosie, go behind the screen and put this on. Wear it just like the girls do downstairs. That's how you'll look on the road with us."

Draper and I paled in unison while Lot stammered incoherently. The others were in the second bedroom, and didn't witness this, thank goodness. "But Lane, I c-can't wear this!"

"Go on, baby. Your brother picked it out for you. Don't be ungrateful."

Draper clutched his forehead with one hand and his stomach with the other. "I'm going to be sick. Give me that." He yanked the skirt out of my hands and threw it into the fireplace, which hadn't been lit for the day yet. "No sister of mine will be caught dead in that skirt. You should know better than to joke like that, Laney."

"Oh, I'm not joking. If it's good enough for your girls, it's good enough for Rosie. You said the other day that you take care of your girls. Do you take care of them like you do Rosie?"

"What? No! I've been nothing but good to you and Rosie! I would never..."

She went to the fireplace and fished out the skirt, brushing off the soot and handing it to me. I blinked up at Draper, my mouth open like a guppy.

Lot moved toward the middle of the room to snatch the skirt out of my hands just as we heard heavy footsteps clomping down the hall toward us. Lot and Lane ducked behind the partition in a blink, but I was too stunned to move when the door swung open. I stood next to the bed, clutching the skirt in horror at being seen by someone who might out me and wreck the whole mission before it properly started.

Draper was livid as he whirled on the intruder. "I said no one was to come on the third floor! Get downstairs, Clovis."

Clovis had dark skin and black hair he wore tied up in a bun like a ballerina. He wore the same dark, smudgy makeup around his eyes like I'd seen on a few of the girls when we'd snuck in. Clovis' gaze fell on me and he winced apologetically. "Oh! I didn't realize you were breaking in a new girl." He looked me up and down appraisingly. "She'll do well. Nice and young. Good thinking to find one who looks a little like Morgan le Fae. They'll pay top coin to give it to her." Clovis' gaze combed downward over my body, giving me the creeps. "Amazing tits. Adelaide's got some competition now. Send her over to me once you're done."

Draper was purple with rage. I feared he might explode if I didn't act quickly. He made to charge at Clovis and strangle him, but I ran to cut him off, popping my hand to his chest and giving him a look that told him to back down. I looked over my shoulder, hating myself as my mouth opened. "Sure. I'll go see you once Draper's finished training me."

"What's your name, sugar?"

"I'm Posh. Posh Spice." I winced at the first name that popped into my head.

Clovis jerked his thumb over his shoulder. "We've got an Untouchable downstairs. Link the Terrifying, from Éireland. If we can get him to take an interest in her, he might stay for a while. That'd be good for business, boss. People love to gawk at the Untouchables. Whoever Link chooses, the regulars will pay double for just to say they bedded the same woman as an Untouchable." Clovis looked me up and down appreciatively once more, and then adjusted his britches none too subtly. "Link wasn't taking to any of the girls, but if we offer him a crack at this little piece, he might stick around."

"Posh Spice is not available. Out." Draper barely worked the simple command from his lips before he slammed the door in Clovis' face. His hands were shaking as he cupped my cheeks to make sure I heard every word he whispered. "You are not my whore!" He gave a slight jerk to my cheeks with every syllable. "Don't you ever put on that skirt. Don't you ever pretend that."

I looked up into his horrified and broken expression, not bothering to hold back my anxiety. "You were about to yell at him for saying your sister's got nice tits. You can't do that. I have to stay hidden. It's better I'm your whore than they figure out who I really am."

Draper closed his eyes, his hands migrating to the back of my head to pull me in for a tight hug that crushed the air out of me. "You're breaking my heart, pumpkin."

"Better that than Morgan take me away from you. That's what she'll do if she finds out I'm here."

Lane and Lot moved out from behind the partition. Lot had a look of extreme disapproval, mingled with a "Whew! That was a close one" gust of relief.

Lane was angry, but quiet about it. "Now do you see how messed up your life here is? Do you get how awful it is, what you're doing? Every girl down there might have a brother who's ready to fight to the death any guy who looks at their sister and says 'nice tits.' Poor Damond had to do who knows what just to get to see you. Your sister had to turn herself into a whore to keep safe around you. Is that what you want for them? Is that what you want for you?" She moved to Draper and touched her heart. "Know who you are, son. I know you, and this life isn't it."

Draper pointed to the door. "Gather the others and go down to the stables. I can't even look at you. Putting Rosie through that just to teach me a lesson? You made your point, but you used your daughter to get there. That's low, Laney. *You* should know who *you* are. I know you, and using Rosie like that isn't you."

This seemed to strike a chord with Lane. "Draper, that's not what I..."

Draper was livid. "Just go! We'll be down in a minute."

"We'll meet you in the barn." Lane left with Lot, her tail between her legs.

Draper waited until the door shut before he sat on the edge of his bed, letting out a heavy sigh that felt like it started from his toes and had about twenty-one years of stress laced in it. "It's all messed up, isn't it."

I softened, moving to stand before him. I put my hands on his shoulders to steady the poor guy, and jerk him out of the funk he was falling into. "Hey, it's just a little off-track. Nothing that's not fixable." Though as I said this, I wasn't sure it was true.

"You have to understand, I thought you and Lane were dead! There wasn't any reason to be more, to try harder."

I tapped my chest, recalling the thousands of times Lane had done this exact speech on me. "Know who you are, Draper. Look at your life and make sure you belong in it. If you don't, then do something to fix what's broken."

He gave a dry laugh. "You sound like Lane."

"Yeah? Well, she raised me, so there's no jumping off that ship."

He looked up at me, utterly lost. His hair was messy to match his disheveled life. I smoothed back the wayward follicles, and then touched his nose as if he was the younger brother, and I was the much wiser, older sister. "How do I fix this?" he asked quietly.

I bent over so I was eye level with him. "You shut it down. Shut the whole place down and come with us."

I could see his hesitance at being caught in a tough spot. "Couldn't I just come with you and leave the place with Clovis?"

"You think he'd give me a job? I'm a decent dancer." I did the Running Man just to make him smile. "Clovis hasn't broken me in yet, but I've got nice tits. I think I'd fit in okay here."

He scowled at me. "Stop it. Don't even joke like that."

"Shut it down," I repeated, pausing my dance. I was resolute that my new brother wouldn't be king of selling women to make a profit. "Shut it all down."

Draper leaned forward from his spot as I straightened. He rested his temple to my stomach, and hugged my hips as if I was precious to him. "Okay, Posh Spice. I'll do it."

WITHOUT DADDY

$\mathcal{B}$ayard was grouchy, which is to say, business as usual. He always got a little crabby when he was hungry, so I made sure to bring all the extra apples and rolls I could stuff into my bag. "I can't believe this is the best plan you guys could think of. You're all idiots."

Draper and I were the last to arrive, so I wasn't totally sure what they were fighting about. It was Bayard, so, you know, it could've been anything. Draper kept my hand in his like a security blanket, but stepped forward and held up his free arm to garner everyone's attention. "Argue later. I shut the doors to the business, and Clovis is sending the girls back to their families. The regulars will be coming in soon, and we should be gone before it gets ugly. Let's go."

Bayard's arms were crossed over his chest as he stood next to his horse (who was only slightly less hairy than he). Their chestnut shagginess matched, which I thought was cute. "That's the thing. We don't actually know where we're going."

"Oh, right. This is the part where I'm supposed to Compass us right to Roland's front doorstep, huh. Could anyone tell me a little bit about him? Like, any detail might help. If I know what I'm looking for, that usually gives my green light a tap."

Reyn looked infinitely better since he'd stopped using his magic. He was a little jumpier, but he looked himself again. "Roland's got your color hair, Rosie, only it's shorter, like mine. He's obsessed with wagons; always trying to get his to move faster, more efficiently, hold more stuff. He lived in the Province 4 palace. He was always tinkering with stuff, fixing things that the servants could've just for the fun of it." He smiled, and the fond memory looked good on him. "This one time, Bastien, Roland and I were trying to get across the lake so Roland could meet some important merchant from another province, and we were running late. Roland got out of the boat in his full royal gear, dove into the water and swam, saying he was a faster swimmer than Bastien was a paddler." Reyn chuckled at the mental picture I could see clear enough. "He beat us to the other end, too. The merchant was not quite as impressed, but Roland didn't care. He's stubborn, and usually sticks to a path once he's on it."

Lot chimed in, "Dogged, actually. Whether he's right or wrong, he'll fight to the death. We were all shocked that

Morgan was able to convince him to give up his throne for the Forgotten Forest."

Reyn scratched Hamish's neck, who poked his head up from Reyn's breast pocket. "Does that help?"

My gut started pulling me east, so I took that as a sign. "Yeah. Now, I've never done this Compass thing for real before, so be cool if I get it wrong. I'm trying my best."

Lot tied his pack to his saddle. "Where's Bastien? It's time we left."

Reyn went to open his mouth, but I beat him to it. "Bastien left. He's not coming with us any farther."

Despite the moderate levels of hurry everyone had until then, they all stopped and stared at me, all except Reyn, who didn't look all that surprised. Reyn held my gaze. "I'll go find him. He's probably just blowing off some steam at a pub. He's used to living alone. Needs his space sometimes. He always comes back, though."

I ignored Lane's hand on my back, meant to soothe me. I kept my chin high and my eyes clear of any crushed schoolgirl emotion. "What a nice luxury, to be able to ditch the mission on a whim. He told me he was out, and it's been four days. Anyone seen him lately?" I looked around at the grim expressions. "That's what I thought. Let's shift it, fellas."

"I thought he was at least checking in with you," Lot said, voicing what everyone else was thinking. Only Lane, Draper and probably Reyn knew enough of the whole story not to be too confused. "You two seemed so close. I can't believe he'd just leave the group like that. Searching for you was his idea! He's been obsessed with finding Roland for over a year. Now he wants out? Now that we've got the Compass and might actually find Roland? It makes no sense."

"*I can guess what's going on,*" Remy said knowingly. "*You two had a fight, and either you pushed him away or he ran out when it got tough. Which was it?*"

"It's fine, Remy. Everyone, this is what Bastien wants. This isn't his responsibility. Roland's my cousin, so finding him is my job. Bastien can do whatever he wants with his life, and he wants to be away from this scene. Respect it. Any of you are welcome to the same easy out whenever you like." I went to grab Abraham Lincoln to hand him to Lane once she got situated on the horse she was mounting, but he backed away.

"*Daddy! Where's my daddy? I need my daddy!*"

I steeled my mushy insides, willing myself not to devolve into a puddle of emotions. "Bastien's not your daddy, and he's not coming with us."

"*My daddy!*" He moaned, letting out a howl that made Draper wince.

"We really have to go," Draper reminded me, pulling his tall gray horse out of its stall. The others were either on their horses or almost there, and I was having an argument with a bear, who behaved like a toddler.

"Look, we're all leaving. Bastien's probably gone home now. I can't get him for you, and he's not coming back." I knelt down and hugged Abraham Lincoln while he whimpered, echoing the sadness of abandonment I tried not to feel.

"I have to find him! I won't go without him!"

I pulled back, blinking in surprise. "Well, then you can stay here by yourself and try to find him, but that's the tune of it. Either come with me or go off on your own. It's your choice." I couldn't believe my eyes when Abraham Lincoln walked away from me, circled three times and laid on the floor, his head resting on his paws like he was watching TV and waiting for something good to come on. "But... But, I'm your mama!" I said quietly, remaining on my knees a few meters away.

"I won't leave without my daddy."

First Bastien walked out, and now Abraham Lincoln was jumping ship. The gut-punch hit me harder than I'd been expecting.

Lane's voice was calm through my heartbreak. "You have to let him go, hun. You've been through this before. Wild animals belong in the wild."

"But he's not leaving to go back to the wild! He's waiting for Bastien, and Bastien's not coming back." I forced the painful words out, flinching only slightly at the hard truth. I turned to Abraham Lincoln, staying on my knees to remain on his level. "He's not coming for us, buddy. He left us, and we have to move on."

Reyn was uneasy. "I think we should wait for him.

Bastien's always running off and then coming back once he's gotten some perspective."

"He's gone, and we're not waiting around for him to grace us with his presence." Lane's tone was clipped and finite, though she gave Reyn an apologetic bow of her head for overruling him so definitively. "We're going. Leave Abraham Lincoln, Rosie. He'll be fine."

"He'll be heartbroken when Bastien never comes for him!"

"And somehow, he'll survive the heartbreak. That's how this kind of thing goes, baby girl." She tapped her chest, reminding me to remember who I was, and that being dumped smack in the middle of my first kiss didn't change the important things about me. Then she and Reyn gave me identical looks laced with pity, so I knew it was time for me to suck it up. I hated that she'd told Reyn my dirt, but at least he didn't ask any questions about the drama.

Hamish scurried down from Reyn's pocket and jumped on top of his furry friend, telling him he would miss him and pretty much hitting me in the gut with all the sweetness. Then he ran back up to Reyn, ready to move on far quicker than I was. He had the attention span of, well, a squirrel.

"Come now, pumpkin. Up you get." Draper watched the exchange between my bear and I, studying my reaction and the connection no one but me, Lane and Judah totally understood. Draper was soft with me when I was on the verge of leaning toward broken. I've found that no matter what world you're in, the bad things could be fixed if only there were more people who valued softness.

Maybe Bastien could've understood my quirks, but he was gone. I'd cried once the night Bastien left in the quiet and solitude of Draper's bedroom, and that was all I would allow myself. Anything more would be more than he deserved.

I stood and walked to my bear with heavy feet, giving him one last hug and kiss before turning my back on him and walking away. Lane blew my bear a kiss and rolled him an apple to tide him over. He hadn't had to go hunting all that much since he started living with us.

Everyone was lined up at the stable door, waiting for Draper to help me onto his horse. My new brother hoisted me up, being quiet to respect my sadness. Then he got on the saddle behind me. Bayard rode out first in plain view of the villagers who passed by. They looked confused that their favorite tension release was closed that morning.

Seven was perched on Lot's shoulder, and kept up a steady stream of angst that her former master would see her once they went out into the open. I called out to her once we veered down a road without foot traffic. "It's okay, Seven. Your old master's dead. Lot knows to cover your ear if he hears any other flutes playing. No big deal. Just stick with Lot, or you'll be seen."

Draper shifted his weight behind me on the horse, hugging me close as he gripped the reins with both hands, encasing me in that cozy feeling of protection you need when you're about to fall apart. He was good like that. Though we were still getting to know each other, Draper let me lean on him. As I rested against his chest while he rode us slowly through the town, I realized that though I was leaving behind bits of me I wished I could take on the journey, having someone to lean on through the transition was a small miracle I was wise enough not to be ungrateful for. When I winced at Abraham Lincoln's heartbroken roar in the distance, Draper nudged his cheek to mine. "It's alright, pumpkin. Everything will work out in the end."

"What if you're wrong?"

"Then it must not be the end."

I knew he was making stuff up to pacify me, but I decided to believe him as much as I was able.

When we reached the edge of the city with no real upset, Bayard drove his horse forward in a run, his tail flapping out with the beast's, and floating through the air like a chestnut waterfall. Draper snapped the reins and set us for the open road, out toward the east where I prayed my gut wasn't leading me over a cliff.

10

AVALON'S WOLF YETI

When the sun fell over the horizon, I was exhausted. The others were hungry, so we broke for dinner. "I think we should set up camp here for a while. There's no point traveling in the dark through those woods." Lot motioned to the thick mess of trees we were gearing up to cross through. It had been mostly open fields all day.

Rousseau dismounted, tied his horse to a tree near the narrow stream that separated us from the woods, and stretched his arms over his head. "That's fine. I'll take Desiree into the woods to see if she can't find some food for us. No use plowing through the apples if there's game around."

"Desiree?" Damond asked, touching his toes to stretch out his back after he dismounted.

Rousseau pointed to Seven. "The bird. I thought she

should have a proper name."

Draper slid off the tall horse like it was nothing and held his arms out for me. I quirked my head toward Rousseau. "She told me her name's Seven."

Rousseau let out a derisive exhale. "Seven's her number. These birds are soldiers to the army, not pets. Seeing as she's not enslaved no more, I thought she might like a name." He stroked her leathery feathers, marveling at the black beauty. "Had a lady friend by the name of Desiree a long time ago. She was lovely, smart. If I could take anyone on a long ride, it woulda been her."

"What happened to her?" I asked, though I knew I shouldn't. I slid down into Draper's arms, giving him a squeeze after my feet hit the ground. He was tense, and kept looking at the woods with a wary expression.

Rousseau kept his eyes on the bird under the darkening sky, the blue moon lending itself to storytelling and waxing poetic. He pulled out his panpipes and blew a few notes that instantly pushed a wave of calm over me. I watched the bird's wings relax, too. He pulled the pipes from his lips to study the effect the simple few notes had on Desiree. "The Queen's Army happened. They took her crops as a tax – *all* her crops – and when she tried to stand up to them, they knocked her down." His eyes were far away as the others quietly took their canteens out to refill in the stream. "That's the thing about the ones worth holding on to. Nothing gets them down, so she got back up. Fought hard until they knocked her down again. If I'd been there, I would've told her to stay down, but then she wouldn'ta been my Desiree, and I wouldn't miss her as much as I do." He nuzzled bird-Desiree with his cheek. "I almost wish she was forgettable. Would make everything loads easier."

Bayard coughed twice in a "dude, you're killing the fun" kind of way. Rousseau glared at Bayard, and then went back to his panpipes. He cleared his throat and wiped off the tips of the small wooden pipes, giving Desiree stern instruction not to be afraid of the instrument that could control her. Despite the gruff demeanor I thought to be permanent, Rousseau was sweet to the bird. After all she'd been through? A little sweetness was exactly what Desiree needed. Though he perpetually smelled like fresh farts, she bumped her feathers to his hairy cheek affectionately.

Rousseau set off to go into the woods, but Draper stopped him. "You can't go in there. None of us can. We'll go around."

I couldn't even see the sides of the woods to gauge how long a trip that would make this. Lot voiced what Remy and I were wondering. "Why can't we go into the woods?"

"That's the Désespéré Woods. The Gévaudan lives there."

The many gasps and hesitant steps backward informed me of the only logical conclusion: the Gévaudan was some sort of Yeti Boogeyman.

"Then we go around," Lot ruled. "I'll not try my luck against that. It'll be a few extra days to travel the long way, but we'll arrive with our heads still on. In the end, that's what matters."

"Then we shouldn't stop long. Let's eat and keep moving through the night," Bayard suggested, leading his horse to the stream to drink.

Something felt wrong about that plan, but I didn't know enough about anything going on to be able to voice my opinion. I drank a bit of my water and refilled my canteen with Damond, who wouldn't take his eyes off the Désespéré Woods even as he dipped his canteen into the stream. "I don't like being this close to the Gévaudan. We should hurry." He got up and went back to his horse. We'd all been grateful to get off our mounts, but now they were itching to ride again only a few minutes later.

Even Lane looked worried as she peered into the woods. "Rosie, stay with Draper. I mean it. Draper, don't leave her side."

I was alone at the stream, I realized. Everyone else was getting ready to ride through the night after they watered their horses. "Hurry up, Rosie," Bayard called over his shoulder without looking at me. "You don't want to be so far from your horse when the Gévaudan comes looking for a fresh kill."

I screwed the cap back on my canteen and stood to find Draper standing right behind me, his hands at the ready, like a goalie preparing to be fired at. "Dude, I've got no idea what a Gévaudan is. I'm guessing we don't invite him to our little tea party?"

Bayard steered his horse over to me, squaring his shoulders and puffing out his chest, as if I needed to be intimidated by him. "The Gévaudan is a wolf that tears out the throats of its victims. It lives in those woods and hibernates until it smells fresh prey." He gave me a dark look that was laced with a bit of his loathing for me and my apparent higher position than his. *Whatever.* "The Gévaudan will take one whiff of your little princess blood and come running for you. Some bodies are found with their heads torn clean off."

Draper glowered at Bayard. "Do you have to put it like that?"

"Like what? The truth? Why not? You might coddle her, but I don't have to. Now that Bastien's gone, there's no need to pretend to get along. We'll do the job and go our separate ways."

"A wolf? That's what we're dealing with? Can't I just talk to him? Maybe ask him to let us pass?"

Lane spoke up, already on her horse with Reyn, and ready to go. "No, Rosie. Bayard's calling it a wolf, but it's really not. It's bigger than an elephant, and it's not a normal animal. It's a monster, and as good as your abilities work on animals, I won't gamble whether or not they'll work on a monster by testing it out on Gévaudan. We'll go around."

"Okay." Everyone was ready to go, except for me. Draper lifted me up, but I couldn't tell my leg to hook over the horse. It felt wrong somehow. "Hey, put me down for a second." Draper obliged, but I could tell he didn't want to.

"We should get going, Rosie. The Gévaudan doesn't come out of the woods, but it's still a risk we're taking, being so close like this. He'll be able to smell us a mile away."

With my feet planted firmly in the grass, I shook my head, unable to make myself obey. "Guys? I don't know how to explain it, but we can't go around the woods. That whole Compass thing? I think it's telling me we have to go straight through." I pointed to the exact spot we needed to enter the woods. "Right there, actually."

This broke out a steady stream of protests and arguments, none of which I was willing to engage in.

I held up my hands. "Look, you all brought me in on this to tell you where to go. I'm not saying it's a good idea; I'm saying it's where we need to go to find Roland. Take it or leave it, but I'm not defending my gut any more than that. It's never been wrong before."

The others argued, while Draper pulled me aside. "Rosie, what you're asking us to do is beyond dangerous. We might all die in there. Horrible, gruesome deaths." He put both his hands on my shoulders. "I don't want to doubt you, but I've got to know, how sure is this Compass thing?"

I looked up into his eyes apologetically. "I don't know exactly. I only just learned it was a legit gift when I got into Avalon. But my whole life, if I wanted to find something, there it was. I don't need maps, but it's kind of more than that." I lowered my voice, digging deeper into the things I'd tried not to examine too closely. "This one time when I was in junior high, I overheard Lane begging the landlord to give us a few more days to come up with the rent. She was crying, and it was awful. I felt that tug in my gut." I slapped my abdomen. "I snuck out my window and went on a walk wherever it led me. I just so happened upon a hundred dollar bill." I remembered the shock and the glee of that day. "Then I felt another pull in a different direction, and I walked for a bit and found a twenty. Then the same thing brought me to a few more bills, some change, and by the time I got home at dawn and snuck back in, I'd found enough to pay our rent and buy groceries to fill the cupboard." I smiled at the memory. "That was a good day. I think I scared Lane a little. Scared myself. So I know what I'm saying sounds crazy, and I'm not thinking it's a great idea or totally safe or anything, but that's where my gut's pulling me. Take it or leave it."

Draper studied my face in the moonlight, and I let him, not looking away or trying to hide myself from the scrutiny. "If you're sure this is where we need to go, then okay. I'll follow you to my death, if that's what's needed."

I butted the crown of my head to his sternum, banding my arms around my stomach. Somehow we'd gotten to the place where that felt natural. "I don't understand how you can say giant things like that. This is what it's like to have a brother?"

I could hear the slight smile in Draper's reply. "No. This is what it's like to have me."

The others started listening in to our conversation, so I took a small step back and chose my words carefully. "Why don't I go in by myself? If it's this dangerous, I don't want to get everyone killed. How about I travel through while you guys go around, and I'll meet you on the other side?"

This did nothing to ease the tension. Draper frowned, standing straighter and crossing his arms over his chest. "Absolutely not. You're not to be out of my sight. The last time I took my eyes off you, I lost you for twenty-one years. I won't make the same mistake again. You're my responsibility."

"Splitting into two teams isn't a bad idea," Rousseau commented, looking around the group and then to the woods warily. "If the gems and Roland are in the woods, then she can bring him out to us on the other side. No point in us all going."

"Two teams, then?" Lot suggested. "Draper's most familiar with the area, so he can lead one team."

Draper postured, his voice seeming to deepen a few notes. "I'll lead the team with Rosie straight through the woods. All other royalty should take the long route around. If anything goes sideways on this, I don't want a kingdom falling because of it." He held up his hands at the protests from Damond and Lot. "Say what you want, but beyond honor and all that, most of you have got a whole province that depends on you being alive. If you die,

Morgan might absorb your land. The whole point of this is to defeat Morgan, not hand the lands over to her on a silver platter."

That seemed reasonable to me, but Lane, Lot and Damond had something to say about it. "I'm not leaving my daughter," she said, resolute. "Or my son."

Remy moved to stand beside Damond. *"He's a boy, Rosie. Don't let him go into the woods."*

I spoke up, "Damond can lead the second team. He led us to Draper, so I know he can handle leading the group. Can you make sure you all make good time, Damond? Our journey's shorter, so you guys will have to ride kinda quick."

Draper exhaled, and Damond seemed slightly mollified since he was heading up a team, and not kicked out of the cool kids' club for not being old enough. "I can do that."

"Everyone take your teams, and let's go," Bayard complained. "Moving through the woods with no light will be tricky enough. We won't be able to take the horses in. The trees are too close together, and no one can see well enough to make sure the horses can navigate."

I batted my lashes up at Bayard. "Does that mean your charming mouth is coming with us?"

"Like I'll leave an asset unprotected. You're going to be the death of me, Rosie. Here's hoping I get in a few good jabs before that day comes."

Internally I groaned. Bayard was such a pill. "Awesome. Let's go, then."

Lot hopped off his horse and stood before me, gearing up to say his piece privately. "If I'm being sent away with the other group, I want you to take my sword." He pulled out his giant sword that went up to my waist. When he handed it to me by the ornately decorated hilt, I grimaced. I could barely hold it correctly; it was so long and heavy. I handed it back, shaking my head. "Look, thanks, but I'm alright. It's a little too big for me. I can't really use that thing, and you might need it."

He took the sword back and pulled a dagger from his belt. "Take this, then." He closed my fingers around it, pulling me closer to look into my eyes with his Prince Charming smolder that made me bite my lower lip. His voice was quiet as he instructed me. "If you come across the monster, show no mercy. Don't hesitate to gut him if you can. Running will do you no good in these woods." He jerked the dagger in my hands toward his flat stomach. "Stick him and tear upwards." He moved the dagger slowly up toward his clavicle.

"Stick and rip? I think I can remember that."

Lot shook his head. "It doesn't feel right, leaving you."

"I won't let you get hurt if I can help it, so go with Damond. Make sure the whole group gets there without anything bad happening. You don't want to know how many times killer flamingos from outer space come down out of nowhere and attack."

He cracked a small smile. "I'll be on the lookout for such harrowing assaults."

Lane tried to dismount to go over to our group that was going on foot, but Reyn grabbed her from behind, holding her tight in the saddle. "Where you go, I go," he said like a vow.

She was hesitant, but quietly said her piece that I tried not to overhear. "You can't, Reyn. Think of your condition. We might come across the Gévaudan. Then what?"

Reyn's tongue ran over his teeth, his anger evident. "Just because my magic is broken doesn't mean my sword is. I can fight alongside anyone just as good as the next man. I won't leave you. So either we both go through the woods, or we both go around."

Draper held up his hand. "You'll both go around. As much as the thought of you leaving for even an hour scares me, I know you won't abandon Rosie. I know you'll come through for her and meet us on the other side." He didn't say it like a bitter jab, but Lane looked gutted all the same. "You're royalty, whether you like it or not. Whether you sit on a throne or not. If we don't make it, you have to find a way to take Morgan down and unite the provinces. You're one of the only people I know who stand a chance at being able to deliver on that."

"No, Draper! You're my children."

Draper's rebuttal was calm, as one who understood he would win the fight. "The people need someone to rally around, and we all know it's you. You're the sister who lived. You're the sister who stole something valuable from the queen. You bested Morgan le Fae. They need you."

Her passion came out as fury, but I knew it stemmed from her broken heart. "I won't leave you! I won't leave my daughter! I won't send the two people I love most in the world straight for the Gévaudan without me there to make sure you get out okay!"

Draper kept his voice low and steady. "You don't have a choice. Either go with the others, or I'll tie you to a horse myself and send it off. You have a kingdom to think about. Royalty goes around, non-royals go through."

There was much heated back and forth I tried to distance myself from. The thought of leaving Lane always brought about a small amount of panic in me, but the idea of her lying in the woods with her throat torn out was unthinkable. I was on whatever side kept her safe, even if it meant I wouldn't be under her wing for a time.

Remy checked my leg to make sure it was up for the task, marveling on the good job he did, considering how much trauma my body had been through. I could walk just fine now, and while I didn't expect to be running down soccer fields anytime soon, I felt confident my leg was nearly good as new, which was a relief of epic proportions.

"I've never seen the Gévaudan before, but I was once brought a man who'd been torn apart by one. Not sure what they expected me to be able to do; the man was dead long before he reached me. We must be careful as we move through the woods."

"'We'? No, Remy. You need to go with the others."

Remy's face soured. *"I'm not royalty. A kingdom doesn't depend on my survival."*

"Lane needs a doctor she can trust." I kept my eyes on the middle button of his shirt and shook my head slowly from side to side. "And I need to know you're safe, far from the monsters."

Remy softened. *"No, no. That's not how this works. I'm the knight, remember? I'm to protect you."*

"Not this time. It's my turn to be the knight, and protect you. Go with Lane." I tried to keep the quiver out of my voice, and failed worse than a hippo trying to attempt ballet. "I need someone I trust to take care of my mom. You have to keep her safe, Remy. If she doesn't live through the mission, I won't be... I can't..." I shoved my hands into my pockets and kept my head down. "I just can't."

Remy's thoughts flickered through his mind, varying from awed to arguing. Finally he landed on falling in line. *"If that's what you wish, then I'll do as you ask. I'll protect Duchess Elaine with my life. But know that you only have to ask, and my sword would defend you, no matter where you led."*

Remy gave me words of wisdom that were, let's face it, a little obvious. Run from the monster, stay with Draper and Bayard, keep my footsteps light in the woods – stuff like that. I cut his advice short by throwing my arms around his neck, pulling him close. I knew it was weird for his culture, but I didn't care. I heard him splutter before landing on a soothing, *"There, there. It's alright, Princess. I'll see you again in just a few days.*" He pointed to the east while keeping me in his arms. "*Do you see that? That's where the sun will come up. By the time the sun rises in three days, I'll be back by your side, sweet girl.*"

"And then we'll talk each other's ears off?"

Remy swallowed, looking down at me with unfathomable affection for someone I'd only known barely a month. "*I'll miss having anyone hear me like you do. It'll be hard to go through the journey without a voice. I look forward to the sunrise three days from now, when I'll be back by your side again.*"

"Me, too. Be safe, and make sure Hamish stays with Reyn. Don't let him go scampering off after us." I hugged Remy once more before giving Rousseau a perfunctory one-armed hug we both muscled our way through. When I gave him a light squeeze, he farted, so I knew I was making him nervous with my embrace. Damond got a big hug I could tell he needed, but was too well-bred to ask for. I moved on to Lane so that Draper could pull his brother aside for some last-minute love and instruction.

"I can't leave you," Lane insisted, tears shining in her green eyes. She was still in the saddle, encased in Reyn's arms. I couldn't tell if he was being sweet to her, or prepping to restrain her in case she tried to run after me.

I kicked my toe at the grass and shoved my hands back into my pockets. "You said the same thing when you dropped me off at college freshman year."

"Yeah, and I stayed with you that whole first week! And

that was just college! This is literally life and death, and I'm being sent away by my own kids?"

"If it was the other way around, no way would you let me come. Draper's right; you're important to Avalon."

"What if I don't want to be important to Avalon? What if I only want to be important to you? What if I want to take you, Reyn and Draper to Common so we can watch bad romantic comedies and make nachos?" I noticed Reyn's arms tightening around her at being included in her shiny fantasy day.

I looked at her with all the love I had in my heart. "That's your idea of paradise? That's your perfect day?"

"Of course it is. My guy, my son, my best friend and nacho cheese. What more could a girl want?"

"I love you. When this is all over, I'll do whatever I can to give you that perfect day. A whole lifetime of them. I'll move back closer to home and finish school there so we can be together."

Lane closed her eyes as she held onto the horn of the saddle. Reyn rubbed soothing circles into her back, giving me a look that told me he was grateful I was sending her away. There was too much emotion and longing jerking Lane around, teasing her with a life I could tell she wanted so badly, but knew she might never get. "I want that, Rosie. I want all of it."

I wrapped my arms around her leg that dangled off the horse, and she sobbed. "Then that's what you'll get. I'll make sure of it. I'll put it on your Christmas list and make sure Santa comes through for you this time." My eyes landed on Reyn. "Though something tells me you've been more naughty than nice, Mrs. Robinson."

Lane laughed through her tears as she leaned down to grip my head to her calf. "It's just a few nights apart. Your Compass has never been off before. It wouldn't lead you straight into danger." She was pep-talking herself more so than me. "I love you, Ro."

"I love you, Lane." She gripped my head tighter, crying in Reyn's arms while I tried to hold in my tears. I didn't want her to see how scared I actually was.

"Screw Avalon! Screw it all! You're my girl. You're my world." She shook her head, and my shoulders fell. I knew the resolve that crackled in her chartreuse eyes. It was like embers of a fire that needed only the slightest provocation to burn the house down. She'd used that same steel on the principal when he'd tried to fail me in the second grade. And the third. "No. I'm going with you, and that's the end of it." She twisted on the saddle to face Reyn, her hand up. "You'll go with them. If we die, someone's got to find Roland, and you know him better than anyone."

I moved away from the onslaught of emotion and arguing that Reyn and Lane devolved into. I wasn't so great at the public romance stuff, but it turns out Lane was. She kissed him so good and hard, I all but ran to Draper's side, staring at my shoes to hide my discomfort. Judah and Jill did the public kiss every now and again, but it was nothing like the Scarlet O'Hara sweeping makeout that Reyn and

Lane invoked to interrupt their squabble. Intense. I had to escape it.

Despite what we were about to go do, Draper chuckled at my squirm, pinching my cheek as if I was three and wore pigtails like a uniform. "Aw, that's cute. I guess part of you is still young. That's nice to know. Thought I'd missed your whole trip to adulthood."

"Dude, I'm twenty-two. When I'm fifty-two, I'll still feel the same way about the public tongue tango nonsense."

Draper wrapped his arm around my head, bringing me into an embrace where he could squeeze my cranium with both his arms, pressing my forehead to his chest. "Oh, Rosie. You won't always feel that way about getting swept off your feet."

Judging by how my first kiss had gone down, I didn't have much hope that Draper knew what he was talking about.

Reyn took his opportunity and cracked the reins, driving them away from us while Lane howled for him to let her stay with me. It broke my heart to turn away from her pain, but it was for the best. If Lane was safe, then I could walk into the monster's lair with a little more swagger.

11

SHARKNADO WITH DRAPER

It's a funny thing, walking into the woods you know there's a distinct possibility you might die in. It screws with your gut. My stomach was churning, making my internal Compass harder to follow. A few times I had to stop and close my eyes, centering myself before taking another step.

Bayard gave a dramatic exhale, his horse tail kicking up in frustration. "I thought you were supposed to know where you were going. This is what we get for putting our faith in a child with no magical training or aptitude."

"Dude, how about we tie you to a tree and see how much you beg for my magical aptitude after that? Come to think of it, that's not a bad idea. It would draw the Gévaudan out and give him a little hairy snack to distract him while we find Roland and the gems."

"Hilarious. I can tell you have no friends up in

Common, or they would've told you how annoying your sorry attempt at humor is."

"Oh, I wasn't joking," I said as I started walking a little to the right, stepping over knotted roots. They looked like dead green fingers and thick garden hoses sprouting up from the ground. Though I'd seen my fair share of Avalon trees by now, it still amazed me that they were scaly and green from root to tip, as if armoring themselves from all Avalon had inflicted upon them. I held up my hand to help Draper over one of the roots that looked like a real ankle-breaker. "What I wouldn't give for some duct tape. That stuff works wonders. It could keep you tied to the tree for days. Rain, snow, doesn't matter. Maybe I'd take your sword. You know, give it a good workout. My hair's getting a bit long. Maybe I could use it for that."

Bayard blanched. "You're joking again. I hate it when you do that."

"No, seriously. I usually keep my hair an inch or so shorter."

Bayard touched the hilt of his sword that hung on his belt. "Look, Princess, this sword has seen battles that would make you scream out during that precious little sleep you seem to need so much of. It wasn't meant for use as a little girl's toy."

"Fine. Then I'll use it for art. When you're tied to the tree with duct tape, saving all our lives by being the bait, I'll take your sword and make sure it's camouflaged so the wolf doesn't see it. I'll paint it different shades of green and put some flowers on it so it blends well. Do you have a preference on which kind of flower I should tape to your sword? I'll let you pick."

Bayard grumbled, knowing that as much hatred as he spewed at me, I had about ninety pounds per square inch of BS to match him.

Draper's voice was quiet, but steady. "Alright, kids. Settle down. Maybe we should be quieter, so the Gévaudan doesn't hear us coming a mile away."

"So no singing?" I asked with a dramatic frown.

"No singing, pumpkin."

"What about Lost and Forgotten? I can't believe you'd silence them. They're mine and Lane's favorite band. You should hear her rock *The Last I Saw of You*. She does a mean air guitar."

"After we find the gems and Roland, you can sing all you want."

"What if I started dancing, too?" I started a silly jig just to break the tension I could tell was eating at him.

Draper cast me a small smile. "Mute dancing is fine."

I put my hand on a trunk to balance as I climbed over a fallen tree that came up to my knees. "It's at least part wolf, right? He probably already knows we're here."

Draper held my hand to balance over the fallen tree. "She's right. We can only hope he's not hungry, or that he's found some other prey." His quieter voice set the low volume at which we were permitted to converse. "I think your back and forth with Lane is funny. You two sound exactly alike. Aside from the Commoner references, it feels like home." He helped me over the next obstacle nature had for us. "And I haven't felt at home in a long time."

We walked for at least an hour, listening to Draper's story of what we'd missed in the twenty-one years we were gone. Most of the references to places and people went over my head, and the stuff I understood was the part he'd already told us. I could tell he was giving us the PG version of how he'd landed himself in the Lost Village, cleaning it up for my sake. It was adorable how much he acted like I was a little child, watching his language and being extra careful with me. "What about you guys? I've been talking away. Tell me what your life is like now up in Common."

I filled in more color to the basics we'd already told him. Lane was a personal trainer, and I was in college. It was all the basic job interview stats until Draper asked about my friends, wanting the backdoor sneak peek into my oh-so-glamorous life. "I live with my best friend in a tiny apartment off-campus." I tapped my heart. "I miss Judah pretty bad still. You'll love him. Totally good guy."

"You live with a man?" Draper inquired, his eyebrow raised in unveiled disapproval.

"Sure. It's nothing to the dozen or so women you were living with, but you've got to start your brothel some-where," I joked. When Draper did not seem to cotton on that I was kidding about renting Judah out to the highest bidder, I toned down my humor a little. "I'm only kidding. Judah's great. Nothing to worry about. He's got a girlfriend." I grimaced, wondering if that was still true, or if Jill had kicked him to the curb when he showed up days late to their anniversary without a ring.

"That sounds... complicated. Commoner life seems quite different than Avalon."

"It is. Some things are better, some things are worse. Wait until I introduce you to root beer floats. You'll be all, 'Rosie, you're the most amazing creature on the planet for showing me the wonders of your miraculous universe!' and I'll be all, 'Draper, you have no idea.' We'll spend a whole afternoon watching *Sharknado*, and then *Jaws*. Then we'll spend the evening at the beach, freaking ourselves out that we're going to get eaten alive by sharks in the water."

Draper's grin was wide. "That sounds pretty specific. You're already making plans for spending time with your old brother?"

"That's like, number thirty on my list of things to do together."

Draper reached for my hand, using it to pull me to his side. "Whatever you like, pumpkin. You keep making that list, and I'll make it my business in life to cross every event off, one by one. I'm in this. I'm permanent."

A smile that had too many kilowatts beamed across my face at his declaration that I would get to keep my new brother. "That's only the greatest thing you could've said to me."

His arm went around my shoulders and took on a

protective hold. I could tell that beneath his laughter, he was nervous at being in the Désespéré Woods. I wasn't used to the male affection he lavished on me. Judah and I were more into the fist bump than the snuggling. Though, admittedly, sometimes when we woke up, we found ourselves holding hands. Eye contact was avoided for a full five minutes during those mornings.

"You're firm on living with this Judah boy, then?"

"While I'm in school, yeah, but if I move back home, I'll stay with you and Lane. Though, Judah's pretty non-negotiable. When he moves back to stay with his mom for the summers, he usually spends at least five nights a week with Lane and me."

"Tell me more about this boy, Rosie. Make me feel better about the man in your bed."

I thought for a bit, flipping through the mental file I had on all the shenanigans Judah and I got up to over the years. "Well, there was this one time when a wicked tornado swept through our area, and we were both a little on edge. We were in the fourth grade and he was my tutor and my friend, but we were still getting the hang of each other. His mom was working late, locked in at the restaurant she waited tables at because all the roads were closed."

When Bayard asked for clarification on what a tornado was, I think I may have scared them a little too much with the truth. Apparently they didn't have tornadoes in Avalon. *Whoops.*

"You're saying whole houses literally get sucked into the sky?" Bayard gaped at me.

I made a face at my own misstep. I didn't want to scare Draper away. "People hardly ever get sucked into the sky. It's not something that happens all that often." I shot Draper a look of concern. "Please still come up to Common with us."

Draper's worry melted into an affectionate smile. "It'll take more than a tornado to take me away from you and Lane. Tell me more. I promise, you won't scare me off. I told you, I'm permanent."

I tried to remember where I was in the story as we made our way up a slight incline, Draper's arm right around me as we ducked under branches along the way. "After a quick phone call from the restaurant, Lane bolted across the street through the storm and got Judah out of his house. She brought him over to our place to wait out the worst of the weather. We stayed up way too late listening to the news to make sure it passed before we turned in our jeans for PJs." I remembered it all like it was yesterday. "Judah was scared. He was worried for his mom, and for so many things." When my timid hand had found Judah's in the dark after the power went out, he turned to me and started crying. I hated it when Judah cried. I would wrestle all the giant wolf creatures in the world if it would keep Judah from breaking down. Being a kid of a single parent ramped up the worry factor when a natural disaster kept you separated from your source of comfort. "I held him in my bed until he cried himself to sleep on my pillow. I didn't let go until the sun rose and his mom came to pry him out of my arms."

"How old were you?"

"I was twelve. Judah was eleven. He started sleeping over during school nights after that, so his mom could work double shifts and Lane could take us to school. Been inseparable ever since."

I didn't tell Draper about the times the kids in my class teased me for being stupid, and Judah was always the only voice who came to my defense. I returned the favor when a few jags started making anti-semitic jokes (I mean, seriously. This is the twenty-first century. Who even does that anymore?), and I came to his defense. It was my first suspension, and my only regret was that I'd had to stay at home for three days for fighting, and Judah'd had to go back to school and face those jackholes without me. You break one bully's nose, and everyone acts like you're a serial killer. *Whatever.* Lane never grounded me for it, and spent the three days I was suspended baking cookies for Judah with me. It was one of the many reasons I loved her. We threw him an "I Wish I was Judah" party when he came home from school, boosting him up when life got him down. My Judah costume was dead on. I'd even made myself glasses out of pipe cleaners.

I cleared my throat, hoping no one was messing with Judah for being bookish and sweet. College kids were better at leaving each other be, so I knew I didn't have much to worry about. "Judah's a great guy. Wouldn't have made it through school without him."

"I guess I won't have to beat on him, then, if it's as innocent as you claim."

Other than the extreme circumstances, I wasn't a hand-holder. Apparently Draper was. It was kind of nice. I'd never had a brother before, other than the one I'd made in Judah. I was determined not to screw this up. If Draper was a hand-holder, then I would get on board with that. I squeezed his hand just to assure him I was good at being a little sister. He bought it, and gave me a smile to cover over his growing fear at traipsing through the Désespéré Woods. "You want to tell me more about what I've got to look forward to when we go to Common?"

"Electricity's going to blow your mind. You flip a switch, and there's light. It's our own brand of magic. You'll love it." It was easier to walk now, with many of the trees felled in this particular area.

"Sounds great. I've heard stories about things the Fae used to be able to do before my time – make light with a click of our fingers – but much of the magic's gone out of Avalon since then."

"What other kinds of magic did there used to be?"

"Oh, the Fae could fly, make their fingers light up by snapping them, some of the more powerful ones could walk through walls, hold their breath for hours underwater. You know, things like that. Now we can keep nature going around us, but it's a greater effort than it used to be. I wonder when that too will be gone."

"Hold the phone. The Fae could fly?" I tried to picture the oddity, and then looked down at my hands to see if they appeared any different to me with this new information factored in. "That's crazy awesome."

Bayard was gruff when he interjected. "Yes, well it wasn't 'crazy awesome' when the magic went out from the world. The higher magic went away one day with no reason, no warning. The more dangerous creatures were taken clean out of Faîte along with it. Maybe we could've had a fresh start, but I don't think we're all that better off."

Draper gripped my hand tighter and kept up a steady pace. "Tell me, do they have a wide variety of animals in your world?"

"Oh, yeah. Wait till you see an anteater for the first time. You'll be like, 'Ro, that's insane. You should've warned me.' And I'll be like, 'Remember that time in the Désespéré Woods? I totally did.'"

Draper chuckled at my stellar impression of him. "Do you have large animals?"

"Sure. Elephants are pretty huge." I motioned to a tree about the right height. "As tall as that one there."

I flinched when Bayard pulled his sword out and looked around with caution, his shoulders tensed. He sniffed the air, glancing behind him, and then in front curiously.

"You don't have anything taller? Say, twice as tall?"

I shrugged. "Not sure. Giraffes, maybe."

"The Gévaudan is quite large. I don't want you to be caught by surprise." Draper's voice lowered. "I've never been this far into the Désespéré Woods." He picked up our joined hands and pointed toward a clearing that had a whole mess of sticks, feathers and nature all jammed up in there. It almost looked like a giant nest, fit for Big Bird. Draper stopped and held his free fist up, his voice quieting to a whisper. "Let's go around. That's where its home is."

Goosebumps broke out on my skin. Not to get all crazy on you, but my goosebumps are never wrong. They urged me forward, and I knew I couldn't disobey the command my body gave. I dropped Draper's hand and moved toward the nest. "Go on around. I'll catch up. I need to see what's in there."

Draper caught my arm, and Bayard surprised me by moving to block my path. "Pups," he whispered, pointing to the left to indicate we were going around, instead of nearer the danger. I mean, I got it, but my gut was pulling me forward.

"How many?" Draper asked, bringing me under his arm so I was sheltered in his wing of protection.

Bayard turned, standing on his toes and craning his neck to count. "I can make out five, but they're all piled in together, so it's hard to tell."

Draper met his eye. "We can't let them run free. There'll be no end to the slaughter." His eyebrows furrowed. "I didn't realize there were two adult Gévaudans.

We may not be able to contain the adults, but we can handle the pups."

"Contain? Handle? Draper, what are you talking about?" I whispered.

"Stay here. Bayard and I can deal with the problem easy enough."

Panic seeped into my pores, and now I understood what my goosebumps had been warning me about. I grabbed onto Bayard and Draper, shaking my head as I fought to maintain the whisper that had been established. "No! You can't kill sleeping babies!"

Draper motioned with his finger for me to turn my head away from the oncoming carnage. "It's got to be this way. Bayard's right. It's five animal lives versus possibly hundreds of people they'll kill once they mature. We can't leave the people of Avalon to fight a battle like that. They can barely take care of themselves. This is how it has to be, Rosie." He swirled his finger in the air. "Turn around, pumpkin. I don't want you to see this."

12

THE GÉVAUDAN PUPS

Bayard's footsteps roused one of the pups as he stepped into the nest of branches, bramble and feathers, and I heard a distinct whine for his mama. My heart pulled inside my chest, desperation rising up as words deserted me. *"Where's mama?"* one of the pups said. *"Who..."*

It was too much. I broke out of the obedient hold I had on myself and bolted to the nest, reaching the pups too late. Draper and Bayard acted quick. They were pulling their bloody swords from the pups, one by one. The last baby started howling, giving away our location and our dark deed.

I hopped over the edge and threw myself into the nest, shielding the only live pup that was left. Though he was a baby, he was as big as a Shetland pony, and looked sort of like a wolf mixed with a fox. "No! I can hear them! They're just babies, and you're murdering them in their sleep!" The pup in my arms howled as I tried to remove him from his brothers and sisters, who were bleeding out in the nest. He was so heavy and large; I couldn't get him to budge, frozen in his fear as he was.

Draper had his arms raised to calm me down. "Rosie, be reasonable. This is their size as babies. Fully grown? You have no idea the damage they can do."

"But I can hear them! You all said they were monsters, not animals, and that I wouldn't be able to hear them, but I can! They're crying for their mama while they die!" I glared at Draper. "Don't you know what it's like to cry for your mama? Is that what you want to do to another living being that has feelings and sentient thoughts?"

Pain pulled at Draper's wide mouth, tugging the corners downward. "It has to be done, pumpkin."

Bayard stepped on the freshly dead bodies to get to my wolf puppy, so I laid on top of the baby, shielding him as best I could. I heard a stream of confusion, fear and boiling anger rising up in the baby's conflicting thoughts, so I ran my fingers down his side, feeling the soft brown hair that was several inches long, and thicker than your average fur coat. "It's okay, sweetheart. I've got you. You can stay with me." He was just starting to calm, but then howled when Bayard gripped my hair and ripped me up, leaving the pup exposed. There was a quick flash of the sword, and it plunged downward into the baby's chest. Bayard pulled it out coated in thick red goo.

My mouth fell open, gearing up to let out a scream that started in my toes and echoed up my body. Draper's palm cupped my mouth, trapping the sound inside. He pulled me backwards out of the nest and lowered me to the ground, holding me to his side as we knelt by the nest until my muffled scream dissolved into bitter sobs. "How could you do that to a baby?" I accused, horrified.

Draper scooped my head to his chest with more love than I could understand. "I'm sorry, Rosie. But they weren't babies; they're little monsters. They'll tear your head off as soon as look at you. I won't let you get killed because you like to play with monsters. You have me now, so you don't need to resort to that anymore."

I knew he was being reasonable, and if I were in his shoes, I might feel the same way. But hearing their thoughts just as they died made them feel less like monsters and more like sweet little babies who just needed someone to take care of them. Maybe I could've helped them not murder so much. Maybe they could've learned to be docile, like Abraham Lincoln.

Bayard wiped his sword off on the grass, offering his hand to Draper, who released me from our huddle. "This is what we're in for, traveling with womenfolk. Let's go, before the mother smells the blood."

I wiped off my wet eyes and gave Bayard an I-don't-forgive-you shove as I passed, moving where my gut led me to the other side of the nest. The three of us froze as a howl that was deeper and grander reached us from what sounded like not too far away.

"Run!" Bayard bellowed, sheathing his sword and taking the lead. He bolted forward, trying to distance himself from the smell of blood that would surely be his undoing. *Our* undoing.

Draper was attached to my hand, setting a pace I could only just keep up with. His grip was hard, and he was panting as we moved through the sparse expanse of trees. They were thicker up ahead, but I could hear nature being crashed through from behind us, and knew we'd never reach the covering in time.

"You've led us to our deaths!" Bayard accused, whirling around when he heard what sounded like an tyrannosaurus rex crashing through nature behind us into the clearing.

We turned as one and gasped at the monster that revealed herself in the open space. With a body almost twice as tall as an elephant, reddish brown hair, and a foaming maw nearly as long as my body, I finally understood why they'd insisted the babies had to die.

"Blood! Blood! No!" I heard the mama's howl as she took in the carnage. My heart broke for her, and as much as I wanted to live through this, I knew we deserved a good thrashing for what the guys had done to her. The Gévaudan salivated, huge buckets of slobber dripping down onto the grass as she began to slip into kill mode.

Draper, Bayard and I ducked behind a cluster of trees,

but the scent of blood was too fresh not to be noticed. Instead of fleeing, the three of us hunkered down behind a few trees, holding hands and praying we'd make it out with our heads intact. The mama's thoughts grew more and more incoherent through her grieving, which was mingled with snorted vendetta of *"Die! Die! Rip! Kill!"*

I thought for sure she'd find us. I mean, I probably smelled like her baby, and Bayard and Draper for sure had traces of blood that could be tracked easily enough by such a predator. But when she sniffed the air, she seemed torn which way to go – behind her or toward us.

Draper drew me slightly behind him, so his shoulder was shielding the right half of my body. Something about that bravery and unswerving loyalty in the face of such real danger made me attach to him far deeper than I'd anticipated this soon. It felt like family. I kissed the back of Draper's shoulder, holding tight to him. For this briefest of moments, I had a family. I had a mom and an overprotective big brother. In our pretend life together, we'd all live in the apartment. I'd go to school. Lane and Draper would go off to work, and then at the end of the day we'd make spaghetti together when Judah and I got home from class. Lane and I always crafted our own pasta when we wanted to feel extra fancy. We didn't have a big kitchen to hang it in to dry, so we hung the long noodles on coat hangers all over the apartment. In my pretend life, we could eat hand-made pasta while we watched shark movies. We could force Draper to suffer through our musicals that Judah always made an excuse to go home during. I'd be sand-wiched between my brother and my mother, fighting Draper for popcorn. On that couch I would know I was loved – much like I knew now.

My arms wrapped around Draper's middle, letting him know that where he went, I would follow.

13

THE GÉVAUDAN'S REVENGE

*M*y eyes were closed as I willed the Gévaudan to find an errant cow (it could happen, right?) or something more delicious than eating us in revenge. We were completely still, but somehow that wasn't good enough. The Gévaudan's nose was keen, and sniffed us out like the good tracking animal it was.

It let out a loud howl of angst and anger that tore at my insides. Her thoughts were harder to pick out whole sentences, but I heard a distinct waft of desperation and horror. My eyes misted over, but I tried not to let the tears fall. Listening to animals grieve was the worst. They didn't have all the words for it, so it came out like a punch of angst. She loved her babies. They were her everything. I was afraid of her alerting the daddy Gévaudan, but she didn't seem to be calling for him. She was caught in her worst nightmare.

I heard hooves coming toward the clearing. I wanted to warn the rider to get lost, but when the pure black horse pranced before the Gévaudan, no one was on his saddled back telling him where to go. There was a white lightning bolt shape running down his flank.

It was the horse – the one we'd been searching for. The Horse to Nowhere who only showed up to take Avalonians to the Forgotten Forest when they'd given up on living. I gasped at the revelation that my gut had led us to the babies, only to have us kill them, which would drive their mother to such heartbreak that the Cheval Mallet would come for her with his offer for solace and escape.

I could hear the horse far clearer than the Gévaudan. He started with a grim greeting that rang in my ears with a deep baritone. *"You have nothing left. Follow me, and I'll take you to a place you can rest."*

"You did it," Draper began, his mouth dropping open.

Bayard's hand went over his heart in a pledge, his whisper barely audible through his awe. "I don't believe it. I've never seen him before. I hoped your Compass wasn't wrong, but I admit, I didn't believe it would happen. Not like this, at least."

"I'll take that as your apology, but I'm going to want flowers and a song after this is all settled," I groused to Bayard.

His eyes were on the horse in reverence. "You can have whatever you like. You did it!"

The Gévaudan howled out a reply that explained in

broken phrasing that her babies were dead, and she had to kill the murderers first. The horse bowed, said he'd wait, and moved to the edge of the clearing, laying down in the grass to watch the show.

The Gévaudan knew where we were. She could smell us a mile away. Her eyes zeroed in on our stretch of the woods, hidden though we were, and she slowly began stalking toward us. My plan was to get us to the Cheval Mallet. I hadn't banked on our killing the babies being the thing that drew him out, and I certainly didn't have a plan for how we'd survive this.

Bayard placed his hairy hand on my shoulder. "I'll fight the Gévaudan. She'll be satisfied with my death, since I smell like blood. Use the distraction to escape on the Cheval Mallet. Don't let my death be for nothing. Leave my body and save Avalon!" he whispered, his grip tight.

"No!" I replied, horrified. "We're not serving you up for dinner." I began to see how deep the love for their homeland ran, and how far they were willing to go to save it. It was noble, which wasn't something I expected to say about Bayard. "Maybe I can try talking to her. Her language is a little broken, but it's worth a shot."

Draper's hand folded over the grip I had on his ribs from behind. "Don't you dare, Rosie." He leaned over me and shook Bayard's hand. "Thank you, Bayard. Your bravery won't go untold."

"Save Roland and find the gems. Be safe, Princess," Bayard whispered, readying himself with steely eyes. He leaned over and pinched my chin. He drew my face to his and planted a firm kiss to my lips, which was so confusing, I nearly spat out the kiss on instinct.

It all felt so very wrong. I didn't know how to solve the problem, so I decided to take my chance with revealing myself and reasoning with the gigantic monster. At my first movement away from them, Draper dragged me to his front and held me tight in his arms, covering my mouth with strength that almost felt threatening. He was a sweet, mushy love muffin up until that point in my mind. My arms were pinned to my sides by his crushing grip, and his hand over my mouth was unyielding. His words came out through gritted teeth. "Don't even think about it. I won't get you back and have you die in the same week."

For all the bruising nature of his hold on me, I saw the love that drove the force. My fingers were free to roam, so I stroked the leg of his jeans with my thumb. I wanted to soothe the ache that being left alone in Avalon had bored through his soul. I went limp, doing my best to show that I wouldn't leave him. The arm that banded around my ribs began to loosen, his hand brushing up and down on my arm to convince me that he wasn't really a brutal man, just a desperate one.

My heart stuttered when Bayard moved out from our hiding place, revealing himself to the Gévaudan. He stalked steadily forward and to the right of us to lead the beast away from where we stood, huddled. Bayard drew his sword, looking fierce through his fear as he faced his certain death. His center of gravity lowered, and his signature sneer stretched across his lips under his facial hair. "Come and get me, you hairy beast!" he growled like a true badass. I could see decades of muscle earned defending his province culminating in the fight that I prayed wouldn't be his last.

The Gévaudan didn't need the invitation. She stalked steadily closer, snorting out words like *"die"* and *"pay for this."* I picked up my struggle against Draper's tight hold on my body, not ready to let someone go to the mat for me. I might've been able to shake Draper off if my mind wasn't so thoroughly blown by the monstrous size of the Gévaudan.

I was expecting a swift death. I was expecting Bayard to last the span of a single sentence before the monster tore him clean in half. What I was not expecting was for the Gévaudan to cry out in pain before the fight even began.

Blood flowed from her hamstring on her left leg, and she howled through the agony. My head whipped around to figure out how Bayard had managed to cut her from the way other side of things. He hadn't strategically thrown any kind of sharp weapon that hooked around like a boomerang. The Gévaudan had the same "what the flip?" face that I did, and she turned around to see who it was she would be mauling next.

But there was no one.

There was no one, and then there was an arrow. The shooter had been waiting for her to turn around to face him or her, and then took aim and sunk an arrow straight through her left eye. I whimpered at the horrific sight as the Gévaudan tried to blink, but couldn't close her eye around the arrow. Another flew as soon as her mouth opened in a loud cry of distress. The tip aimed true, driving straight into her mouth, and I'm guessing sticking in the back of her throat.

Bayard didn't understand either, but he took his window of opportunity and ran at the Gévaudan with his sword raised.

It happened so quickly, it was barely a fight. The Gévaudan turned, her giant paw swooshing through the air and catching Bayard's midsection. He was flung backwards, flying several feet in the air, and landed with a thud in the clearing not too far from where Draper and I were hiding. Blood bloomed over Bayard's shirt, and his gasps sounded like they rattled with a dying man's desperation.

I ducked out of Draper's stunned hold and ran to Bayard, revealing my presence so I could stand over him, chin raised. I had to shield him from the Gévaudan, who wasn't finished with him yet. "Leave him alone!" I shouted with my dagger drawn, scared and angry.

"Die. Kill. Eat."

My heart spluttered when the face I expected never to see again burst out from the woods behind the Gévaudan.

14

NOT SO LOST

Bastien the Bold was fierce in his focus, shooting three more arrows that each landed strategically in various painful and unignorable spots. I wanted to run both to him and away from him at the same time. I wanted to shake him and also to hold him a little bit. I wanted to throttle him, but was terrified at having someone who'd dinged my heart so thoroughly too near the oversized beast. Draper had Bayard by the ankles, and was dragging him back into the woods for some semblance of cover. When I finally found my voice, the cry of my heart was a resounding, "Run, Bastien!"

Bastien didn't seem surprised at all to hear my warning, but his grip on the bow tightened as he aimed another arrow. "I've got this, Daisy! Just stay put."

The beast, caught in the worst day of her life, turned

around in confusion as it dawned on her that this would also be the last of her days. Bastien ran at the beast when she started to topple. He jumped up with his long retractable knives at the ready, slashing and stabbing as often as he could while he climbed up her side and mounted her like she was a horse.

The horse!

My eyes flicked to the Cheval Mallet, and I heard his inner debate that judged whether or not the Gévaudan would make it out of this alive. If the beast died, he didn't need to stick around. I knew if we waited until it was completely safe, we would lose our shot at the Horse to Nowhere.

Draper was tending to Bayard's supine form. He didn't have a chance at restraining me when I bolted toward the horse, hoping I'd make it before I was noticed by the flailing Gévaudan.

"No, Rosie!" Draper was fast, but I was faster.

I flew to the Cheval Mallet, throwing myself over his seated body and hugging his neck. "You can't go yet! I need you to take me with you."

"*You?*" The horse spluttered, distracted from the fight by the only person who could speak to him in a language he knew. "*The* Voix? *You're the* Voix?"

I nodded into his sleek black mane. "Yes, and you took my cousin away. Roland. I need to find him and bring him back. I need you to take me to him, and then let Roland

and me come back to Avalon. Please, Cheval. Please!" My mind raced as the piercing cry of the Gévaudan echoed out behind me. "And the pouch of jewels that belonged to Duchess Heloise, Gliten, and Elaine of Avalon. Master Kerdik gave them to you and sent you off with them twenty-one years ago. I need those! I need you to take me to them so I can bring them back and help the people of Avalon. Please?"

The horse seemed shocked, but still too hesitant for compliance. *"I don't know, I..."*

I heard Bastien cry out, and my head whipped around at the horrible sound. His shoulder was bleeding, but he was still in the clear winner's spot atop the flailing giant wolf monster, who was down on her knees now. I wanted to help them; it wasn't in my nature to sit back while the people who belonged to me were attacked. But I couldn't bring myself to lash out at a grieving mother. I just couldn't do it.

Draper ran out to the fight and drew a slice across the Gévaudan's throat with Bayard's sword. The two men were sweating, grunting and letting out the occasional noise of terror when the oversized wolf-monster reared up or fought back in its last attempts at survival.

Bastien's forearms were bulging with sweat and strain as he fought to see which of them was the bigger beast. I was caught between running out to help the guys slay the beast, and clinging to Cheval's mane. The Gévaudan's cries of pain and grief struck my heart with far too many deep arrows. I curled my toes inside my sneakers and gripped my horse around the neck, willing the tears not to fall at the anguish I couldn't unhear.

My arms gripped the Cheval Mallet at first to make sure he didn't run off on me, but as I watched the harrowing stabbing and war cries, it grew to be more than that. The hold became a hug I desperately needed when Cheval hooked his maw over my shoulder. This wasn't the journey I signed on for. Come to think of it, I'd been kidnapped in the beginning, so there wasn't much signing on I could've done at that point. I buried my face in Cheval's mane when Bastien howled. I wanted to go to him, to help the guys, but I knew making sure the horse stayed was the whole point of this. I wouldn't let us go through all this again.

Bastien had come back. He'd run out on me, but he'd come back. I wasn't sure how to feel about that, so I tucked it away and reasoned I would decide later when I could talk it out with Lane over raw cookie dough and green tea. We always drank green tea when we gorged on something totally unhealthy. In our minds, it balanced everything out if we ingested a mug of tea with the garbage. More than anything, I wanted that mug of terrible tasting tea to balance out all the rubbish in my life. I wanted the blue couch with white stripes that Lane and I sat on either end of with our toes touching in the middle under the afghan we'd made together. I say "together", but really it was me trying to copy Lane's stitches, getting frustrated and creating more work for her to undo and redo while I slept.

Cheval leaned his head to mine to comfort me, the sweetheart. His silky black mane was soft and almost felt like water, but it wasn't wet at all. I buried my cheek in his long neck, marveling at the luxurious texture of his velvety skin. *"There, there,"* he said to me, sounding like a patient sage. *"Sometimes this is the way of it. Death or despair is how these things end. For some, death is a welcome release. For others, I take them so their despair is contained. They can heal far away from the battle they couldn't escape. I'm their escape."*

"That's really beautiful." We were snuggling, and I didn't feel one bit of ashamed at how much I needed the comfort. "Do you remember my cousin? Roland?"

"I never know their names. It's possible I took your cousin."

"Do you remember the gems?"

Cheval stiffened and nodded, resting the underside of his head atop mine. *"I do. I'll only surrender them to you, Elaine of Avalon or Master Kerdik, though. They belong to Master Kerdik. He told me to take them away until the time was right. That you're here now? That must mean it's time."*

I hugged his neck tighter, a ball of nerves growing in the pit of my stomach at the level of expectation everyone was putting on me. "Can I tell you a secret?" I clung to him while the battle started coming to a crest.

"I keep many things; secrets are safe with me."

I closed my eyes and squeezed him tight, digging my fingers into his mane. "I don't know what I'm doing.

Everyone wants me to stand up to Morgan and make their crops grow, but I don't know how to do any of that. I was barely passing my classes at school. Now I'm supposed to be some awesome princess? Find things and people that can't be found? Find treasures I've never even seen?"

Cheval was quiet a few seconds, mulling over my confession. *"I'm not sure many people know the breadth of what they do. Your very best effort will have to suffice."*

I heard Bastien announce with an evil villainous laugh that they defeated the Gévaudan. A triumphant shout from Draper forced out an exhale I didn't realize I was holding in. They were safe. We survived. Cheval nuzzled the side of his face to my cheek as I clung to his neck on the grass of the woods. It somehow felt like we were the only two there for the briefest of moments. His voice was quiet when he spoke to me. *"I can tell you for certain that nobody knows what they're doing all the time. This is your moment to feel lost. Even the greatest leaders go through that. You have to learn to trust the road that leads you there."* His tone was warm toward me, soothing the ache that had settled in my breast. Cheval had a sense of calm about him that was infectious. Like he'd seen too many battles to think of them as anything but ordinary at this point. Death was nothing new for him, but having a conversation with a person was. *"My job is to find people who are lost and bring them to safety. Take it from me, Princess, you are not so lost."*

My eyes closed as my face buried itself further in his silky raven mane. "Sometimes I need to hear that."

"The company I keep is usually the broken down or left for dead. I don't often get to speak, since the other animals avoid me. They assume I bring destruction. This... Being with you is peaceful." He paused as he surveyed the fallen Gévaudan, and then took on a note of affection that broke through his solemn demeanor. *"When you feel like a lost girl again, I'll find you. Then we can be lost together."*

It was the sweetest pledge I'd ever gotten from an animal. The love sizzled in my heart, leaving a mark there that couldn't be glossed over. It was funny how animals could do that. They could take one look at you and get a true sense of who you are, and tie their loyalties to you or attack in the next breath. People needed far more convincing. There were nuances and hidden pitfalls that were harder to put a finger on. Love was simple with animals. "I'd like that," I whispered. "Please don't leave me."

"Not until you're ready. I'll stay with you so you know you're not lost. After we find Roland and I get you the gems, I'll bring you back to your life."

"Thanks." I kissed his cheek, and I could tell he'd been starved for affection. His usual company was people on the verge of suicide.

"We've got an audience," Cheval informed me.

"They're all going to want to come with me to get Roland and the gems."

"I'm afraid that's not possible. I can carry two, but no more. Now that I've met the Voix? I see the good in your heart. I'll only hand the gems over to you."

I turned my head and saw Draper and Bastien standing behind me, gawking at the most beautiful black horse they'd ever seen. Blood and sweat were dripping from them, but they wore the breathless and accomplished grins of the victor.

15

STALKED BY BASTIEN THE NOT-SO-BOLD

"You found him!" Draper breathed in amazement, his sword still dripping at his side. He limped forward, his leg bleeding through his pants. He clumsily knelt on one knee, showing his reverence to the mythical creature. "I've heard stories of him, but I've never seen him for myself. Beautiful."

I kissed Cheval's neck. "Is everyone okay?" I kept my eyes from Bastien, knowing if I looked at him for too long, some kind of emotion would bubble up like vomit. I wasn't in the mood for emotional chunk-blowing.

Draper's voice dropped with sadness. "Bayard's body is in the trees over there. I couldn't save him."

Bastien's jaw stiffened, and he turned on his heel to go to Bayard. I stood with Cheval, and walked with my horse toward the place in the trees we'd hidden from the Gévaudan.

Sure enough, there was Bayard, lifeless eyes staring up at the underside of the trees, as if he was contemplating the meaning of life. The slashes across his chest were deep, but the one over his stomach had been lethal. I could see clear into his innards, some of which had spilled out onto the grass at his sides. I covered my mouth with my hand, catching the scream in my palm.

Bastien knelt down and closed Bayard's eyes. He lifted Bayard's limp hand and sandwiched it between his own. I bowed my head in respect as Bastien recited the soldier's farewell I'd heard twice before already. If things kept going this way, we would bury more bodies than we saved. "'Beyond the clouds there lies a home for the brave at heart to rest and roam. Your weapon's sure, your body best, but now you've earned a warrior's rest.'" He stood and glanced around. "I don't have a shovel to bury him."

Draper shook his head and picked up Bayard's ankles. "In the nest. If anyone happens into these woods, they should know Bayard's fight to defeat the Gévaudan."

Bastien nodded once, and picked up Bayard's upper half. The two carried him over to the nest, and gently lowered him inside. Bastien positioned his arms to cross over his chest, looking more heroic than tragic this way. He spoke to Draper without making eye contact. "Send his sword back to his people. Province 3 should know they lost a hero."

Cheval led me away from the carnage, sensing my impending breakdown. Bastien and Draper soon followed, and we sat on the other side of the clearing, the guys taking a few minutes to inspect their various injuries.

Draper frowned, and then pulled Remy's first aid kit out of my backpack, setting to work on Bastien's shoulder. "Looks like this and my leg got the brunt of it. Not bad, guys." Bastien wouldn't remove his shirt to make stitching up the wound easier on Draper, but rather tugged the collar down to expose the gash. I watched him suture the wound in silence, and then he muttered something that sounded like an incantation over the wound. His eyes cut to me to explain. "That's me disinfecting the wound. I used a bit of my magic. It can't heal everything. Obviously, I still had to stitch him, but it fends off infection."

When Draper finished, he sat in the grass, rolling up his pant leg to reveal a long gash from a claw with too much precision. Bastien took the needle and thread and started on Draper's leg. I moved over to my brother, holding his hands through the stitches that made him grimace. When Bastien did the same incantation over Draper's leg after the needle and thread were put away, Draper reached out and grasped Bastien's hand in a firm lock of men who'd fought a battle together. "I thought that would be our last moment. That you came for us? Thank you."

Bastien had none of his usual swagger, though if any occasion warranted his brash attitude, this was the one. "Yup," he mumbled.

"How long have you been tracking us?" Draper asked quietly.

"Since you left the Lost Village. I've been with you all the whole time, just keeping watch from a distance. I was afraid your bird might spot me, but Seven stayed with you guys, so I lucked out." His eyes flicked over at me with some hidden meaning I couldn't place. What's more, I didn't want to decipher it. I'd given him my very first kiss, and he ran off with it. Come back though he did, the betrayal still ran deep.

I pointed to the other end of the woods. "You guys should go back. Cheval's going to take me to find Roland and the gems, and he'll bring me back to you afterwards. You want to meet at a spot on the other side of the woods or something? Might take me a few days, but you can all rest and chill there while you wait. Probably should get out of the forest at some point."

Draper shook his head, sifting through the first aid kit. "No way, Rosie. I'm coming with you. Two can fit on that horse." Draper's voice of reason had a hint of anxiety to it.

Bastien finally spoke in my direction. "If Roland went with the Cheval Mallet, he may not want to be found. Someone has to go who he'll trust."

"Draper can take me," I said quietly, hoping I'd missed a conversation where Draper was really Roland's best friend or something.

"Duke Roland hates me because of who my father is," Draper admitted, his hard gaze falling on Bastien. "He'd have no reason to trust me enough to come back to Avalon."

Bastien nodded, and I buried my face in Cheval's neck, angry and so very embarrassed that we were being forced to work together. Bastien's voice was quiet and humble. "I'll go with you, then. Is that alright, Rosie?"

I don't know why my traitor heart pulled in my chest when he said my name. "You don't have to pretend like I get a vote. I can go by myself, but I know no one will listen to me."

Draper remembered his role as my greatest protector when he stood and rolled his pants back down his leg. He stood up and cuffed the nape of Bastien's neck, leading the surprisingly submissive ruffian away from our group like a naughty schoolboy. All I heard was, "If you're going anywhere with my sister, we're setting a few things straight first."

I kept my head down until Draper came back. "Bastien's refilling the canteens, then he'll take you with the Cheval Mallet."

Draper sat down beside me, leaning against Cheval with a hint of trepidation at being so chummy with the coolest horse in history. He rubbed my back to relax me, and I wished he'd had a better relationship with Roland, so he could come with me instead. "I don't want to go with Bastien," I whispered.

"I don't want you to go with Bastien, either. He's scum for running out on you like that."

"Yeah? Well, you're a jag for making me go with him after he did that to me."

Draper's hand stilled on my back, but after a few beats, he resumed rubbing slow, soothing circles into the fabric of my shirt. "I suppose you're right. Would it help if I said I was sorry, but this was the only way?"

"No. Just get me out of Avalon as fast you can after this. I mean it. I bring back Roland, we return the gems, and they can handle it from there. You, me and Lane are going up to Common, and we're not looking back."

"You got it, pumpkin."

Bastien came back with his tail between his legs and freshly filled canteens, looking thoroughly put in his place. With a heart heavier than a bowling ball, I stood, putting a leg over the side of the horse before he rose to standing. It wasn't nearly as startling to ride Cheval as it was the other horses. His movements were fluid, and felt designed to fit to my level of experience – which was none. I kept my eyes on the back of Cheval's head, unwilling to let the hollowness in my heart be known.

Draper gave Bastien a leg up behind me. His arms were awkward, and nothing like the sweet seduction we'd had before when we rode together. Bastien looked around in confusion. "I need reins. How am I supposed to direct him?"

"You don't direct him," I answered quietly. "He leads. We follow."

"Oh. Right. That makes sense. Where would I lead him? I don't even know where we're going."

"Exactly." I cast Draper a look of complete dread. I didn't like this arrangement one bit. "Lane's going to freak."

"I'll explain it to Lane. She'll be alright. Does the horse know how long you'll be?"

"When do you think we'll be back?" I asked Cheval, stroking his mane.

"I can make it there in two days, if we don't stop."

"Two days there, two back, but I'll need to sleep in there, so probably longer." As the words rolled out of me, doom set in. Five, possibly six days stuck with the one person I couldn't get away from fast enough. I hung my head, lifting it only to cast Draper a "how could you do this to me" look that I hoped he truly felt guilty for. "I'm ready," I lied to Cheval.

"I can feel your despair," Cheval said to me, jerking my vulnerability to the forefront. *"I'm here. You're not a lost girl if I can find you."*

"Thanks, man. I'm not sure I believe you, but thanks all the same." Draper handed me my backpack, and I put it on so it hung off my front like a baby carrier. Bastien had his pack, his bow and quiver, and what looked like a world of regret in his eyes. "What about you? I don't want to leave you alone in the woods."

Draper motioned to the sky. "I can find my way out of the forest if I follow the sun. I'm alright, pumpkin."

"Please be around when I get back," I pleaded, not liking the idea of being parted from my new brother so soon, and for so many days.

Draper's smile was tender, as if he'd needed to hear that I was a big baby who wanted my big brother around. "I can't imagine anywhere I'd rather be. Quick, now. Come back safe to me."

16

MISSING JUDAH

Cheval started off at a gentle trot, not minding at all that I used his mane to keep myself steady. Bastien fumbled around behind me until his hands finally settled on my waist. "Sorry. I don't know where else to hold on."

"It's fine." It was all so awkward and forced. This was the dude I'd wrapped my legs around while he shoved me to the wall and kissed me until I could barely remember my name. His hands felt wrong around my hips now, but I had no other option for him.

"Tell your Guardien he doesn't need to use his magic along on the ride for healing his shoulder. I can do that well enough on my own. People often come to me injured, and my magic speeds along their healing."

"He's not my..." I wanted to correct Cheval, but it was hard to do that without Bastien listening in. I could feel his breath on the back of my neck, and it was starting to make me jumpy. I turned my chin slightly to the left to talk to Bastien. "Cheval says you don't need to use your magic to keep up the healing mojo on your shoulder. He can do that for us. Save your magic."

"Okay. Thanks."

We were polite and formal. I hated it.

We rode through the woods, and I could tell Bastien didn't like the feeling of not being able to steer. It was too much control out of his hands. Given his proclivity for being on top of things, he was having a hard time. He had to let someone else lead, and for all his accomplishments, submitting was a thing he wasn't all that great at.

Cheval galloped when we broke out from the thick smattering of trees, tearing through a wheat field like it was nothing. He didn't tire, and our legs didn't get ripped at by the long golden stalks.

It was at least an hour before Bastien said anything to me. "I'm sorry I left like that."

"Yup. We don't need to talk about it," I ruled, not wanting to have this or any conversation with him when we couldn't escape each other. I wasn't being a jerk, just honest. At this point, an apology did little good. I didn't need it, and I didn't want him to think his running out on me could be excused with a commitment-phobic "guys will be guys" shrug. I didn't want any part of an excuse that made it sound totally logical why he'd leave me high and dry. If that was his M.O., he could take it to the rest of the fangirls in Avalon. Let them nod understandingly.

He was quiet for a long time, which suited me just fine. My eyelids were heavy, but I fought with them as the world grew darker and harder to see through to the horizon. It wasn't until hour three that his arms snaked all the way around my stomach under my front-worn backpack, tracing my sides with his knuckles. It would've been sexy, or at the very least cozy, but Bastien felt all wrong on me now. My hands gripped his wrists and moved them back onto my hips. "Knock it off. We don't know each other well enough for you to do that."

Bastien hung his head behind me, bumping his forehead to the back of my shoulder. "I said I was sorry, Rosie. Don't punish me more than I'm punishing myself."

"If you think you should be let off the hook for what you did to me, then you're not punishing yourself nearly enough." Resentment started to creep into my voice, so I ironed it out. It wasn't worth fighting about. Our little... whatever it was, wasn't worth saving. "It doesn't matter. I don't care. It never happened. Just don't hold me like you know how. You don't. Or you shouldn't, anyways."

"Will you just hear my side of it?"

"You don't get a side of it. Your side of it is that you left. The time to air your grievances was days ago. Literal days. Almost a week. It's too late now. It's done."

"You say that like you know how big a deal what almost happened actually was, but you don't. That was our first kiss, and right in the middle of it, you almost give me your *lueur*? It's like getting married on the first date."

My teeth ground together as I counted to ten before answering. "You are such a jaggoff. I obviously don't know what any of that is, so you know I wasn't trying to trap you into all that. Instead of talking me through it, you left me while I was choking on the floor! I could barely breathe, and you were more concerned about your precious bachelorhood than the oxygen in my lungs." Emotion crept into my voice, forcing accusations out of me before I could remind us both that I'd said I didn't want to talk to him about any of this. "I don't care about your commitment issues. That was my first kiss ever, and you ruined it! You took it and ran!" I stiffened, shaking my head as I tried to diffuse the bomb that I was. "It doesn't matter. I don't care. I'm over it. So very over it. I'm like, the Lost Princess of Over It. I care zero about your side of things, and I don't want to talk about it. It never happened."

"I'm trying to apologize!"

"I don't need it. I need space. I need to not be around you. Why'd you even come back? Lurking in the shadows instead of facing the mess you left."

"I killed the Gévaudan to save you!"

"You had days to talk to me about it, but now that I'm on the cool horse after you faced the cool monster, now you're all chatty. Now you want to be seen because you think I'll swoon after you slayed the dragon."

"It's not like that. I needed time to sort things out. And I wanted to get a feel for Draper. If he's going to be in your life, I wanted to spend some time watching him when he didn't know I was there. Make sure he's a good guy."

"How very fatherly of you. Draper's for Lane to vet, not you. You didn't spend four days vetting him. Where were you then?"

He paused, and for a second, I didn't think he was going to answer. "I needed a drink. It's okay for me to blow off some steam."

"Drinking for four days? Sounds like you've got a problem." I said it in jest, but part of me wondered if Bastien had, in fact, drank himself stupid for four days straight to avoid talking to me.

Bastien let a growl of frustration build in his throat. "You sound exactly like Reyn. I don't have a drinking problem. That was a big deal, what almost happened. I didn't mean to get so comfortable with you that I forgot the basics. I wouldn't be a good *Guardien*."

"I wouldn't let you be my guard if you begged. I don't need one. I'm twenty-two, not five. I don't need a babysitter. I'm fine with Lane and Draper."

Bastien scoffed. "Lane hasn't lived in Avalon for twenty-one years, and Draper? Well, he's been hiding in the gutter too long. He doesn't know what he's doing."

I closed my mouth, knowing only venom would spew out. I sorely missed Judah. Judah would never make me sit through this conversation. I stayed quiet and kept my eyes forward, wishing Cheval was just taking us another block.

Maybe he was taking us to a hotel with a big old bed and a whole mess of tacos. And a milkshake. And some donuts. With a warm blanket. And Judah, who wouldn't make me talk about this. My shoulders sagged at how badly I missed the guy who knew me best. I didn't need confusing romance; I needed someone I could count on to never make me feel this turned around. I liked my life better when I was the ugly girl.

"Come on, Rosie. We've got to get past this. Tell me what I can say."

"Nothing. I don't need anything from you. After we find Roland and you get the gems, I'm going home."

He paused, his hands tightening on my hips before dropping the gavel. "You can't go back. Morgan sent her spies after you. When you go home, they'll find you for sure. They won't stop until they bring you to her. Then she'll put you to work relocating the gems to bring them to her."

I stiffened, not having worked out that mess of crap that lay like spilled spaghetti at my feet as we rode through the darkness. "Then what am I supposed to do? How does this end for me?"

He swallowed, and despite my warnings to keep his hands on my hips, his arms encircled my waist underneath my backpack again, hugging me from behind. "It ends when we kill Morgan and put someone worth the hype on the throne. Then you can go live up in Common again."

A heaviness pressed down on my shoulders that I

couldn't shake off or even breathe properly through. I leaned over my backpack, my hand moving to my chest to hold my heart inside my ribs, lest it plummet down into my stomach and fall out my shoes. It was a swift punch, delivered right to the sore spot I knew would never heal.

Cheval felt my sudden shift downward and slowed to a trot before stopping in the wheat field. We were surrounded by acres and acres of golden wheat in the dark. *"It's a good time for you to rest,"* Cheval said to me. *"You should sleep before I have to take you to my forest. You'll need your rest for other reasons than to bring someone back. There are many people and animals who will accidentally drain your magic to get a chance to speak with the Voix."*

"Um, why's he stopping? I don't see Roland. Is this where the gems are?"

"I'm getting off," I announced. "You first. I can't swing my leg over with you behind me."

"Oh, right. The sleeping thing. You could've just leaned on me and slept on the horse. I would've kept you from falling."

"That's not how sleep works. Why don't you go stretch your legs or something?"

"I'm fine." Bastien dismounted and held his hands up to me.

I hated the idea of him helping me down, so I dropped my backpack onto the ground and carefully slid off Cheval's other side. I felt bowlegged and shaky and so very sad. "Go play in the wheat or whatever. I'll come get you when I wake up."

"Just lay down. I'll keep watch."

My temper had been stretched thin before, but it snapped like an overused rubber band at this. "Would you just go? I know you all want to murder my mother, but I've never even met the woman! I don't even know what she looks like! I don't know if I have her eyes or her hair, and I probably won't ever know any of it before she starts using me like the tool I am to all of you. How horrible that she wants to use me for my abilities. If only I didn't have a whole Council to beat her to the punch."

Bastien took a step back, his hands raised at my verbal blow of defense. "Whoa! I didn't mean to make you go there. I thought you knew that was the plan all along."

"I did, I think. I probably did." I deflated. "Look, I'm a mess. I'm overly exhausted, I just watched a man who was following my lead die, and you're a stranger to me. Just go. Get some air. Let me deal by myself."

Bastien's face turned surly, his strong hands flying out with attitude. "You know what? No! I run, and you rip me a new one. You push me away, and you get a pass? Where do you get off?"

"Here!" I motioned around wildly to the wheat. "Here's where I get off the whole friggin' train! Here's where I give you a free pass to go be the hermit in the woods you've always dreamed of. Go be Bastien the Untouchable. Such a perfect title, since I got way too close. Untouchable, indeed."

Cheval sat down in the wheat, giving us both a derisive harrumph at our dramatics. Bastien turned to Cheval as if gearing up to ask him if he minded, but then thought better of it. He turned back to me, his voice quieter to stem our arguing that never seemed to end. "Look, you're pissed at me. I get it. But I'm not leaving you for a second. You were mad when I left before?" He jutted his chin out in defiance. "Now you'll never be rid of me. Suck on that, Princess."

I blinked twice at him, stunned. "Honestly? Stupidest hill to plant your flag on. You're not my *Guardien*. Watching me isn't your job. Go back and be the village idiot. That seems a well-suited post no one will fire you from."

Bastien ignored my "village idiot" comment, which was probably best. My insults weren't at their peak when I was pushed to the edge like this. "Maybe watching you isn't my job, but I know better than to leave some naïve little princess alone in the middle of the night in a world she knows nothing about."

"I hate you so much right now."

Bastien pretended to get choked up, wiping his eyes and letting out a dramatic sob before straightening and snapping at me. "Fine by me! That makes everything easier without you getting all confused."

I wanted to scream at him. I wanted to storm his castle and beat on him until he admitted he was a spineless jackfish who feigned experience with women, but ran away at the first sight of one who demanded he be a man.

I turned on my heel and stomped a few paces until I found a patch of bent wheat stalks to lie down on. I barked at him like a dog when he took a step toward me, making my point clear without the use of words (which would only be nonsensical cussing at this point). I pulled out a few shoots of wheat by the roots, wishing I wasn't wasting some farmer's crop like this, but knowing I couldn't sleep on such an unforgiving surface.

I curled up on my side away from Cheval, whom I didn't want to see me break down, and away from Bastien, whom I didn't want to see at all. I hugged myself in the dark, waiting only a handful of quiet minutes before the tears began to moisten the corners of my eyes. I made sure to keep my breathing steady so Bastien wouldn't see me fall apart. I felt so young and foolish, letting myself get carried away with my budding feelings for him. I shouldn't have let my imagination run away with me to concoct a whole scenario in which a selfish loner jackhole magically became a gallant prince overnight.

I missed Judah, and hated sleeping without him. I knew he didn't like sleeping alone, either. Though without me there, he and Jill probably weren't doing much sleeping... on my bed. In my sheets. I cringed at the thought. The longest relationship I'd ever had was with a totally platonic guy who would probably marry his high school sweetheart. They'd sleep in their own bed together, as they should, and I'd go live by myself somewhere, or I'd move back home and be the mama's girl I was. I'd toss and turn at night, as I often did when Judah slept elsewhere.

I closed my eyes, but images of Bayard's torn body threw themselves in my face. I steadied my anxiety-riddled breaths into my hand so my tears didn't fall too noticeably. I was a freak who talked to animals, but couldn't get it right with people.

As if on cue, Cheval moved to my side and laid down so his flank was at my back to keep me warm. He was sweet, and didn't say anything to cheer me up. He just sat with me while I cried myself to sleep, assuring me that he could still find me, so I wasn't the lost girl I feared I might always be.

17

THE JERK AND THE BRAT

I awoke to the gentle rays of the sun warming my face and coaxing me to life. My neck was stiff, and I smelled like horse, but I didn't care. I opened my eyes, startled to find Bastien sitting right next to my head, watching me sleep. "Dude, how long have you been sitting there?"

"I dunno. A few hours. It's boring when you sleep."

"Here's a new rule: don't watch me sleep. It creeps me out."

He sighed as I sat up, a man's flannel shirt falling off my arms that I hadn't realized was there. "I don't want to fight anymore. I was a jerk, and you were a brat. That's the end of it."

"Is this your first apology?"

"It's not an apology at all. We've got a lot to do, and I don't want to waste time fighting. Do you?"

"I guess not. This yours?" I handed him the green and brown flannel that smelled like heartbreak and Christmas.

"Yeah. You were tossing and turning half the night. Thought you might be cold. You calmed down once I covered you with it." He opened his pack, rolled the shirt and shoved it inside. He wore only his white undershirt, looking far too good in it to have such a surly personality. The taut material stretched across his muscles, daring me to ogle, which I refused to do.

I rubbed the back of my neck, trying to make sense of his rollercoaster-sized mood swings. "Thanks. Yeah, I get acrobatic sometimes when I sleep by myself."

He handed me an apple from his pack. "You and Lane share a bed?"

"Not since elementary school. No, Judah's my roommate. You know that."

He scoffed, his shiny truce easily broken. "Are you trying to make me jealous?"

I rolled my eyes, exasperated. "Would that even be possible?"

"No," he replied, taking a succinct bite from his apple.

I frowned, wiping the sleep from my eyes. "Then that's clearly not what I was trying to do. I thought you didn't want to fight. Threw in the towel on that one easy enough. I was just making conversation. Letting you know I don't toss because I'm cold. Next time you don't have to make yourself uncomfortable by loaning me your shirt, if you don't want. But thank you for the gesture. It really was nice of you to do that."

He didn't know what to do with my non-antagonistic demeanor. "Whatever. It's my job to make sure you don't die out here. Stop reading into everything."

My face soured. "Reading into what? I called you nice. Jeez! Lesson learned. Bastien's a raging butthole. Tread lightly. I don't know why I'm always surprised when you turn, but you get me every time." I stood in unison with Cheval, who snorted and shook out his legs to get some life flowing through them again. "Let's go."

Bastien stood in front of me, his backpack and quiver fixed on his shoulders as he handed me my pack with a little less attitude. "I was a jerk," he admitted, shoulders drooping. "I really didn't want to start the day fighting with you." He turned me around and hoisted me up. Once I was in position, I extended my arm to help him get on the horse behind me. When Cheval started trotting, I tried to ignore Bastien's hands on my hips. "So, you and Judah live together, but you're not married? That's different than how it works in Avalon."

"Uh-huh. You mentioned."

Bastien waited for a more eloquent response, but I couldn't give him one. He pressed onward, trying to keep everything conversational and light. "Here it's all very serious with talks of intentions on the first sign of attraction. It's a lot of pressure. Sounds nice in your world."

"Yup."

Cheval picked up speed, running through the wheat until the golden crops turned to a flat prairie stretching to a gray bit of land in the distance. Bastien tried a few more attempts at conversation that failed miserably, due to my monosyllabic responses. He let the silence settle the feud between us as much as it was able for half an hour or so, and then picked it up again. "So, you were in school?"

"Yeah."

"Our schooling only goes until we're sixteen. Then we either go into a profession, join the Queen's Army, or start an apprenticeship. Is that how it works with Commoners? Just a longer time in school?"

I sighed, wishing he hadn't learned not to ask yes or no questions. I had to actually answer this one. "In the country I'm from, we go to school until we're eighteen, then it's a lot of the same options. Job, military, loaf around or go to college, which I guess would be a little like your apprenticeship, but more studying and less hands-on. I was in college, but I also worked."

"What were you going to be?"

I bristled. "I didn't drop out of school. I'll go back once I can go home. I'm *still* going to be a veterinarian. That's a healer for animals."

"That makes sense with what you can do."

"Uh-huh."

He paused, squeezing my hips too playfully for my liking. "You're really going to make me work this hard to smooth things over?"

I batted at his mischievous hand. "I don't really feel pressure to make your life any easier. We're coworkers. You accused me of getting confused, and now I'm not. You don't need to care about my life, and I don't need to know about yours. One day you'll look back on all this and barely remember my name. You'll call me 'that girl I met from Common,' and that'll be the name of that tune. How it should be."

He shook his head, bumping his forehead to the back of my shoulder. "I've never had this much trouble with a woman before."

"Oh, now. Let's not tell lies. You suck with all women equally, I'm sure."

He sniggered, thinking I was joking. I was not.

I tried not to lean into him, so as not to get too comfortable. "What happened to Abraham Lincoln? He said he was waiting for you." A pang of worry shot through me that Bastien had found me, but not my bear.

"I saw you split off from Lane, so I went after you, and I sent Abraham Lincoln to go watch over Lane. I thought you'd prefer her to have the extra backup."

"That was smart." I didn't want to be a jerk, so I offered up a quiet, "Thank you."

"Of course."

Cheval slowed down when we reached a stream that separated the grassy prairie from the gray rocky earth on the other side. *"Get a drink. Refill your canteens. There won't be water for a while once we cross,"* he warned me.

I relayed the message to Bastien, taking my spot a fair distance from his. I washed my face and drank my fill, refilling both canteens after scooping water onto my arms to liven up my skin. The sun overhead wasn't oppressive, but the long ride certainly was. "Is the ride always this long?"

"How should I know?" Bastien replied, and then pointed his finger to Cheval. "Right. Not me. You were talking to the horse."

Cheval nuzzled me affectionately with his head. *"It's long so the person has much time to consider going back to their life. They rarely do, but it's worth the offer. We're making good time. You only slept for two hours."*

"You're telling me. Could we break for longer tonight?"

Bastien opened his mouth to answer, but closed it again to let Cheval respond. *"It's your timeline. We can stop for however long you want."*

"You can take a nap once we find Roland and get the gems," Bastien ruled. "That's the most important thing. You're going to have to suck it up until then."

I kept my eyes on the water and nodded, expecting as much from someone who didn't need sleep, and barely understood the concept. I made a promise to myself not to talk to Cheval excessively in hopes of not using up my magic so I didn't need so much sleep. My heart sank at the thought. I really liked Cheval. He was nice to me, and had a lot he could teach me about Avalon. But no, I would be a team player and get through Avalon as quick as possible.

This was easier said than done. From that moment until night fell again, Cheval kept up a steady stream of conversation that was too interesting to resist. He told me about Master Kerdik, who gave him the abilities he had so that the people of Avalon could have a way out that wasn't suicide. He both feared and revered Master Kerdik, and wanted to introduce me to him, but dude hadn't been seen in decades.

We rode through the dark without stopping until the sun cracked over the horizon, spreading light for my bleary eyes. The sun awakened my senses that felt beyond repair and schizophrenically jumpy. My skin felt thin, having been blown by the breeze for too many hours. The sun kept rising until Bastien interrupted the midmorning by breaking in on Cheval's rant about the rocky terrain he didn't care for. "I've got to pee, and we should probably eat something. You hungry? We can stop for a couple minutes."

I nodded, I think. Cheval slowed down, stopping near a clear-ish space of rocky terrain between two larger gray mountains. Everything had been gray since last night, giving my brain nothing new to latch onto.

Bastien dismounted, shaking out his legs and stretching before holding out his arms to me. I wanted to go down the other side, but knew I couldn't manage that in my bedraggled state. I dropped my backpack onto the crushed rock ground, and then I reached down and let myself fall into his arms, trusting he'd catch me.

Bastien gave me a quick hug before releasing me, no doubt sensing I would push him away. Only this time, I wouldn't have pushed him. I needed him in order to stay upright. I swayed where I stood, reaching for Cheval with a drunken hand. The world had been moving at such a rapid pace for too long. My vision swam, now that my feet were touched down. I didn't mean to take a step towards the ground, but I felt the rocky surface yank me toward it, sucking me in with an enormous dose of gravity that hit me out of nowhere. I tried to right myself, but it was no use. My eyes closed as my body careened toward the ground. Gratitude swept through my body, relieved that finally sleep was claiming me.

18

NOT THINKING

I awoke to a large hand lightly slapping my face. Then water was poured over me, making me choke and splutter as the world came back. I wasn't in my bed, and the hand was much too big to be Judah's. "Rosie! Rosie, wake up! Come on, honey. Talk to me!"

I was on the hard ground with a rock sticking into my spine. I shifted my body, grateful when Bastien helped me to sit up. "What happened?"

"You fainted! You fainted and scraped up your hand on the way down. You're lucky you didn't hit your head. Why didn't you tell me you needed to sleep?"

"I did." My whole face frowned, unable to keep up with his speed of talking. "You know I need to sleep. You didn't care. You said I could sleep after the gems and the Roland, and the whole big thing."

"Well, I didn't mean for you to faint on me! You have to

stop talking to the animals. It's wearing you out."

I rubbed my forehead. "Cheval's nice to me. He cares about my thoughts and he trusts me with his."

"Was it worth it? Honestly, Rosie."

"I need to matter to someone, so I take what I can get!" I cut myself off too late. I hated getting openly emotional, especially in front of Bastien, who turned acerbic on a dime. "I just fainted, dude! Back off!"

Bastien took a chance and held me, kneeling by my side and pulling my torso tight to his chest. "You're right. I wasn't paying attention. I was too focused on the job. Reyn's always bugging me about that. Here, take a nap. I'll keep watch."

I wanted to weep for a million reasons, but knew I couldn't shed a tear. I was exhausted and hungry, and wished anyone or anything felt familiar. My hands trembled as I pulled away from him, crawling to a space without too many rocks beneath me so I could collapse somewhere comfortable.

"Oh, man. You're shaking. I'm sorry, Daisy."

My voice was quiet, but sharp. "Do *not* call me that. I'm not your Daisy."

Bastien paused instead of arguing, and then continued. "I keep thinking you can turn it on and off, but you can't. People don't sleep all that often here. Only the Brownies who take on a household do, or people who are very sick. I've never actually seen a woman sleep, other than you. I'm a little out of my element. I wasn't thinking."

It couldn't have been more obvious Bastien didn't think about me, but I didn't say as much. I didn't even push him back when he cleared away a few rocks for me and guided my weary head to rest on the ground. He pulled out a shirt from his pack and lifted my head, sliding the folded material under so I had a thin pillow. It was nice. It was so nice that I burst into embarrassing tears, turning away from him to hide my face. "Thanks. You c-c-can go now."

Bastien softened, his hand on my shoulder. "Rosie. Honey, I'm so sorry."

"Just go!" I cried, horrified that my emotions were taking me over when Lane was gone. The one person I didn't want to break down in front of wouldn't give me any space, in a land filled with plenty of it.

The next thing I knew, I was scooped up in his arms, blubbering and apologizing incoherently. My hands alternated between pushing him away and clinging to his shirt to pull him closer. I didn't know why he held on tight; I would've pushed me away a long time ago.

Finally my trembling arm found its way around his neck, gripping his skin so tight, I knew it had to be uncomfortable. "I've got you," he whispered. "It's my fault you're crazy right now. I kissed you and ran, then I came back and made you go till you collapsed, picking fights with you the whole way." He looked into my tear-filled eyes with such frustration, it temporarily stilled my sobs. "I don't know why I do that, push when I want to pull, run when I want to stay in one place and hold on tight. Reyn's always telling me I have a problem." He gathered me closer in his arms, squeezing me to his chest. "I'm sorry, Rosie. I don't know how to do this – to be around someone like you. Someone who makes me feel things I've got no business feeling."

He traced my wet and filthy face, seeing something there that I couldn't in that moment. All I saw in myself was someone unlovable, unsmart, unattractive and un... just *un*. I held my breath when I saw his resolve shift, his lips aiming for mine. I inhaled sharply, turning my cheek when his lips lowered to my face. The kiss that had undone me a week ago grazed the crest of my cheekbone, stealing my heart when he didn't have a right to come near it.

He buried his face in the crook of my neck, inhaling my unbathed skin like it was a bouquet of fresh flowers. "I haven't earned a real kiss yet, but I will. I promise you, Rosie. I'll be better."

Then Bastien lowered us both to the hard earth. He shifted his body so my head could rest on his arm that curled me to him. "You sleep better with someone next to you? I can't fix everything, but I can fix that." My face landed on his chest, and he picked up the shirt he'd gotten out to use for my pillow and draped it over my arms. "That's right. Just rest. I've got you."

The simple kindness won me over, if only by the smallest amount. I cried myself to sleep in his arms, not sure how to feel or what to do, other than give up on consciousness.

19

THE MOST HYDRATED WOMAN IN AVALON

I awoke to the feeling of someone staring at me. When my eyes fluttered open, I was greeted to the sight of Bastien inches from my face.

"Finally!" he exhaled, filling me with his Christmasy scent. "I've had to pee for hours!" He kissed my nose and slid his arm out from under me, shaking it and rubbing the muscle with a grimace. "Oh! My arm's asleep. It's burning! It's tingling! Ah!"

I wiped my mouth off, chagrinned that I'd been drooling all over his white t-shirt. I stretched, giggling at his upper body dance that had him groaning dramatically as sensation crept back into his arm. "You alright there, chief?"

"Yeah. Hand me my shirt, will you? You drooled all over this one."

"Gross! I was hoping you wouldn't notice. Yeah, I drool when I'm in a deep sleep. Not cool to comment on it."

He walked around behind a rock to relieve himself, and I was reminded how much I sorely missed indoor plumbing. "Sorry, Princess," he jabbed not unkindly. "I don't know much about bedtime etiquette." He came out from behind the rock and fished through his pack for a few hard rolls, sat down on my right and handed one to me.

My stomach lurched, and I almost vomited right then and there. "Here's a tip: I have to sleep around eight hours every night. I can power through for a little bit, but not forever. Gotta pay the piper."

"We have that saying, but we have actual pipers. Wildmen with the panpipes. How'd you learn the phrase?"

I shrugged. "Dunno. Don't listen to me. I'm still waking up." I chewed my roll, trying to take my time with it so my stomach didn't go berserk on me. "So what'd you do while I was out?"

"I laid on my back and tried to recite all the names of the soldiers I served with. It's a long list."

"But what did you do? Did you and Cheval go exploring?"

Bastien paused with half a roll in his mouth. "I didn't go anywhere. I stayed right with you the whole time. You said you slept better when you were next to someone, like how you are with Judah." He looked down as he rubbed the nape of his neck, his voice surprisingly humble. "Look,

I feel awful I didn't take your whole sleeping thing seriously. I mean, I worked you until you passed out. Not good. I used to be better at the details, but I haven't been responsible for anyone but myself in forever. Smack me around next time."

"The one thing I didn't try." I cleared my throat. "You stayed with me the whole night?"

"I did."

I tapped my heart. "That's a big deal. I know you don't have many sleep rules in this world, but staying with me like that? Way more decent than I thought you'd ever be."

He met my eyes, and though there was a foot of space between us, the gaze felt very intimate. "I should've stayed after things went sideways during our first kiss. I keep kicking myself for it. I panicked, and it was childish."

I nodded, not willing to defend him on that point. "I can understand freaking out. Can you understand that I wasn't trying to give you my *lueur*? Can you be cool and get that all of this is new to me?"

Bastien touched his knuckles to my cheekbone. "I figured all that out about an hour after I ran. I just didn't think you'd take me back." He took another meaty bite of his roll and handed the crust to me. "You still hungry?"

"Yeah, but I know you are, too. Plus, you're bigger than me. I'm not going to take your fuel."

He dropped the crust in my hand, as if the decision had been settled upon. "Eat it. Seriously, hun. It's going to be a long day."

My fingers closed around the gift that felt like the fresh start we both needed. "You didn't have to do that."

"Oh, I'm in deep groveling mode."

I chuckled, in a more amiable mood, now that I'd slept. "Is that so?" I shoved the rest of the roll in my mouth and rubbed my palms together to demonstrate the pure evilness of my plans for him. "I may have some shoes that need shining."

"Later. Gotta go get Roland first. The horse told me we're twenty minutes away."

I raised my eyebrow at him. "Cheval told you what?"

Bastien grinned, then turned around to change his shirt. He was still self-conscious about his sculpted, yet scarred, body. He buttoned the flannel and shoved the drooled-on undershirt into his pack. "Nah. I was only kidding. How much would it freak you out if that was true, though?"

"Like, nine."

"Nine?"

"It would freak me out nine. That's pretty big."

He snorted, shaking out his limbs while I took my time behind the rock and readied myself to get back on the horse. "You ready?" he asked, holding his arms out to me next to Cheval.

"I think so. Man, I'm gonna be permanently bowlegged after this is all said and done." I moved into his body space, expecting him to hoist me up so I could throw my leg over the tall horse.

Instead of lifting me high enough to reach Cheval, he only lifted my toes off the ground so he could bring us nose to nose. "I've been staring at your lips all day long. Just one kiss, Daisy," he begged, his voice low, though no one was nearby.

I wasn't sure what to do; either choice felt like a mistake. But I wanted him, and I knew we wouldn't be afforded with privacy many more times on the mission. I nodded timidly, reminding myself not to let the kiss go on as long as it had before. "Just one."

His mouth didn't waste a single second. He tugged at my lower lip, bringing my walls down with too much force. I felt my defenses shatter around us as I melted in his arms. He lowered my feet to the floor, in case I got too swept away in my swoon. There were two kisses, then three, and then I lost count. I wanted dozens more, and like the glutton I was becoming, I took exactly what I wanted. My fingers furled in his collar, tugging him closer so I could swallow his low groans that matched my scared noises of passion.

"Even better than the first time," he murmured, caressing his lips with mine again. "I didn't think that was possible. More," he pled, keeping one arm wrapped around my hips and running the other up my spine. My head tilted up while my back arched, molding myself to him in scandalous ways I was glad no one else could witness. He was warm and inviting, and I didn't miss his prickly nature at all. His facial hair had thickened over the past two days, and I ran my fingers over the growth to experiment with the feel of him. My lips made a perfect mess of my resolve to keep my heart free and clear. My heart started to warm, fending off the coldness I'd thought I needed. In the span of a few more kisses, I was flooded with all kinds of delicious heat, and also the unwelcome kind.

That familiar ball of fire started to form in my belly, so I jerked away from Bastien, stumbling as I went. He looked hurt that I would rip away from him with such force, but when he saw me start to cough, he understood. I expected him to run. I expected him to panic. What I didn't expect was for him to come closer, to offer his canteen with a steel in his eyes that told me he wasn't going to bolt this time. I turned my head so I didn't cough directly onto him, choking down a few gulps of water that cooled the flames in my abdomen, so they didn't rise up anymore.

Bastien's arms went around me once I stopped coughing. He pulled my head to his chest and rubbed my back to soothe us both. "You alright?"

I nodded, bunching his shirt so I could hold onto him. I needed to remind myself that he hadn't run out on me this time. "You stayed," I commented lamely. "Thank you."

He kissed my hair before tipping my chin up so he could kiss me once more. This time his lips were gentle and barely brushed against mine. The kiss was slow, melting me all over again, this time at a more languorous pace. Like the others, we couldn't indulge in just one. They stayed soft and beckoning, assuring me there were good things worth investigating between us.

When his tongue found mine, the fire in my stomach started getting worked up again, so I broke the kiss what felt like hours too soon, shaking my head and burying my face in his chest. "We're getting the hang of it," he said over my coughing. He tipped the canteen to my lips, chasing away my hacking with a few swallows.

"At this rate, I'll be the most hydrated woman in Avalon." I leaned up on my toes and blessed him with one more simple kiss. "Let's go find Roland."

Bastien hoisted me up on Cheval, who'd been patiently waiting for us to finish up. His hands lingered on my leg as he gazed up at me with what could only be explained as enraptured affection. "I like us better when we're not fighting."

I helped him up with a smile. "Are you sure? Let's try fighting again and see which is better. Here," I raised my fist in the air as he got situated behind me. "I'm super way mad at you for untold reasons!"

Bastien responded by rolling the hem of my shirt up, exposing a few inches of my stomach to the world. His fingers stroked the skin, trailing along my side to my navel as Cheval started trotting forward. "We're done fighting," he ruled, his tone finite as he thrilled and relaxed me with his summoning touch. "This is how we should always ride together." Bastien leaned down and pressed his lips to my shoulder. He yanked a gasp from my mouth when he sucked on a tender spot. My eyes rolled deliciously as my back arched against him.

"We could try this I guess," I said, biting off a moan that dripped out of me as we rode onward.

20

WELCOME TO THE FORGOTTEN FOREST

e rode glued to each other for another day, stopping only for short breaks to stretch and refill our canteens. Our banter was comfortable and surprisingly light, once we'd established that we could kiss without imploding, and Bastien could converse without turning surly.

Cheval kept apologizing for talking to me too much and exhausting me, but I told him I didn't mind. I mean, poor dude. The only company he ever got was suicidal people living through the last of their worst moments. Cheval enjoyed listening to Bastien and me go back and forth with our goofy flirtation.

When the seemingly endless expanse of gray rock gave way to a cheery green, my spine perked up. Soon the introduction of sparse patches of grass was accompanied by tall, full trees that stretched higher than a brontosaurus into the blue sky. Everything was flowers and chartreuse bushes with frothy leaves. It was a wonderland paradise, and smelled like a haven. Nature seemed at its most radiant here, offering peace and loveliness as a welcome mat for us to rub our feet into. I wanted nothing more than to throw out my arms and belt out a chorus of "'The hills are alive with the Sound of Music!'" but thought that might be perceived as slightly strange.

Birds sang joyfully, announcing us with a tune of welcome to the cozy forest. One of them commented to the others that my hair had perfect curls. Another said my hair looked like a mix between honey and the earth. I kind of loved them all, and bathed in the compliments I wasn't expecting after being on a horse for who knows how long. *"What pretty nests that would make. Just a few curls."*

I batted my hand up at them, knowing they didn't think I could understand their back and forth. "Oh, you're just trying to make a girl blush."

"Huh?" Bastien inquired, never sure when I was talking to him or conversing with animals.

"It's the birds. They like my hair."

Bastien's response to this was to grip my ponytail possessively and use it to yank my head back against his shoulder. *"I like your hair."* His mouth suctioned to my neck, working my lucky spot right good until I was writhing and moaning while my brain took a vacation, and my libido started calling the shots. "We're in the Forgotten Forest," he commented darkly. "I want to kiss you in the Forgotten Forest. Who else can say they've done that?"

A dozen birds landed atop Cheval's head, combing out his mane for him with their claws. They chirped animatedly in their excitement that I had heard them. I was the *Voix*, and they had a million things to tell me, each of them talking in unison.

I wanted to answer them, but some things just couldn't be put on hold. I twisted as best I could in the saddle, Bastien's mouth catching mine with no hesitation. His lips were hungry for me, and devoured greedily while his knuckles brushed down my cheek. It was like we'd been intimate for years, and knew just how to get down to business. His hand on my face made my dirty skin feel soft and creamy, warming me to his touch. His other hand grazed my stomach under my shirt, caressing the line above my low rise jeans just to drive me wild.

I was hot all over, but the déjà vu feeling of heat culminating in my belly slowed my need for the taste of him. "Bastien," I whispered, cautioning him about the coughing I knew wasn't too far off.

He didn't hear the warning in my voice, only the sound of his name on my lips, which apparently unhinged the last vestiges of his control. He deepened the kiss with his tongue teasing mine, gripping my stomach possessively and tightening his hold on my hair. "I want you," he replied in a low growl that made me arch my back, shoving my stomach into his hand while he thumbed my navel.

I wanted him too, but my body started warring with my heart, until finally my desires took over. The heat began to rise up my esophagus, an ominous slow roll that told me to slow my roll.

If you've never kissed someone while coughing into their mouth, I highly recommend it for the entertainment value alone. Bastien's eyes bugged when he finally reared back, wiping his mouth and fumbling for the canteen so I didn't vomit a metaphorical wedding ring all over him by accident.

I gulped down the water, blushing at the birds, who chirped animatedly that the *Voix* had taken a husband. "No, no," I corrected them, my eyes still watering. "Not my husband. Just Bastien."

"'Just'? How would you like it if I introduced you as 'just my Daisy?'"

I ducked my head, my cheeks going from pink to deep red at the declaration that I was his. "Alright, alright. Excuse me, everyone. This is the incredible Untouchable, Bastien the Bold."

He glanced to one of the brown-feathered birds with a confident grin and a firm hand on my belly. "And this is my Rosie."

Bastien dismounted, stretching from head to toe before holding his arms up to me so I could slide down. I expected him to move back, but his arms wrapped tight around me, venturing another kiss. It was lighter this time, a sweet blessing that reminded me we had two sides to our dueling natures. There would always be the fight, but only we could bring out the sweetness in each other.

Sexy me that I am, coughed in his face again. Bastien chuckled at our affliction. "It's a good thing you've got that hacking thing built in, otherwise I don't think I'd be able to stop kissing you. Call me Bastien the Bold again." His thumb drew a lazy circle at the base of my spine.

"I wasn't hitting on you. Reyn said that was your title."

"It is, but I only like it on your lips."

My head cranked to the side when the birds started chirping at the top of their lungs that the *Voix* had come to the Forgotten Forest. My eyes scanned the woods, and found a few uni-deer peering around trunks to get a better look at us. Three two-headed pit bulls came bounding forward, their tongues wagging like puppies on a treasure hunt, and I was the juicy bone. I waved at them and smiled when Bastien reached for the knife on his belt. "Hey, everyone. This forest is gorgeous. Is this your home?"

Too many voices answered at once, but the one I had to address first was the two-headed dog who was growling at Bastien's knife with too much intention. I put my hand over Bastien's and guided the weapon back into his belt. He frowned, not taking his eyes off the dogs. "These aren't harmless, hun."

"You handled the Gévaudan; I'll handle these guys." I ignored Bastien's grumble and bent down to scratch the backs of their heads, smiling when they softened immediately under my touch. I looked over my shoulder to

Cheval, who had been trying to keep his conversation to a minimum so as not to exhaust me. "Cheval, I'm not sure I should wait around and socialize, as much as I want to. Roland and the gems, and then we should probably split. Is that alright?"

"Whatever you like, Princess. I can take you to the heart of the village where most of the people are. I don't remember all their names, so I don't know which one he is. Is he an Untouchable, like your keeper?"

I glanced over to Bastien, who was wary at all the encroaching wildlife, his eyebrows pushed together in consternation. "Is Roland an Untouchable? Cheval's trying to narrow down where to look for him."

Bastien's scarred eyebrow raised slowly. "Roland's royalty, but not an Untouchable. Is there an Untouchable here?"

Cheval confirmed that there was, and I relayed the message while I scratched the pit bulls' belly when he rolled onto his back.

"Aim for royalty, but we don't go back without seeing the Untouchable." His eyes seemed to darken. "I was up in Common for a year, and I haven't checked in with the Brotherhood since I got back. Who would've given up like that?"

I spoke to Bastien for Cheval. "Cheval can take us to both people, but it's a few minutes' ride still to get to the village where most of the Fae are."

"Let's go now," Bastien ruled, his playful side gone.

This was Business Bastien, and he was on a mission. With a sad farewell to my new friends, I climbed back atop Cheval, with Bastien behind me. He gripped my stomach, thumbing my navel to assure me that we were in this together, even if the mission just got a little more complicated. I'd been worried he would shut down, but apparently he was capable of growth.

"What's the Brotherhood?" I asked.

I didn't think Bastien was going to answer me; the silence went on so long. "It's a group of us. All Untouchables."

"You mean there are more of you who fought your way out of the army and survived? I thought you were the only one."

"I'm the only Untouchable from Avalon. There aren't many more. A few that escaped from the Éireland Army, that's a separate country in Faîte. We're a grim bunch, but after you go through something like that, it's hard to be around other people. We check in on each other, do jobs together when more muscle is needed. Things like that." He scratched the tattoo on his neck, and then tightened his grip on me.

"I guess it didn't even dawn on me that there was military outside of Morgan's Army."

He raised an eyebrow at me like I was stupid. "The Queen's Army only fights for Avalon. The other country is entitled to protect themselves, too."

"How many other countries are there?"

"Just the two. Duchess Lane really didn't tell you any of this?"

"Hello, she told me exactly zero things about your world. She didn't want me anywhere near Avalon. Everything is new to me."

"Two countries, but most of our wars are internal. Éireland usually doesn't bother with Avalon. We've both got enough problems of our own."

"Huh. So, your Brotherhood, they're not pissed you're from Avalon?"

Bastien gave a curt shake of his head that I only just saw over my shoulder. "No matter our countries' statuses, we see each other as men with no ties. Loyalty to the Brotherhood trumps any affinity for our country. Our tie is that we survived the brutality of our nation, so we're under no one's thumb anymore."

Cheval cantered at a mild pace, so the woodland animals who were gathering behind us could keep up. "I feel like I should be nervous. Are they cool? Like, are they nice?" I didn't know how to ask if they were a bunch of jaded, homicidal maniacs.

"Nice? Um, no. Just hang back while I see which one of us it is. Some of them are great, but... well, let's just say breaking out of an army leaves lasting damage that some can handle, and others can't."

My hand fell to his that was pressed to my stomach, while my other hand reached up over my shoulder to stroke his stubble. I loved the feel of his scruffy cheek gliding over the nerve endings in my fingertips. It was intimate in a way I didn't often get to be. I craned my neck and pressed a kiss to his cheek, not expecting him to nuzzle his face closer to my lips so the kiss could linger. "I'm sorry you had to go through that. I don't like the thought of someone hurting you."

"You're such a softy." I don't know why this made him snigger, but his cheek lifted against my lips. "It was just a couple scratches. Nothing to get upset about."

I snorted at the G-rated explanation of the event that made his torso look like it had been shredded, and then sewn back together. "Darn those nasty kittens, swiping at you." I angled my chin up to look into his eyes, communicating that I knew it was more than a few scratches, and that it wasn't right for them to hurt him so brutally.

"Don't look at me like that," Bastien scolded, his voice firm, but without attitude. "Look at me like I'm strong, not like I've been broken apart."

Instead of addressing this, I opted for deflection. "You think you're strong? Pfft. I'd like to see an actual display of muscle, then. I mean, I'm starting to think this 'Bastien the Bold' stuff is all for show. Defeat the Gévaudan, sure, but I mean, Draper and Bayard did most of the work there. And was the Gévaudan really *that* terrifying? I don't think so. Practically like wrestling a puppy. You should've just thrown her a treat."

Bastien scoffed, his mouth falling open at my teasing.

"You've got some mouth on you. I've got half a mind to kiss that snark right out of you."

"All talk and no action." There weren't any people around, so I tangled my fingers in his hair and tugged him down to indulge in another kiss. His lips were soft, but he put pressure to the kiss that brought us from testing the waters to a feeling of claiming each other. That kiss took us from sneaking the occasional flirt to a deeper, more familiar connection that we would keep coming back to. His tongue teased mine, the slow seduction different from our previous crashes of passion. This kiss unfolded and melted like honey, dripping from the bottle at a torturously slow pace. Like we had all the time in the world to explore each other, like the world wasn't Faîte or Common, but it was just us. The nation could fall to ruins and crumble beneath us, but we wouldn't notice, because we would be locked into this luxury of desire. Bastien let out an impassioned bleat that sounded like fear and vulnerability. Bastien the Bold was afraid of me, his barely audible whimpers escaping his control.

Bastien pulled back, and then straightened, turning me so I was facing forward, instead of twisting to get a little bit more of his lips. "You can't kiss me like that." His command came out with a finality to it that confused me.

"Like what?"

"Like you mean it." His body was stiff, his hand on my stomach taut instead of teasing. "I'm not good for you."

I shook my head more at myself than him. I could taste

his helplessness and trust in that kiss; I should've known he'd bite. "Don't be a donkey. Don't take something beautiful and make it mean. I don't know why you do that."

He ran a hand down his face to rid his lips of me. "Let's just do the job. I'm engaged, Rosie. Some of the people here might know that. I don't want them to think Reyn's sister is a joke. I offered my hand to her to preserve her reputation, not wreck it more."

I didn't answer; he didn't need me to. He'd already shut down on me, and closed the door on us.

Cheval waited the obligatory few seconds before consoling me with a stream of, *"He's confused. It's not worth the tears,"* and more things of that sort. Cheval was around despondent people a great deal of the time, so he was sweet to me and said the things a human might if they'd been a fly on the wall to watch it all go down.

I'm not sure why I was surprised our connection crashed so easily, or how I'd let myself get tricked into thinking something flimsy at best was solid enough to lean on. I sucked down a steadying breath, keeping my chin high as my *lueur* settled back in my belly.

21

AUNT AVRIL

Cheval trotted through the woods for a good twenty minutes of quiet tension before we reached a clearing. My eyes widened when I saw that it wasn't just a few huts in the woods, but a whole city of one-story apartment cells. The two mile-long buildings on either side of the main path were made from wood, and stretched down for at least half a mile. Some doorways had a straw-braided thatched doormat laying down to wipe your feet on. Others had wreaths of thistles and various flowers twisted on the knocker. A few had boxes of herbs sitting under the one window each cell seemed to be equipped with.

It was a cozy little city tucked inside the woods. A few dozen people were milling about, exchanging pleasantries and giving the Cheval Mallet furtive looks at bringing in two people at a time on this run.

Bastien dismounted behind me and reached up to help me down. "I got it," I responded, not unkindly. I swung my leg over the saddle and hopped down on the opposite side. I wondered how good I would get at riding horses by the time everything in Avalon was said and done. I switched my backpack from my front to my back, and kissed Cheval's long cheek so he could stop his lengthy *"Young love can be tricky"* speech. I didn't really want to hear anything more on the subject. "Can you take us to where the royals stay?"

Cheval respected my change of topic and led us down the long rows of apartments toward the very end. *"This is where the royalty live,"* Cheval informed me, nodding his head toward the few cells on the left at the end.

I motioned for Bastien to start at the last apartment and make his way down. I really wasn't all that useful here, since I didn't have a clue what Roland looked like. I was nervous, tucking back my flyaways into my ponytail and straightening my clothes as best I could. It was the first time I would be meeting my cousin, and I wanted to make a good impression. Damond and Draper had taken to me easily enough, but Gwen and Uncle Duke Henri hadn't wanted me too near. I was determined Roland would break the tie, and tip the scales in the favor of "Rosie's totally a cool branch to have on our family tree."

When the door on the end swung open at Bastien's knock, I knew we had the wrong place. A woman blinked at Bastien with confusion that someone was disturbing her. Then a wave of recognition swept over her dainty features. She looked to be in her early forties, had a pinched nose, a few freckles on one cheek, dark brown hair that was pulled back into a crown of braids, and wore a simple dress that hung to her toes. "Bastien the Bold?" she inquired, gaping. "What are you doing in the Forgotten Forest?" Her eyes widened further and her mouth popped open. "No! You can't be here! If you're here, then there's no one to stand up to Morgan! Avalon had a chance with you there to fight. What happened that made you give up and come here?"

Bastien dropped down to one knee like a knight before her. "Your majesty, I've come to find Duke Roland. I didn't know you'd be here. I thought you'd gone into the mist."

She placed her hand atop his head, which seemed to be the international way of saying, "Cool. You bowed, so now you can get up and keep your life." Bastien rose, towering over her stature that wasn't too much different than Lane's. She managed a polite smile for him at having to talk about the life she'd left behind. "That's what was about to happen. Morgan's soldiers were inches away from ending my life, but the Cheval Mallet found me in the garden they were chasing me through. It was either die or live here, so I chose the Forest." Her nose scrunched. "The people really think me dead? How is that possible? I didn't leave behind a body to bury."

"A year and a half ago, there was a formal funeral, but the story spun was that your body had been pecked on by vultures, and wasn't fit for the kingdom to see. So your body wasn't put on display. I had no idea, your majesty." He looked around. "Are there other rulers here?"

She shook her head. "There's Duke Roland and me. My nephew lives next door, but he's out hunting right now. He should be back soon."

Bastien moved to the side and motioned me forward. "I brought someone you might be interested in meeting. Come on," he said to me when my feet didn't move.

I was starstruck, for lack of a better term. As soon as I learned that Lane had eight sisters, and all but the evil one were dead, it didn't occur to me to wish I had another aunt, other than Lane. Jill had an aunt who took her shopping once a month. They got their nails done and gossiped about which celebrity dude had a better butt in a tux (No lie. I've sat in on several of these conversations. In case you were wondering, it's The Rock).

I wanted to go to this woman, but my feet were frozen, so I stood there gaping like a fish with a low IQ. I had another aunt.

Bastien watched me freeze up and crawl into my turtle shell, confused that this was who I actually was. I hadn't had the option of hiding myself around him. He'd been so infuriating, I couldn't help but talk back. But faced with a new family member? I felt like I had my hump and lazy eye, and that she'd take one look at me and wonder where it all went so wrong. Bastien's eyebrows tented, and he moved over to me, reaching for my hand to pull me forward.

That snapped me out of my reverie. I didn't want him holding my hand. Not after destroying a kiss as beautiful as our last one. I finally took a step forward when Cheval nudged me toward her, informing me that he would be back soon with the jewels.

"Hey. Good to meet you," I offered up lamely. I wasn't sure if I was supposed to bow. She was wearing a dress, and I was a dirty girl in jeans. She'd grown up in a palace, and I, well, had not. She was going to hate me; I just knew it.

"This is Duchess Avril of Province 8." When I said nothing further after Bastien's introduction, he grumbled, "Why are you being like this?"

Avril waited patiently for Bastien and I to duke it out quietly. "I thought we were keeping me a secret," I whispered to him.

"From your family? She's not with Morgan, Ro. We can trust her." He motioned to the now hundreds of animals who were gathered behind Cheval, waiting on tiptoe and hoof for me to turn around and chat with them all. "And I hardly think people aren't going to figure out who you are here. It's not like I can keep all these animals away from you."

I took another tentative step forward, noting the similarities in her face to Lane's, and a little bit mine. "I, um, I'm Rosie Avalon." I swallowed the lump in my throat, remembering that my last name had been fabricated. "I think I might be your niece, Ma'am."

Avril reeled back in confusion until Bastien filled in the gaps about my parentage. I wasn't sure what to expect, but when Avril threw her arms around my neck and hugged me tight to her, I exhaled about ten percent of my nerves. "Rosalie? The Lost Princess of Avalon? Are you truly her?"

My fumbling arms found their way around her hourglass waist. It was the same shape as mine and Lane's. "Um, that seems to be the consensus."

Bastien groaned, as if my lack of royal awesomeness pained him. "She's Morgan le Fae's daughter, and she's been living up in Common with Duchess Elaine since the two of them went missing. She only just learned about Avalon in the last two months."

When Avril finally pulled back, her arms remained around me while she examined my features. "You have my nose. All the sisters did. And the wavy brown hair, of course. You're stunning, my dear. Lane? My baby sister is really alive? We all thought she must have died a Commoner. I mean, a duchess losing her magic in that world would be devastating. We never expected her to survive."

I nodded. "She's alive and well. She raised me in Common and kept a roof over my head. We came back to Avalon because Morgan's soldiers found me there, and they tried to kidnap me."

Avril stiffened, her emotional expression icing over

with a queenly air. "You must stay here, and far away from Morgan. This is perhaps the only place you are safe. You can stay with me, or if you prefer, you can take the cell next door. Roland, I'm sure, wouldn't be opposed to moving down to make room for you. Is that why you came here? To escape Morgan?"

I looked around and noticed a couple dozen villagers wandering out of their homes. They gaped at my collection of animals, and then whispered about me, pointing with uncertain fingers at my face that looked, apparently, a lot like Morgan's. I ducked my head and shoved my hands into my pockets. "I, um, can we talk about this somewhere private?"

"Of course. Where are my manners? Come inside, darling." She wiped a few tears on her sleeve. "Your *Guardien* can come in, as well."

I answered before Bastien could shoot me through the heart. "He's not my *Guardien*. Just a guy Lane trusts to see me through Avalon, since I don't know the area."

Avril nodded, as if it all made sense. "Ah. That rings more true. I didn't guess Bastien the Bold would ever tie himself to one person. You're welcome to come inside, Bastien. Thank you for escorting my niece safely through Avalon, and helping her stay hidden from Morgan. A true hero if ever I saw one."

Bastien grunted in response, miffed about something that crawled up his butt. I wasn't interested in researching what he was annoyed about this time. It was hard to keep up with his mood swings.

We went into the simple apartment that had one large main room with a kitchen and a living space, and a bedroom with a bath tub inside off to the right. The wooden floor was clean, and the apartment had no frills. Thinking further on that topic, I wondered how they would acquire things like paint, rugs, vases and whatnot. There wasn't exactly a store where they could buy stuff. Everything was made by the people living here, which was kind of cool. Frontier life at its finest.

Avril led us to the table, motioning for me to sit down. There were only two chairs, so Bastien stood behind me like a sentry. I scooted my handmade wooden chair to the side, so at least he could be part of the conversation, but he compensated and moved behind my chair again. "You don't have to stand behind me, Bastien."

Bastien's arms were tucked behind his back, like he was a military man readying for a command. "This is how a soldier behaves among royals, your grace," he informed me.

I cast him up a look of mild frustration. "Well, it gives me the creeps to have someone standing directly behind me. Could you just be normal?"

A small smile played on Avril's pink lips. "You're welcome to take a chair from Roland's place next door, if that would make the princess more comfortable."

"Yes, your majesty." Bastien left and came back with no

flair or backtalk. I barely recognized him. He sat in his chair next to me, angling it so he could be the first one to fend off an attack, should one come tramping through the front door.

Avril directed the conversation back to me. "You came here to escape Morgan, then? But where is Lane? Can I assume Morgan's found her?"

I shook my head, and started in on the mission. Finding the jewels, restoring the provinces, and the inevitable overthrowing of Morgan, if that's what it came to.

Avril's jaw was on the floor. "But then how are you here? If you have such a plan, who's to carry it out, now that you've ended yourself in the Forgotten Forest?"

"Oh, we will. We're going back just as soon as we find Roland, and Cheval brings the jewels Master Kerdik and Lane gave him to hide."

Avril held her forehead in dismay. "Oh, child. That's not how this place works. Once you've entered, you can't leave here!" Her eyes cut to Bastien in a glare. "How could you let her come to this place? Did you not think to educate her on the rules of the world? I brought my jewel with me here, so Morgan would never get her hands on it. This is truly the only safe place from her clutches."

Bastien didn't bother defending himself, but left that to me. "Cheval promised to take us back. That you've still got your jewel? That's very good news. Is it safe?"

"Of course it is." Avril's face had fallen to piteous disbelief, but then her posture stiffened. "You're the Compass! And you have a hidden language. I know the animals always flocked to you when you were a baby, but is that your language? You can talk to animals?"

"Yes, Ma'am." I hoped that didn't make me too big a freak to remain on her family tree. I jumped when the door on the apartment next to us banged.

Avril waved off the interruption. "That'll just be Roland coming back from his hunt."

Bastien was completely stiff in his chair, but didn't move. His eyes shot to me, as if waiting for me to say something. "Um, did you want to go get your friend?"

"Yes, your majesty. I'll return shortly."

I wouldn't have believed he was referring to me unless I'd seen the words come out of his perfect lips myself. Before I could comment on it, Bastien was already out the door.

22

SPAWN OF MORGAN

I answered Avril's questions as best I could, relieved when Bastien came back in several minutes later with a brown-haired dude whom I could only assume was Roland. Bastien's wide grin at being reunited with his friend melted into polite stoicism when Roland took his chair, and Bastien resumed his post behind me. Like, right behind me.

Roland gaped at me like I had a chicken laying eggs on my head. "You're really her? You're the Lost Princess of Avalon? Morgan's daughter?"

I worked up a smile that I hoped shone through my nerves. "That's the rumor. Hey, man. Good to meet you. Rosie." I stuck out my hand for him to shake, but he just stared at my offer, like it had offended him.

"Morgan's daughter has the nerve to walk in here and

shake my hand? Do you even know how your mother destroyed my mother's land?" He stood from the chair, looking impossibly tall and suddenly forbidding as he puffed out his chest and anchored his fist to the table. His shoulders were broader than Reyn's, his musculature lean but still forbidding. He was easily six feet tall, and had a clean-shaven, dimpled jaw that looked built for intimidation.

Avril's reproof was gentle, but firm. "Now, Roland. Rosalie hasn't been in Avalon since she was a year old. She knows nothing of her mother's crimes, so she'll not be punished by your anger for them."

Roland whirled on Bastien. "This? This is who you bring to me? Most of the people here came to escape Morgan, and you bring her daughter right to our doorstep? You know what that witch did to my mother! You know she stole my entire province out from under me. Province 4 doesn't exist anymore because of her!"

Bastien looked just as taken aback as I was at Roland's fervent hatred of me. "Roland, Rosie's never even seen Morgan beyond her first birthday. Morgan's been after her, too, trying to capture her so she can use Rosie's Compass ability to find the lost gemstones."

Roland spat on my shoe in disgust. His spatter of spit stuck to the toe, but the insult didn't seem to pacify him. "Pity she wasn't killed. It would save us all the trouble of having Morgan's spawn roaming about Avalon."

My mouth fell open in horror. If someone had spat on Lane's shoe, no way would I have just sat there mutely. If anyone had implied that the world should be minus one Judah, they'd have to explain their theory to my fist. I'm not sure if it was because I couldn't bring myself to speak in my defense, or because I hadn't been expecting such vitriolic hatred from my cousin, but I found myself without words.

Avril had plenty. "Roland, you'll sit down and control your temper. Rosalie had nothing to do with your parents' death. Heloise and Isengrim were murdered by Morgan le Fae, not her daughter. Punish the criminal, not everyone who's ever heard of the criminal. Be sensible."

Roland glared up at Bastien. "You brought her here, knowing who she was. Tell me this plan of yours that gets me out of the Forgotten Forest. I would've stayed here forever, but now that Morgan's spawn is here? I won't make it another minute."

My lower lip started to tremble, but I would sooner cut off my own hand than cry in front of Roland. "Aunt Avril, could I have a minute in your room to unwind? Just need a second to collect myself."

Avril nodded, compassion and sadness in her eyes. "Of course, dear. My home is yours."

Roland snatched at my arm when I stood, punishing my bicep with his firm grip. "Oh, no you don't. I'll not leave Morgan le Fae's daughter in a room alone to do any number of spells. Did she collect a sample of your hair, Aunt Avril?" He sneered down at me. "And you don't call her that. This is Duchess Avril to you."

Maybe I was struck dumb when my cousin spat on my shoe, but no way was I going to let some dude with a temper put his hands on me. I shoved my fist into his gut, and then let loose a swift uppercut the second his grip on me went slack. It wasn't meant to do any lasting damage; I just wanted to disorient him so he wouldn't grab at me.

Finally, Bastien came to life, jerking me away from Roland and standing between us, his hands outstretched and his eyes wide. "Enough! Rosie, go to the bedroom and lock the door. Roland, are you kidding me with this?"

Roland was still bent over, holding his gut. "You try having your land taken by that witch and see how under-standing you are. Leaving the spawn alone in a room? When did you get so careless, Bastien? A daughter of Morgan's is lethal! With all the magic Morgan's got in her? We're housing a catastrophe waiting to happen with that girl under this roof. There's no telling what she's capable of destroying with all that magic flowing through her."

I ran into the windowless bedroom and locked the door behind me, my chest heaving. I fought with my confusion and hurt, trying my best to stuff it all down so I didn't burst into tears. If Roland came charging through that door to throttle me, I couldn't be an emotional wreck. I clenched my fists at my sides, scolding myself for hoping in a fairytale. Perfect families weren't real, and as much as I wanted my new family to like me, I had Lane, and she was enough. I tapped my heart with a shaking finger, reminding myself in Lane's voice that I know who I am. I wasn't an evil witch, and I wasn't someone who could be jerked around and spit on by some jaggoff who didn't have a clue. I imagined Lane next to me, engulfing me in her hug to steady my nerves and remind me that I was her daughter, and that was enough to get me through any tough situation.

I listened to the shouts filtering in from the main room. Roland's voice rose above the others', his angst mingling with his fury. "If you love me at all, brother, you'll take that spawn to the woods and burn her right now!"

Bastien's reply was incredulous. "If I love you? *If* I love you? I spent a year tracking her down, fought Morgan's soldiers just to find the Compass so I could come here and bring you home! *If* I love you? I brought you your ticket home on a silver platter, and you spit at it?"

"I never asked you to come find me! I failed my people, Bastien. You're responsible for you, so you have no idea what this feels like."

Bastien's voice softened. "Morgan forced you to choose between leaving or dying."

"Then I chose wrong!" Roland roared, and then after a few beats, he quieted. "As much as I love you for coming to find me, it was a wasted effort. I cannot go back. I'm too ashamed I left in the first place."

A key jiggled in the door, and Avril let herself into the

room where I was eavesdropping. Her lashes were wet, but she was composed when she spoke. "You'll not listen to a word of this, child. Roland's always been a bit emotional. This isn't about you at all, so dismiss it from your mind. Are you alright? Did he hurt your arm?"

"I'm fine." I took a deep breath. "Duchess Avril, I promise you I'm not a witch. I can do that Compass thing and talk to animals, but it's nothing evil. I don't even know what Morgan looks like! Honest, I'm not working for her. I came here to help give Avalon back to its rulers."

"You may call me Aunt Avril, if you like. Pay no mind to Roland's anger. He has much of it to spew at the world. You are not the first to catch his temper." She paused and extended her hand to me. "I see you clearly."

I nodded, grateful she hadn't come in here to attack. I took her hand and squeezed it, trusting her enough to let her feel my nerves.

The shouts picked up outside the door, until a childish "Fine!" ended the feud temporarily. Aunt Avril shielded me with her arm, and opened the door to let us out. "Gentlemen, I trust there's not going to be a problem anymore?" Roland didn't answer, and neither did Bastien, who looked a mixture of hurt and livid. "Very well. We'll sit at the table like a civilized family and discuss our options."

"She punched me," Roland said like a petulant tattletale.

"Put your hands on me again, and you'll catch my right

hook," I retorted, taking my seat. I sorely missed my hoodie. Now seemed the perfect time for my magical disappearing act, where I sat in plain sight, but with a flip of my hood over my hair, I became invisible to jags who wanted to pick fights.

"I'll not fault a woman for fighting back when a man grabs at her," Aunt Avril responded, sitting in her chair like a queen with her chin raised. "Conduct yourself like your mother's son, Roland. Heloise would not tolerate such unfounded hatred. Do not exasperate me." She cleared her throat and leveled her gaze at me. "So you've come to the Forgotten Forest. Tell us why."

I explained the whole bit about Master Kerdik for Roland's benefit, and that we were going to take the gemstones to the provinces. Cheval promised to take us back, and that's the name of that tune.

Roland's arms were crossed over his chest, a sneer on his face. "I suppose no one's going to question that Morgan's daughter wants to waltz in here and grab the stones Morgan's been after for decades. No one thinks that's odd? Of course she won't go running to mummy dearest."

I didn't bother defending myself. There wasn't a thing I could say that he would believe anyway.

Aunt Avril raised her finger. "If the Cheval Mallet will take me back, I'll resume my post. I've not seen magic like yours in far too long."

"I wouldn't be able to give you back your stone. Right

now, I'm thinking Cheval's only got Lane's, Gliten's and Heloise's. But it's better than nothing."

"What?" Roland shouted.

Then I had to explain that Lane, Roland's mother and his Aunt Gliten gave their jewels back, and they'd been somewhere in the Forgotten Forest this entire time. "So I don't know where your jewel is, Aunt Avril. Maybe you can stay in Lane's province for a while until you get back on your feet. I don't really know how all of that works, but it's worth a discussion when we take you back."

"Lane is well, then?"

I nodded. "I can't speak to the last few days, since we've been separated, but yeah. She's doing great." I mulled over how I could get my hands on Morgan's other gemstones, but came up empty. I mean, short of storming her castle, I didn't see how I could return them to the provinces. *That's a problem for another day. If we can get the three gems back, that's a good start.*

Bastien relayed a little more of the plan, until the two were all caught up.

"Wow. What could possibly go wrong?" Roland flatlined, begging for another punch to the gut.

"You can stay here, then," Aunt Avril replied, her delicate nose in the air. "This conversation doesn't concern you, if you're so bent on condemning an innocent girl."

"Innocent? Morgan's daughter, innocent? Oh, Auntie. I almost feel sorry for you. I'm going with you, if only to make sure the little witch doesn't kill you while your back is turned."

Great.

Bastien looked wary at having Roland come with us, but was also reticent to have traveled all this way only to leave him behind. Bastien let Roland spit on my shoe. He'd stood there while Roland grabbed my arm. He didn't bother correcting him when Roland referred to me in any number of derogatory ways. Bastien was bold alright, just not around his buddies.

I stood when Cheval called me from outside. I'd been trying to block out all the animals that were talking to each other excitedly about the *Voix* being in the Duchess' home. Bastien was right behind me when I opened the door to literally hundreds of animals, who were all waiting to greet me – hopping, chittering and flying excitedly. Cheval dropped a pouch from his mouth into my hand, for which I kissed his maw. "Thank you," I whispered to him, handing the gems to Bastien so I wasn't seen as a thieving daughter of Morgan. "Can I take a minute to say hi, and then we get out of here?"

Bastien spoke up at my side. "First, the Untouchable. Then we get out of here." He looked warily down the lane to the others who were gaping at us. "It's only a matter of time before they all put this together. If any of them feel the same way Roland does, we're in trouble. So only a minute, Rosie. Then send the animals away."

Roland scoffed from inside. "No, she's not a sorceress. That's completely normal."

I nodded, my knees wobbling with nerves as I stepped forward. "Hey, guys. This is such a gorgeous forest. You all live here? Lucky ducks."

Too many of them answered at once. I don't know if it's just because I was shaken from Roland's aggression, or if it was because I wasn't used to hundreds of animals vying for my attention, but the whole thing was a little overwhelming. Usually animals put me at ease, but not this time. I could barely understand them, but tried to pick out a question at random to answer. "I'm not staying here, guys. I wish I could spend more time with all of you, but I only came for a little visit." I dropped to my knees and scooped up a few bunnies, birds and a black cat, touching as many of them as I could. "I'm so sorry I can't stay."

I nodded with my eyebrows in full-on concentration mode as I tried to listen to all of them, speaking whenever I was given a second to answer. When my minute was up, Bastien placed his hand on my shoulder. "We have to go. You're causing a scene."

I stood solemnly, not bothering to look up at Bastien. "I've got to get going, guys. I'm real sorry. And you have to go back to your normal day. I think we're freaking out the locals." Animals always saw through my bravery to the heartbreak beneath, and they wouldn't stop commenting on it. Most of them scattered, taking my polite request as a command, but I could still see them poking out from behind bushes, tracking me with their eyes.

The birds didn't listen. They started bringing me flowers, lacing them through my messy ponytail and smoothing back the flyaways that taunted my forehead and neck. They even teamed up and wound my ponytail into a ballerina's bun, assuring me this style looked more regal. This amused Aunt Avril to no end, and turned Roland's face purple.

Bastien took a step back, still not immune to the occasional what-the-crap from my animal connection. "Uh, we should get going, then. Pack your stuff and we're gone."

Packing their stuff took all of one minute, since they had only a sack each of things they'd acquired. I shoved Aunt Avril's other dress into my backpack, and Bastien stuffed a change of clothes belonging to Roland into his.

Cheval could sense how tired I was, and how weighted my soul felt, so he sat down on the ground to let me climb up on him. I was grateful for the offer, and clung to his neck to keep myself from letting the sadness take me over as he stood. Cheval swatted his tail against Bastien's face, letting him know in no uncertain terms that he was not welcome to a free ride this time.

Bastien offered Aunt Avril the spot behind me, but Roland wouldn't hear of it. "I'll not have my aunt on an animal the little witch can control. I'll blink, and they'll be gone."

I kept my eyes straight ahead and didn't bother

defending myself. Cheval kept up a steady stream of encouragement, and then asked me if I wanted him to give Roland a sturdy kick. I patted his neck and whispered, "No, thanks. But I appreciate you sticking up for me."

Bastien shook his head, rubbing the nape of his neck as we started walking past where the trail ended. Their feet and hooves trampled the lush, green grass that carpeted the woods. "Roland, you've got to stop this. Rosie's not a witch. I've been traveling with her for a couple months now. We all knew about the birth blessings she got from Master Kerdik. That's all this is."

"Whatever you need to tell yourself. You've got the gems, right? I don't want her touching them. I mean it. I see them in her hands, I cut them off her body."

"Jeez, Roland. I've got the three, and Avril's got hers."

"Good. I'll want my mother's peridot back once we get to my province. It's safer with you for now, though. This way if she attacks you for them, we can hang her for putting her hands on an Untouchable."

I didn't much care for being threatened, but I knew there was nothing I could say to defend myself that Roland would believe. Instead of making me bristle, his threats made me unbearably sad. An ache started in my chest, making me appreciate how wonderful a thing it was that Lane had taken a chance on me not turning out evil. She loved me, even though I was Morgan's daughter. She never once looked at me like I was something to be afraid of, or that there was wickedness lurking inside of me. In fact,

Lane knew all my crazy, yet still had the grace to call me her best friend. The ache grew, feeling like a hole gouged in my chest. There were people out there – family – who would cut off my hands, burn me in the woods, and do who knows what else to end my life after taking one look at me.

And I was stuck on a journey with him.

23

MAD FOR THE BROTHERHOOD

I was completely silent on the way through the woods, letting Cheval narrate as he showed me his favorite parts to escape to. When Bastien asked how much farther we had to go, I relayed Cheval's reply. "The Untouchable doesn't like to live near people. His hut is just up there on the other side of that hill."

Through the entire journey, the birds had taken turns flying overhead to drop flowers down on me. They could sense my despondency, and wanted to cheer me up.

When one bird tucked a flower behind my ear and pranced on my shoulder, Roland let his temper fly loose. "Honestly! How can you not see that she's a witch? She's controlling the birds right now, and we're going to trust her with the stones? We're just going to believe that she's not going to take them and run back to her precious mommy?"

The bird on my shoulder flew at Roland, getting in his

face and chirping sharply a few very vulgar things in my honor. "No, sweetheart," I told the bird. "It's alright. He can have his feelings. I don't need you to do that. Roland's allowed to be afraid."

Aunt Avril postured. "Be that as it may, he's not allowed to mock you. Roland, behave yourself."

The bird flew back to perch on my shoulder, and nuzzled the underside of my chin.

Bastien stalked on ahead to be the first to climb the hill, his head no doubt filled to the brim with upset over Roland hating me. I felt bad for the guy, and didn't want to put him in a tight spot, which was why I wasn't over the moon pissed at Bastien for not defending me when Roland put his hands on me. He'd made it perfectly clear he wasn't my *Guardien*, and super way extra clear that he wasn't my boyfriend. I didn't get angry, but I saw things more clearly. I'd been naïve, thinking I could kiss an engaged man with a temper, and assume I'd get a fairytale ending.

André René Roussimoff would never have been so stupid.

We made it over the hill, my spine completely erect at being so near Roland, who was visibly seething on my left. My eyes fell on a hand-hewn hut in the woods, resting on its own mid-sized hill. Bastien was already knocking on the door, bellowing for his lost friend to come out.

When the door didn't open, I expected to have to wait around a little. I was not expecting a man's head to pop up from atop another hill a few stone's throws away, and shout

out Bastien's name. Bastien turned toward the sound of the voice and put his hands up. "Don't shoot them, Mad! They're with me."

The dude ran down the hill toward Bastien. He was tall, muscular and broad-shouldered, like I would expect an Untouchable to be. He wore black pants tucked into his army boots, and a matching t-shirt. The bow and arrow over his shoulder were ominous, and I was glad Bastien had led the way.

Bastien met his old friend in a bone-crushing hug of affection and relief, but I noticed the man only hugged him back with one hand. "What are you doing in this place, Mad? You should be back home with Link. What happened? I was only gone a year. How'd it get so bad you ended up here?"

When Mad opened his mouth, a thick Irish brogue rolled off his tongue. "Meara died." Before Bastien's shock could give birth to a slew of horror, Madigan held up his hand to stop any questions. "It's a long story, and not one for mixed company. What insanity brought ye here? Ye were always the man with too many plans. What happened tha ye gave up on seeing them through?"

Bastien shook his head as the grief by proxy struck his face, though at Mad's request, he tried to rein it in and stay in the conversation. "I came to get Roland and take him home. I didn't know you were here, but now that I do? No way am I leaving you alone. Meara truly died?"

Madigan nodded, but offered no further explanation.

Bastien seemed to come to himself, posturing as he pushed aside his heartache and took charge. "You don't want to be in the Forgotten Forest."

"No, I don't. Not anymore. But tha's not the way it works in this place. Ye make your decision, and ye live with it."

I noticed Mad had the same tattoo as Bastien cuffing his wrist. He also wore a matching neck tattoo. Bastien didn't let go of Mad, but instead held on tighter. "Not today, brother. Today you come back with me."

Mad craned his head to look at Bastien, breaking the embrace and taking a step back. Bastien was quite tall, but Mad had two inches on him. Mad wasn't quite on par with Andre the Giant, but nobody's perfect. "Are ye off your nut? There's no goin' back from the Forgotten Forest. But at least we have each other now. Tha means no one's looking after Link, though." He jerked his head toward the village. "I don't like them over there. Ye can stay here with me."

Bastien shook his head, a glowing look of gratitude on his face at being reunited with his old friend. "Let's go inside so we can talk." Bastien started toward the hut, but Mad motioned him to the other side of the hill. "Tha's not my house. It's the decoy, in case anyone comes hunting for me."

My mouth gaped that dude had built an entire hut just to throw people off their game. Bastien shook his head in amusement. "Some things never change."

24

CONVINCING THE FORMIDABLE

*M*ad led us to a clearing and motioned for us to sit on the leaves. Dude had a whole hut, but lived out in the open in case... bears? Ninjas? I'm not sure who he was afraid might come to look for him.

I dismounted like a pro and stood a healthy distance from the others, so as not to spook Roland. I banded my arms around my stomach, my shoulders hunched inward to close myself off from the things I didn't understand.

Aunt Avril came to stand at my side and coiled her arm around my shoulders. I willed myself not to crumble in her arms and sob like a baby at the loving contact. It was gentle, and didn't have a hint of I'll-kill-you-in-your-sleep to it. I really needed to get ahold of myself. I didn't want to fall to pieces. Not until I had Lane with me. Then she could make popcorn while we watched overly cheesy romance movies and tried to pick out which of the lead guys would make the stealthiest serial killer (Greg Kinnear, in case you were wondering).

We formed a loose circle while Bastien filled Mad in on everything we'd just broken down for Roland and Aunt Avril. However, this rendition had Roland chiming in every few sentences with, "See? Not suspicious at all, right?" and "What else would you expect from Morgan le Fae's daughter?"

Aunt Avril and Roland went back and forth a few times, but Bastien stuck to the facts, not veering from the truth or using emotion to persuade Mad. He used short sentences, and spoke using only logic to his friend. I kept my mouth shut and my eyes on my shoes throughout the entire ordeal. I didn't need to defend myself. I knew who I was.

"Honestly, I'm in a little over my head with this," Bastien admitted. "Morgan's entire army is looking for her, looking for me, and trying to pin stuff on people who are close to me. So yeah, I could use some help taking the Jewels of Good Fortune to the provinces and figuring out how to steal Morgan's jewels. I don't have much of a plan, and the odds aren't all that great. Staying here is probably the safest option for you."

Mad tilted his head at Bastien, as if safety wasn't a feature he'd ever cared all that much about. "Ye trust her? Morgan le Fae's daughter?" Mad's eyes zeroed in on me, and I tried to keep my chin down and not fidget.

Roland answered for Bastien. "If you think you can

trust anything that comes out of Morgan, you're off your four-leaf clover. She's already proven she's a witch, controlling animals and trying to weasel her way closer to Duchess Avril."

"For the last time, Roland. It's her birth blessing," Aunt Avril said with a heavy sigh. "I trust her, Sir Madigan the Formidable."

"You're a duchess who couldn't hold onto your kingdom," Madigan ruled in a low growl. Then his eyes cut to Roland. "And I didn't ask your opinion, rich boy. I asked Bastien. What say ye?"

Bastien puffed out his chest and nodded once. "I trust her. I trust her enough to bring her here unbound, and I trust her to get us out of here. Coming to the Forgotten Forest at all means I trust her with my life."

Madigan took three long strides and cleared the distance between us. My heart started racing when he drew his long dagger from his belt. I narrowed my eyes at him when he took the hilt and pushed it under my chin, lifting my face so he could stare into my eyes with his blue ones.

Madigan up close was overwhelming. He had tattoos and scars on his arms and coming out of shirt to spill onto his neck. He had light brown hair that was neatly combed, parted on the side. That was the strange thing about him. Bastien's messy hair made sense, but this guy was clean cut, while covered in tattoos. He looked capable of ripping my head clean of my shoulders, but he had the controlled hair of an accountant.

Madigan's eyes bored into mine in while he searched for... something. He tilted my head to the left and the right, examining me while Bastien held his breath. Finally, he nodded, seeing whatever it is he'd been looking for. "Aye. If ye trust her, I'll go. If she steps out of line, I can handle her easy enough. Morgan's had her fun. Time the Brotherhood stepped in."

Bastien exhaled and let out a grateful laugh. "Music to my ears, Mad. You need to pack anything?"

Madigan looked around curiously, as if Bastien had suggested he scoop up a few leaves to put in his pocket for the journey. "Lead the way, brother. I'm ready."

25

RUTHLESS ROLAND

As it turns out, there were actually several legendary horses who were meant to take people from their gloom and deposit them here. They each had a black coat, with a white lightning bolt across their flanks. Nobody knew there were more than one because to see them was such a rarity.

We waited at the far edge of the woods away from the stretch of apartments until two additional mystical horses joined Cheval. Roland and Aunt Avril took one horse, Bastien and I on ours, and Madigan on his own. Honestly, dude was so burly, I couldn't imagine him being able to share a horse with any of us. Though, Bastien was no small kitten, either.

The sun had already set, and the gray of the rocks were lit only by the blue moon that steadily rose overhead. The pounding of the hooves cancelled out the ability to eavesdrop, so Bastien was able to lean in over my shoulder and speak low in my ear. "You alright, honey?"

"Uh-huh." I didn't have it in me to balk that anything about this was okay. "Please don't call me that, though. That's not my name, and I'm not your honey." I didn't speak antagonistically, but rather with a gentle push so we could respect the boundaries we both kept forgetting about. The fact that he was asking how I was holding up was nice, I guess. It was the most he'd spoken to me in hours.

"Good. I don't think they'll want to stop until the horses beg for a break."

I let out a quiet whimper I tried to keep to myself, but the misery broke it loose from my lips. My eyelids had been drooping before he started the conversation.

"It's okay. Just tough it out for the next day or two."

I hung my head, weighted and already beyond the point of emotional and physical exhaustion. "You don't know anything about me," I admitted to myself and to him. It wasn't a nasty accusation, just a fact. "My first kiss was with a guy who knows nothing about me." Lane would never assume I could go for two days without sleeping, but then, she knew me. Bastien and I had only been around each other for a month or two. He was making assumptions about my abilities and limitations that were completely false. "Bastien, I'm barely upright as it is. I'll be lucky to make it another half an hour." I shook my head. "I push myself hard enough, but you're pushing too hard. I have limits that are pretty non-negotiable. It has nothing to do with being tough; it's biology. I get that I'm the tool in all of this, but if you don't care to learn how the tool works, you'll break it."

Bastien exhaled in defeat. "Fine. Yeah, alright. If you can't make it a couple more days, then let's go until the last possible minute right before you drop. Then we'll stop for a break."

I closed my eyes so no tears of exhaustion would well and risk spilling out. I didn't want him seeing me break down. I couldn't weep in front of Roland. I couldn't let Madigan see I was a freak who, you know, slept.

I went through my list of all the periodic elements, trying to picture where they all were on the chart Judah and I had made in high school. He'd invented a rap for us, so we could remember them more easily. When I finished with that, I went through Lost and Forgotten's entire second album in my head, matching the beat to the pounding of the horses' hooves.

Cheval entertained me with errant memories about different people he'd taken back to the Forgotten Forest. The other two horses chimed in with their favorite passengers, giving me three strains of conversation to latch onto. I felt slightly loopy as my consciousness wove in and out of too many conversations. I wanted to hear it all, but the more they spoke, it was like a slow leak to my sanity.

I didn't even realize I was swaying, my body starting to sleep and then jostling awake when it realized I was upright on a horse. "I can't!" I whispered, on the verge of a breakdown. My heart was working too hard, making me feel cold and stretched thin on the inside. "Bastien, I can't make it any farther! I'm sorry."

Bastien hung his head like I'd let him down, and whistled for the others to come to a stop. I could tell Bastien hadn't wanted to explain my affliction to the others, but at this point, it couldn't be helped. He dismounted, as did the others, while he explained the sleeping tax that had to be paid for the use of my birth blessing.

I tried to dismount while they were digging into packs for food, and managed to swing one leg over the saddle. My dexterity was, you know, not so much, and I ended up getting my foot caught in the stirrup while the other was on the ground.

Roland was the only one on this side of my horse, so only he was witness to my clumsy predicament. I struggled to untangle my leg, but just when I was almost there, Roland reared back and slapped the hindquarters of Cheval, making him rear back and start off at a hard gallop.

I screamed as my shoulders hit the ground, my leg still caught in the stirrup. My head skipped over sharp gray rocks, my arms banging and stinging with shallow and deep slices. I tasted blood in my mouth as I cried for Cheval to stop.

Cheval didn't make it far before he slowed and then came to an abrupt halt, turning over his shoulder in horror, thinking I'd been a pack that had gotten stuck on his saddle or something. He tried to get to me, but I was still stuck, so he ended up dragging me in a circle until he realized he couldn't nuzzle me without causing me further injury.

Bastien and Madigan were on me in the next second. Madigan untangled my foot, and gentle as he was when he lowered it to the ground, I let out a tortured scream at the slight movement. I knew that feeling well. My ankle was sprained, for sure. I could only hope it wasn't broken.

Bastien's hands were trembling as they ghosted over my face that was wet with blood. He swore in a steady stream of disjointed noise before coherent words came to him. "I'm sorry. I'm so sorry, Rosie. Do you think anything's broken?"

My ankle? My brain? My heart? My will? I wanted to answer him, but the world was getting fuzzy. There was a dark halo around Bastien, and then the ring slowly closed until there was nothing at all.

26

IN BASTIEN'S ARMS

I awoke to a violent shiver rocking my body. When my eyes opened, I was surprised to find it was daylight out, and we were still in the land of gray rocks. The three black flanks encircled me, with one at my back, propping me up on my side while I'd slept. I tried to stretch, but that was a bad idea. I was sore from head to foot – especially my head, and especially my foot.

My slight movements alerted the horses that I was awake, and they started all talking at once, Cheval's voice the most insistent with too many apologies. "It's okay," I muttered. "I'm alright. Just a few bumps." I carefully sat up, and then leaned forward, wincing at the sting on the right side of my ribs. It was worth it to give Cheval a little kiss on his spine. He craned his neck to stretch over my lap in a gesture of total submission, woeful in his sorrow at his part in it all. Animals could be a little dramatic sometimes, but

I didn't mind the sweetness. I needed someone to be nice to me. "Not your fault," I told him.

Bastien was trying to get to me, but the horses had me closed inside the fort of their bodies. "Rosie, would you tell them to move? I need to check your injuries. Are you alright?"

"They don't trust you," I said flat out. I didn't want to hurt Bastien, but the message was clear from my trio of equine watchmen.

Bastien's jaw clenched. "Be that as it may, I still need to check you."

I nodded, which was a mistake. The right side of my face felt stiff and puffy, and when I ran my fingers over my cheek, I could feel divots and scrapes that I prayed wouldn't leave permanent marks. The horse to my left stood finally to make room for Bastien and Aunt Avril to come check on me. My aunt's fingers were gentle as they fluttered over my hair that was somehow damp. She looked unsure of where or how she should touch me. "Honey, tell me where it hurts."

"It doesn't," I lied. My shoulder felt funny, and my right eye wasn't opening all the way. "We should get going. That's all I needed, just a nap." I turned my head, and my neck cracked horribly. I felt about a hundred years old, but I knew complaining about it wouldn't make anything better.

"Rosie, I know you're in pain," Bastien said mournfully.

I did my best to compose myself, brushing my hand

down my damp shirt. I guessed they'd washed off my hair and clothes with canteen water. "Do you have anything to help with the pain?"

"No," Bastien admitted. "I'm so sorry."

"If you don't have anything for the pain, then it doesn't help anyone for me to be in pain, so therefore, I'm not in pain."

"It doesn't work like that, and you know it. Tell me what I can do. You look awful."

"You can keep a better eye on Roland, and you can stop looking at me if it's such a chore." I kept my voice composed, trying to preserve a little of my dignity. "I don't care what I look like. I don't care if I'm the ugly girl until the day I die. I'm riding a horse through no man's land. I'm not exactly gunning for a beauty pageant." Okay, maybe that was a little grouchy. It was one of my pet peeves when people commented on how I looked. Growing up with a hump, a lazy eye and acne had given me a keen under-standing that the people who cared what you looked like weren't the ones you needed looking your way to begin with. It was super irksome when I was on the soccer field. No one said of my male teammates, "Number 24, Bobby Johnson, scored a point for his team, but his hair's a little messy."

"You're right. I didn't mean it like that. I just meant you look like you've been dragged by a horse."

Cheval whinnied mournfully and apologized again.

"It's all fine. I lived. Is there anything I can eat on the road? We should get going."

Bastien was eager to please. "I saved you an apple." He pulled it out of the pack and sliced off a chunk for me. I managed a few chews that weren't too painful, grateful none of my teeth had been knocked loose.

Madigan started saddling the horses, catching my eye silently with a grim nod of, "Sorry you got dragged by a horse. Our bad."

Aunt Avril and Bastien helped me to stand, and only then did I see Roland. He was sporting a black eye, a gag and rope securing his wrists. Madigan jerked him forward and tied the rope to his horse's saddle, keeping Roland on the outer edge of our group so he couldn't look at me. I tried to take a step toward Cheval, but my ankle was being a baby. I bit off a noise of distress, stopping my almost progress.

Madigan came over to us while Aunt Avril fretted over my hair, fixing it back into its bun. Madigan stooped down to check my ankle. I was just grateful I couldn't see the scope of the damage done to my face. I could pretend I just rolled my ankle going for a goal or something, and that was the only thing wrong in my entire life. Madigan looked up at me with a frown, still holding my ankle. "Just grand. This is tender, then?"

"It'll be fine. But maybe not this morning, though."

The corner of Madigan's mouth twitched upward the slightest inch. It wasn't a smile, but it was something other than his firm don't-look-me-in-the-eyes expression. "You're a tough little princess, aye? Bastien, get up on your horse, and I'll hand her to ye."

"I'm not a…" I started to correct him. "Oh, never mind. Sorry you have to help me. I know you're on the fence about trusting me. I didn't mean for this to happen. I can probably figure out how to get up without the help."

Madigan quirked his thick, light brown eyebrow at me curiously. "You're apologizing to me? I'll let ye know when ye can do tha. This one's on us. I'll watch Duke Roland from now on. Don't ye worry about him another second."

I lowered my head. "Okay." Before I could brace myself, Madigan scooped me up like a bride in his arms, deftly lifting me higher and handing me to Bastien. He instructed me to ride sidesaddle for now, since we would be going slower for a while. None of the horses would permit Roland on their backs, so he had to walk.

I was practically positioned on Bastien's lap, my head on his shoulder and my legs drawn to rest over his left thigh. His arm coiled around my back, so I didn't have to use my sore ribs to keep myself upright. Bastien waited until Madigan mounted his horse and Aunt Avril was climbing up on hers before his lips grazed my forehead. "I'm so sorry, Rosie."

"Yup. Let's just go. Lane's probably worried." Cheval listened to me and started the slow trot. My ribs jarred painfully, but I bit my lip through the worst of it until my body got the hang of the ride and learned to stop tensing.

"Tell me how to make this right," Bastien pleaded, his arms around me.

"Don't let me fall off the horse."

He chuckled, and the sound was deep and velvety. "You got it. What else?"

I shrugged. "Nothing. I don't need a single thing." It was true, to an extent. I didn't need a thing that he could give me. He couldn't be with me. He couldn't protect me. He couldn't understand basic human needs. He couldn't understand *me*, even when I was telling him exactly who I was and what I needed for survival. I wasn't angry, but there was nothing Bastien could do for me, other than take me to Lane.

"Anything, hun. Please."

I was firm in my rebuke. "You can't help me because you have no idea who you are. You'll never help anyone if you can't figure that out. You're lost, but I'm not going to be. I won't be the lost girl. I know who I am."

We rode for too many long hours all stretched together into an unending abyss of loneliness. I tried to go through the rap song Judah and I worked out to teach me all the bones in a dog in order from head to toe, and rapped it to myself over and over with plenty of nineties flare and "yo-yo-yo" shoved into the downbeats for good measure. I couldn't let myself go through any more Lost and Forgotten albums. Those lyrics knew me too well, and I didn't want to break down.

Cheval wanted to talk, so I paused my epic gangsta rap

for him, letting him tell me about his time with his favorite passengers. After a few back and forths that the others listened in on my side of, a lightbulb dinged in my head. "Do you remember meeting that Kerdik guy?" I asked, switching the subject abruptly.

Cheval's answer came back wary. *"Of course. No one could forget meeting him. He created us."*

"Do you see him often?" I felt Bastien stiffen at my question, and I knew the others were listening in.

"Not since he gave me the jewels to hide. It's been twenty-one years, though I can't say I miss him."

"Yikes. That doesn't sound good. Is he a good guy, or not so much?"

"He travels with prosperity, but leaves behind utter ruin. He doesn't like people, so he mostly kept to the animals and nature when he used to visit Avalon."

"Huh. I think I'm supposed to meet up with him at some point. Lane wanted to surrender the jewels to him after we steal them back from Morgan. Said they'd caused more harm than good."

Aunt Avril perked up at this. "Oh, no. We're not going through all this just to give the gems back to Master Kerdik. We're taking them to our provinces, where they belong. Master Kerdik doesn't care about Avalon anymore. If he did, he wouldn't have let it fall to ruin. I wouldn't have had to bury most of my sisters." Her horse trotted up next to us, both she and her mount wincing at the sight of the scrapes on my face. "We have three of the gems back, plus the Lost Princess. That's more hope than Master Kerdik has given Avalon in decades."

"I'm not really big into taking sides on things I know next to nothing about, so I'll let you and Lane duke that one out. Fair warning, I always side with Lane, so you might want to work on persuading her, not me." I managed a wan smile that Aunt Avril returned before she fell back to ride next to Madigan and the prisoner, Roland. They'd been doing that, keeping the rear so Bastien and I could speak privately. The thing is that I hadn't had much to say all day, and Bastien was stuck on permanent apology mode whenever we did manage a meager back and forth.

"That was well-handled," both Bastien and Cheval said in unison. Then Bastien's hand moved on my back. He'd been careful only to touch me as much as needed for traveling safely, so the gratuitous softness soothed me beyond what I was expecting. I snuggled into him, finally exhaling a bit of my unhappiness over the events of yesterday. Bastien matched my exhale, relieved I was finally letting go of the tight hold I had on my body. "That's better. I've got you, honey." He tucked my head under his chin and rubbed the tender inside of my wrist with his thumb. "You can lean on me." His whisper was just for me, lest the others hear it and assume he'd thrown over his unconscious fiancée for the foreigner.

"I promise you, I'm not a witch." I wasn't sure if that was a debate in Bastien's head, but now that I finally felt comfortable talking to him a little, I needed that established before Roland could stuff his head with any other nonsense.

Bastien's chest rumbled with levity. "I know that. Once Roland gets to know you, he'll see it, too. He's a good guy. Worth spending a year up in Common to track you down so I could bring him home."

I stiffened in his arms again, shifting away from the comfort of his solid chest to sit up on my own. My ribs screamed at me, but my independence was worth the pain. "I like to make my own opinions about people. He could've killed me. I hope you get that. If I hadn't been able to talk to Cheval, no way would I have survived a mile of that. I know he's your BFF, and I get the whole bros over hos thing, but dude. I can't walk right now because of Roland, who you think is this great guy." I held up my hand when Bastien tried to say something stupid in Roland's defense. "I'm not telling you how to feel about him; at least give me the same courtesy."

Bastien closed his mouth and swallowed hard before he nodded, pulling me back into his arms. "Here," he whispered. "Right here is where you belong. I've got you, Daisy."

"Do not call me that. I'm not your Daisy."

As the sun passed overhead, we didn't talk much. I conversed with the horses, but let Bastien and me fall into a non-aggressive silence. It had been a long day, and I was a little tired. The sun was starting to dip down, and the monotony of the gray rocks had given way to the golden wheat that climbed up to Cheval's belly. Cheval led us to a stream that ran through part of the wheat field only the horses knew about, so we could refill our canteens and wash off. The dust of the road had coated us thoroughly, making me the most luscious kind of sexy imaginable. With my beat-up body, my scraped face, and covered in filthy clothes I'd worn too many days in a row, I knew I'd be prom queen in no time. I could move my ribs without wincing now, and my shoulder wasn't so stiff. Bonus.

Bastien was reluctant to hand me off, but his look of unquestioning trust in Madigan reassured me a little bit when I was placed in his arms. Madigan was tall and had a menace to his tattooed muscles that made me feel both wary and safe all at once. He carried me to the stream and sat me down beside it, kneeling to refill his canteen. His voice was quiet as the others fished through the packs for food and a change of clothes. "Ye seemed rather comfortable in Bastien's arms," he observed. It wasn't a simple statement or a tease; it was a veiled threat.

"Did *you* want to be the one in Bastien's arms?" I quipped, unwilling to let him accuse me of something I'd have to explain. "How exactly did you want me to ride the horse, banged up like this?"

Madigan eyed me, and then nodded, as if confirming something was there he'd been looking for. "Grand. You're terrible at hiding stuff. Just wanted to know what your face looked like when ye were covering over a secret."

My mouth dropped open, and my voice fell to a whisper. "Nothing's going on. Bastien's engaged."

"Aye. *I* know that. I didn't think *ye* did. He seems to have forgotten, too." He did that knowing nod again, and I wanted to shove him into the creek. "And now I know what ye look like when a lie's twisted your tongue. Remember tha. I never forget what a person's lie looks like."

"You're about to see what you look like after I push you in this creek. Stop trying to figure me out. It's creepy."

"Aye. I've been called tha before."

"Shocking."

He jerked his chin over his shoulder toward the rest of the group. "Know this: the Brotherhood are family. We'd die for each other in a heart's breath, and tha loyalty extends to our ladies. You're not his, though, so don't expect loyalty like tha from me."

My eyebrows pushed together, and I couldn't believe I was letting him rile me up. "Are you trying to say something, dude? Take it up with Bastien." I blew out a long gust of air. "He's engaged. Noted. You're a loose cannon who doesn't give a crap about me unless Bastien's my boyfriend. Got it. Thanks for giving me a day where Roland didn't try to kill me. Totally cool of you. I get that I'm on my own from here on out."

Madigan frowned in confusion, which was actually a pretty amusing look on him. His left eyebrow wrinkled twice as much as the right one, adding an additional note of what-the-crap to his expression. "I didn't say all tha."

"Yeah, you did. It's cool. I know you don't owe me protection. Thanks for the heads-up. I'll watch my back around Roland."

"I'll not leave ye to sit as bait. Tha's not what I meant. I've been with the lad all day. His hatred for ye hasn't calmed at all. I thought a day of walking would give him a wee bit of perspective, but he only seems more determined now."

Great. "Not your problem. You just told me as much. It's fine, Madigan. Thanks for watching him today. I'm good as new." I managed what I hoped was a confident smile when Aunt Avril came to join us with clean(ish) clothes for her and me.

"The men will bathe first. You can come with me while we wait, dear."

"Thanks." I struggled to climb to my feet, and put out my hand to stop Madigan from hoisting me up in his arms. "I got it. Go rinse off. Good talking to you," I lied.

"You're being stubborn. I'll not let ye walk on tha bum ankle. We both know it's useless."

"Not your problem," I repeated. I kept my chin up while I limped off toward the horses, taking Aunt Avril's arm to use as my crutch. The pain in my tender ankle was rough, to be sure, but I reminded myself that it didn't matter. This was the job, and I didn't have any other options.

"Mad!" Bastien barked. "I thought you were watching Rosie. She can't walk on her leg." He trotted to me and scooped me up in his arms, shooting Madigan a look of disappointment mingled with confusion.

Madigan stood and threw up his hands. "I was just... Ah, forget it. Your old lady's just as stubborn as ye are."

I stiffened. "I'm not his old lady."

Bastien frowned down at me like I'd told him he was fat, but didn't correct me. He sat me down next to Cheval and tossed me half a smile that showed off his lickable dimples. "Don't go sneaking peeks, now. Can't sully the Lost Princess with too much lust."

"All I heard was 'blah, blah, blah, I'm about to get naked.' Come on, now. I paid for a good show. Nice and slow, just how I like it." I snapped my fingers like I was a paying customer at a strip club.

Bastien laughed as he slowly lifted the hem of his shirt just to tease me with the ripples in his abdomen. And what a tease they were. It would be so much easier to ignore Bastien and put him out of my mind if he didn't look like an advertisement for masculine soap. I tried not thinking about him all lathered up, and failed miserably.

"You made a joke. I think I needed to hear you do that." He checked to make sure the others weren't looking, and kissed his thumb to brush a little affection over my wounded cheek. His touch was soft, tender and bespoke of fondness that was slightly more stable than the explosive passion we were trying to avoid. "We'll figure this out," he whispered, promising me more than he could be certain of.

I nodded, since being agreeable was simpler than arguing. There wasn't anything to figure out. He was engaged. His BFF was plotting my violent demise. He had commitment issues up his perfect wazoo. The only thing to figure out was how broken I was willing to let my heart get before we inevitably crashed and burned. "Go clean yourself up. You're starting to smell worse than Cheval."

He dimpled, but still tried to communicate with his eyes how much he meant what he'd said, no matter how much I was trying to blow it all off with a joke.

Aunt Avril came to sit with me while Bastien untied Roland and took the gag off with a warning (that sounded more like pleading) not to stir up trouble. I got a chance to sit and eat with my aunt, hearing about the beauty of her kingdom before it all went to ruin when her opal was stolen.

When it was our turn to bathe, I tried not to be weird about it. The locker rooms I changed and showered in didn't have much more privacy than this, but the added difficulty of a busted ankle, the guy I like nearby (and didn't want to see me naked all mangled as I was), and the guy who was waiting for a vulnerable moment to strike made me a little jumpy.

Aunt Avril was positively crimson with the inappropriate nature of bathing so near men. She mentioned she was used to attendants helping her bathe, and had "managed okay" without them in the Forgotten Forest. "I didn't run my house as Morgan does," she said with a schoolmarm shudder I didn't totally understand. She kept her opal in a small sack with her as she bathed, unwilling to be parted from it for a single minute. With how much drama had been caused over the Jewels of Good Fortune, I didn't blame her for being zealous about protecting it.

Bastien was kind and respectful, shooing Madigan away to go find game to hunt for us to eat, and tying Roland to one of the horses a fair distance away.

I heard a rumbling amongst the ranks, but it wasn't the men disagreeing. *"Just run! He's tied to your saddle. It's your one chance, now that the big one is gone hunting. The Voix is all the way over there in the water. She won't even know until you're too far away to be scolded."*

The angry grumble came back quiet, their tone thick with plotting. *"I don't want to leave her, but I think it's worth it to be rid of him. He tried to kill my Voix; he deserves to die the same death he tried to give her. Maybe I can pretend there's a snake that spooks me, so she's not cross with me."* Madigan's horse lowered his head. *"I worry she'll put me out of her graces. She's too fair. Too sweet. Avalon will destroy her spirit, and that's a jewel that can't be replaced."*

Aunt Avril was telling me about the trouble Damond used to get up to in her palace when he was younger, and Duke Henri was overwhelmed with the kingdom and being a single parent. I felt bad for holding up my hand abruptly to stop the girl talk. "Don't you even think about it, guys! I can hear you, you know. It's the drawback of me being able to listen to the things you mean to say. I can also hear the things you don't mean for me to be in on."

The horses started apologizing, afraid, as Remy had been when he realized I couldn't turn my gift off on a dime.

"What's going on?" Bastien asked, whipping his head to investigate my sudden outburst.

"Bastien, untie Roland. The horses are planning on pretending a snake spooks them, so the one you tied Roland to will run off. They want to kill him the way he tried to kill me."

Bastien's face pulled into a grimace, turning to look at the horses with an expression of stunned amusement. One by one, the horses lowered their heads in defeat and submission to my preference that they didn't murder. Bastien undid the rope around the horse and held tight to Roland's restraint to keep him in place. "Sneaky little devils," Bastien teased, ruffling his hands through the guilty horse's mane. He jerked Roland's rope irritably and grumbled, "I hope you see that she just saved your neck. What kind of a witch would do that?"

"The kind who can't prove the horses actually said anything. The kind who wants to get in your good graces by saving your friend."

Wow. Didn't see that one backfiring.

27

HAIL AND LEECHES

The trip through the wheat field felt never-ending, but the fact that I wasn't covered in dust and dirt was a definite plus. I was stable enough not to have to ride sidesaddle anymore, which meant we could gallop through the wheat. By the time night fell, the stiffness on the side of my face had subsided, giving me eyefuls of how beautiful the world was without the usual light pollution I was used to in the city. I never got to see a whole sky of gorgeous stars, highlighted by the blue moon. The giant orb above shaded us in hues of navy and cerulean as we rode through the wheat. The horses were talking about a *tonnerre* coming, but as I didn't know what that was, I remained a patient listener.

Roland had been tied atop Aunt Avril's horse so we could gallop and make better time. Bastien finally started asking to see if I was tired, and then listening to me, which was a welcome change. "Are you sure you don't want to stop for the night now?" he said low in my ear. We were a little ahead of the other horses, which afforded us just enough privacy for a few mild flirtations. His lips brushed the shell of my ear, just to drive me crazy. "Your eyes are starting to glaze over, and you're doing that yawning thing you do before you get snippy."

"I'm not snippy," I bristled, and then caught myself. "Of course I'm tired."

"Talk to me. You're tired, but you don't want to stop?" When I didn't reply, he shifted uncomfortably. "Are you hungry?"

"Sure, but we all are. It's best just to not think about food. You know I always want more."

"Greedy little witch." He meant it as a tease, but my shoulders fell at the label that had caused me to get dragged through dirt. Bastien hissed. "I'm sorry. I didn't mean that. It was a lousy joke."

"It's fine." I was about to make a pun to pass it all off, but Madigan sidled up next to us. My spine straightened, and I ghosted my hand over the front of my gray thermal shirt from Draper, as if I'd been naked and needed to cover the scandal.

"I feel the wind shifting," Madigan noted above the gallop of the horses. How he could feel changes in the breeze at this fast pace amazed me. The wind had been whipping at my face for so long, I barely felt it anymore. "If ye don't have to sleep, we should ride as fast and as far as we can. I don't fancy being stuck in the rain."

"The horses are saying that a *tonnerre* is coming," I said.

Bastien stiffened. "What are you talking about? There aren't any black clouds."

Madigan turned around and gasped. "They're starting to come in behind us. I checked not one minute ago, and the sky didn't have a hint of black to it." He shook his head. "I don't think the duchess is up for the beating tha's going to be coming from above." He appraised my injuries with a careful eye. "This one might have been able to handle it if she wasn't already one manky foot over death's door."

Bastien checked over his shoulder and swore. "Duchess, we have to ride harder if we don't want to get caught in the storm. The *tonnerre* clouds are coming in fast. I wasn't paying attention." His arms stiffened and his body went rigid, as if missing this detail was somehow my fault, and he needed to end our budding sweetness so he could be a good warrior.

I explained the situation to the horses, and asked them to go a little faster, if they could. Cheval rallied, letting out a whinny to inspire the other two and push them on to greater speeds. "What is it, Bastien? If it's just a little rain, then is it worth maxing out the horses like this? They've been going all day. I feel bad that they're pushing themselves like this."

"It'll be far worse if we're stuck in the storm. They know the drill. They understand the risks if we're caught in the storm. They're loyal to you, so they'll run as far and as fast as they can to keep you safe."

"Hello, I'm not going to melt if I get a little water on me. I'm not a real witch, you know."

Bastien's eyebrows furrowed at the *Wizard of Oz* reference that went way over his head. "Huh? It's not a little water, Rosie. It's a rolling storm that lasts for days. The *tonnerre* clouds multiply until they've squeezed everything out, and then the hail starts."

I nodded. "Okay. Hail. I gotcha. We have that in my world. It's a little annoying, granted. Can we find a place to duck and take cover until it passes?" Though as I surveyed the plains, there was nothing but wheat, wheat and more wheat as far as I could see, with not a single tree in sight.

"No, babe. No place to hide. I saw hail in your world once while I was looking for you. It was like fat grains of salt. This isn't the same. Our hail is a ball of ice hurtling down at you." His arms around me demonstrated the size to be that of a softball.

"Oh, yikes. Yeah, that wouldn't be easy to avoid. Sorry, guys," I said to the horses. For our own sakes, we had to keep riding as if our lives depended on it.

Bastien opened his mouth, and I immediately wished he hadn't. "Then there's the leeches."

"Huh? Like, leeches? Little slugs that suck blood from you?"

"What? No, *leeches*," he said, as if I hadn't been paying attention. "Do you not have them in your world? They fall from the clouds after the hail. They're half a foot long critters. They're hairy and have fangs. Their slime leaves a slow poison that scrambles your mind so you have hallucinations."

"What the crap, Bastien? And we've got a storm of them bearing down on us?" I patted Cheval's neck. "Go faster if you can, guys. I don't want any of you going crazy or getting hit with softballs of ice tonight."

"We'll need a plan," Aunt Avril shouted to us, riding on our other side with a look of trepidation on her features. "We can't run the horses forever, and there's no shelter I can see."

I looked overhead and noticed a few clouds migrating to the space in the sky behind us, as if drawn to the culminating storm like a magnet. For not having noticed it before, it sure had collected and grown quickly. Each second I watched over Bastien's shoulder made my eyes widen with how much the epicenter was spreading out. It started to look like thinned black cake batter across the sky. "Oh, Bastien, it's spreading fast."

"Hold tight to me, hun," he warned, giving Cheval a light kick to urge him forward. The wind started picking up more noticeably, turning cold and biting as it nipped at our faces. "We'll find shelter." His words held no certainty, only the promise that if we didn't, we might not survive the storm.

28

MY SHELTER IN THE MIDDLE OF NOWHERE

My ankle jarred painfully as the hard gallop shook it over and over, but I gritted my teeth through the discomfort. Sweat broke out on my forehead, despite the growing cold. Cheval reassured me that he would take care of us as best he could. I wanted to kiss him and feed him apples, but the storm behind us was inching its way closer, daunting us with the inevitability that we could only run for so long.

"I don't want to scare you, but I take this route all the time. There's no shelter anywhere." Cheval's warning was grave. *"Lean forward a little more. I can go faster if you're not as upright."*

I complied, biting my lip against the tug in my ribs and the worry that flooded me. It was one thing to hear Bastien's concern, but another one altogether to have those fears confirmed by the veteran of this area. "Cheval needs us to lean forward, so he can go faster." I tugged him down by his green and blue flannel sleeve. Bastien's torso covered mine, ramping up our attraction that was mingled with trepidation. "He doesn't think we'll make it," I informed Bastien, trying not to sound like I was freaking out.

"Stay under me like this." Bastien's volume rose as Cheval and the other two horses bolted with renewed speed. "If the storm catches us, you won't get hit by the hail if I shield you with my body."

"I don't want you to get pelted with giant hail balls and psychedelic leeches!" Emotion choked my throat at the gallant offer. I pried my fingers from Cheval's mane so I could twine them through Bastien's. My grip pulsed in his, my cheek pressed to his stubble when he squeezed me in return. His heart beat wildly into my back, matching my own erratic rhythm. For all the fighting we did, we rode in perfect harmony when the storm was bearing down on us.

His cheek was warm, giving that small space on my face a respite from the biting wind. His voice had a forced calm about it that scared me. "I told you, I've got you, Daisy."

Panic started to rise up inside of me. My beautiful horse, my new aunt and my first kiss guy were about to get knocked out by giant hail balls. My brain started working overtime, trying to fit a square peg into the round abyss that was Avalon. I had to get us out of this mess. Bastien's body was already scarred enough. I needed to find a safe place.

A familiar trickle of intuition leaked into my veins, lifting my spirits from pure anxiety to determined hope. My gut tugged a little toward the left, and I thanked whatever birth blessing gave me the trump card we needed. I didn't bother questioning it, and spoke up immediately. "My gut's telling me we should head that way," I pointed in the vague direction, hoping that the darkness of night was hiding something sturdy and solid that wasn't too far off. Cheval didn't have a sliver of doubt that I would lead us to safety, even though he was certain there was no shelter in that direction. I prayed my gut didn't fail me, now that the stakes were this high.

Bastien didn't question me, but trusted my internal GPS without me needing to elaborate. "Rosie's Compass is calling the shots now, so try to keep up!" he called out behind us.

When he led the way with the other two horses following behind, I could hear Roland's anger spewing out all over the place. "She'll lead us to our doom! Don't you see what she's doing, Bastien? She's a witch! She's no doubt controlling the storm, driving us right into the heart of it! You can't be this trusting. What happened to you? Are her lips really so sweet you'd let her lead us away from safety?"

Bastien was furious, and for once, it wasn't with me. "Shut up, Roland! Don't talk about her lips. You know I'm engaged to Rachelle. Rosie's the Compass. If she says we should change directions, then that's what we'll do."

"You've turned fool for her!"

Aunt Avril was scolding Roland, but I stopped listening. Bastien stuck up for me. I clung tight to his fingers to show my gratitude. "You're sure about this?" Bastien asked me quietly.

Cheval chimed in before I could answer. *"I've ridden this path thousands of times. There's nothing in your direction, Princess. But we wouldn't make it to shelter even if we kept going the way we were heading, either."*

"I don't know how to explain it; I just know that my gut's tugging me this way. No one has to listen to me. I've got no proof other than that."

Cheval mulled this over in time with Bastien, and together they said, *"That's enough for me."*

We rode hard in the direction I pointed us, and with every racing step, I prayed we were going somewhere safe. I scoured the darkness so that I could find anything we could hide in and wait out the storm that was bearing down on us.

"See? There's nothing! And the storm is gaining on us. I knew the little witch would see us all ended. She's going to take the gems to her mother once we're all dead. How can you not see this, Bastien?"

"We weren't going to outrun the storm the other way either, Roland," Aunt Avril said in my defense.

My stomach felt sick that I was leading the escape in a

world I didn't know, through a terrain I was unfamiliar with, and to a place I wasn't sure existed. I nearly cried with relief when Bastien gripped me around the waist and pointed in the distance. "Is that a person?"

"We can't stop for anyone," Madigan ruled. "We have to find shelter."

As we ran closer, the figure started to take shape. It was a man, calmly walking toward us. Like, strolling through the wheat field as if a storm wasn't brewing, readying to take us all out. The man wore a Newsies cap, chocolate-colored fitted slacks with a gray vest, a white dress shirt rolled up to his elbows and a green shirt underneath.

Bastien swore loudly in time with Madigan, as if they recognized the man. Aunt Avril let out a cry of scandal, but I didn't know who the dude was, so I wasn't sure what the fuss was about. Even Roland was finally speechless, unable to say anything negative to me at the sight of the man. His head was down, his cap shrouding his face (not like I would've known him anyway). We slowed when we came to him, and Bastien dismounted behind me. His hand was on the hilt of his knife, his hackles on high alert as he took a step forward to speak for the group. "Your majesty?"

The man nodded, tilting up his head to offer Aunt Avril a toothy smile. I gasped when I realized he wasn't wearing a green shirt beneath the white one, but his skin was completely chartreuse from head to toe. Like, Kermit green. His lips were full and expressive when his grin turned toward me, unperturbed that the storm was encroaching upon on us. "Hello, *Fleur*," he said to me, his almond-shaped eyes sparking to life when they landed on my face. "How nice to see you."

My mouth fell open, and though the storm was baring down on us, a girlish attraction flitted through my mind. The thirty-something man had full lips, an angular jaw and a confident charm to him that made me wet my lips without meaning to. There was a hint of wickedness to his smile and mischief to his teasing eyes that drew me in. There was no other word for it. Kerdik was sexy – green skin and all.

I chided my libido and tucked those errant thoughts away with a slight blush. "Is your name Kerdik?" I asked, picking the name out of Cheval's head. My horse didn't seem too thrilled to be in such close proximity of the man, and backed up a few steps. "You're the birth blessing dude, right?" He didn't look much older than thirty-three, but I knew that couldn't be right if he'd blessed me twenty-two years ago. He couldn't have been an eleven-year-old wizard or magician or whatever.

Kerdik chuckled at my terminology. "Indeed, I am. I see you've grown up quite nicely since I saw you last. You were just a baby back then."

"It's good to meet you, man." I didn't bother with too many niceties. I could feel the cold wind whipping around us, even at a standstill. It hadn't started raining yet, but the black flat, swirling vortex above us threatened much inescapable damage. "Look, I've got a pretty healthy fear of hairy leeches trying to suck the sanity from me. If you've got the same kind of fear, you can ride with us. We don't really know where we're going, but you shouldn't be caught out in the open like this. Come with us. We'll find somewhere safe to wait out the storm together."

"He doesn't need us for anything," Bastien said quietly between gritted teeth. "That's Master Kerdik."

Kerdik watched my face with an intrigued tilt to his head, as if I'd just said something odd. "You want to keep me safe from the storm?" He said it like he'd never heard of anything so strange. Thick coffee-colored lashes framed his eyes, making each expression something to ponder.

I shrugged. "Well, yeah. You expect us to just leave you here, all alone?"

A slow smile spread across Kerdik's features, making him that much more handsome. "I've got shelter enough for us all. There's nothing else around for miles. You'll never outrun this storm, *Fleur*. Come with me."

"Oh. Seriously? Thank you. I didn't totally have a plan."

I expected him to hop on the back of Madigan's horse or something, but he calmly turned from us and lifted his hands like an orchestra conductor to the wheat field.

The horses spooked, and everyone let out noises of confusion and warning when the ground began to tremble. My mouth fell open when dirt and rocks shot out of the ground like some sort of reverse waterfall. Millions of pebbles started to amass together, acting as one to form a structure of some sort. Wheat flew everywhere, making its own cyclone of confusion until finally a large, towering shape began to take place.

Water flew out from Kerdik's outstretched palms, turning the loose dirt and dust into thick, moldable mud. The gooey brown spackled itself between the pebbles, turning the suggestion of a wall into a solid structure that could withstand... I dunno, hairy leeches, I hoped. The rocks and mud mingled together to form what was starting to look like a giant hand, wider than all three horses lined up end to end. The rock hand looked as if it was grabbing at the air before us. Then there were several cracking sounds, and the mud was extruded from between the fingers of the hand, resting on top to form a coating. I watched in wonder as the pebbles expanded like balloons filling with too much water, morphing into each other as they formed an impenetrable roof and walls.

My brain didn't have the physics explanation to make sense of that. My mouth dropped open like a guppy, but no sound came out.

Roland shouted his wonder that was weighted with fear. Aunt Avril screamed at the too much that none of us were expecting to find out here. Madigan dismounted, his long, arched blade drawn. You know, in case the mud needed fighting.

The moldable rock-hand froze, and the mud and wheat started spackling in between the tips of the fingers, creating a sort of cavern with a long roof. Kerdik turned back to us, a sly smile telling me he enjoyed freaking people out with his super weird elemental magic. If Judah were here, he'd be configuring Kerdik's stats, to see how he'd measure up in a duel against an ogre or something.

Cheval was chanting over and over to me that Master Kerdik could be dangerous, and that such power to twist nature itself wasn't to be trusted. Being that I could converse with animals with my own janky brand of magic, I wasn't sure if I should heed Cheval's advice or not.

29

KERDIK THE DANCING KING

When the impromptu cave was finished, Kerdik stepped inside and motioned for us to follow him. Cheval was wary, but knew we didn't have another option. The rain started to fall behind us, and I looked over my shoulder to confirm that we were half a soccer field away from the torrential mayhem. It looked as if someone had poked a hole in the swirling pancake cloud that filled a hefty bulk of the sky, and buckets of water were being dumped down on the field behind us. Cheval cursed himself as he reluctantly carried me into the cavern with the others. He backed into the furthest corner from Kerdik, as if he didn't want me too near the magical green guy.

The smell of the fresh dirt surrounding us made me feel like I was underground. Though I could hear the rain pelting the field and coming closer, somehow in our cave it didn't feel quite so harrowing. The shelter was surprisingly deep and long, giving us enough room for all the horses and people to stretch out. We'd been granted a reprieve from the chase, and no matter what everyone's conflicted feelings were on Kerdik, I was grateful not to have to run the horses past their breaking point. "Hey, thanks, man," I offered lamely. "That was super way impressive."

"But, of course. Can't have my little Compass lost in the rain." His delighted smile only grew when it touched on my face. He turned to Aunt Avril with a slight dip of his chin. "Avril, dear. It's been too long."

"Far too long." Her reply was laced with accusation. "I tried finding you for nearly two decades. Sent my bravest knights to go looking for you."

"Ah, yes. They were delicious. Thank you for the offering. I'm sure you know I'm only found when I want to be."

"We were desperate," she accused, dismounting and marching toward Kerdik – all pretense of civility lost. "You knew what Morgan would do, and you just sat back and let it happen! My region fell to ruin because of her, and you did nothing! Tell me how she got in your good graces. Tell me how Morgan sold herself to you to gain such favor." Aunt Avril spoke to him like a child mouthing off to an adult who'd let her down, but she was clearly in her forties, and looked far older than him. I didn't totally understand their dynamic.

Bastien backed away and untied Roland, who didn't need to be told not to stir anything up right now. Roland was positively ashen with reverential fear when he took in the green man, matched with a display of his power.

It was like, the millionth weird magical thing I'd been introduced to in less than two months' time, so I was less shocked and more grateful. All the differing brands of enchantment seemed to muddle into one big wave of "Huh, that's pretty crazy." It was hard to pick out which was the truly impressive spellwork, and which was just the everyday. Apparently, what Kerdik had done by forming us a shelter was more than a little terrifying to the average Joe Avalonian.

Bastien reached for me with hands that had an uncharacteristic slight tremble to them. He didn't say a word, but told me with his darting eyes that though we were in a shelter, somehow this might be more dangerous than the storm. I slid down into his arms, grateful to find that I could put a little weight on my bum ankle without pain ricocheting up my leg. Still, Bastien clung to me, forgoing the stoic "she's nothing to me" demeanor he'd worn like armor around his besties. "Stay back," he warned me quietly, his arm slung low around my hips. He held me close and pressed my front to his so that we were breathing in unison.

My hand and head rested on his chest, which puffed and broadened at my touch while the rain neared. It sounded like a deafening wave coming to crash down on our heads, echoing off the rock walls that closed us in.

"Did I lead us somewhere bad?" I asked quietly, scared I would be our undoing.

"We'll see, I guess." Bastien's free hand gripped his dagger, wary of Kerdik's every move.

"I owe Avalon nothing," Kerdik replied to my aunt's accusations, amused at the fight he didn't feel the need to go at whole-hog. "Avalon, on the other hand, owes me years of prosperity."

Aunt Avril guffawed. "Go to my war-torn province and see what prosperity still exists. Your gift was fool's gold. Glittery for a time, but left us with nothing. Your gifts always do that."

Kerdik's tone came back clipped. "Perhaps if you'd taken better care of my gift, it wouldn't have deserted you so easily."

Aunt Avril's nostrils flared. Never had she looked more like a royal than when she pulled back her hand and let it fly, slapping Kerdik across the face.

Despite the chaos of nature outside, the air in the cave was silent and still, afraid to move at all. Madigan didn't step forward to shield Avril, but angled his body so his shoulder was in front of Bastien and me. Though Aunt Avril was the one in the line of fire, the Brotherhood was concerned only with protecting each other.

Kerdik's smile didn't fade, but only widened at the fight in my aunt. He reached out and took her hand almost lovingly. "Oh, Avril. I would say you were sweet and naïve to strike me, but Tyronoe was the sweet one. Gliten was the naïve one. You were perpetually trying to overshadow the first-born. Morgan was always shinier, wasn't she?" He tsked Avril as if she was a petulant child. "You haven't earned the right to strike me. Now I shall have to punish you."

My breath caught in my throat at the light tone that held only mild disapproval, and not the indignation one might foster if they'd just been slapped across the face. "My land was taken from me when Morgan tried to steal my stone, and you did nothing to stop her! I have every right to hit you after what your magic did to my family."

He examined her fingers and then slowly placed her hand on the rock wall in the back of the cave, his grin never faltering when the rock started rippling. Aunt Avril screamed when her hand suddenly sunk into the stone surface, as if it were made of only mud. The stone sealed around her wrist, keeping her locked in place while she screamed and struggled against the immovable wall. "Let me go, you snake!"

I tried to go to her to help, but Bastien's hug mutated into a restraint. His hand went around my mouth when I opened it to shout something foul at Kerdik. "Shh. Kerdik does what he likes. I won't see your hand sealed to the wall next to your aunt's. Quiet now. He won't hurt her. He's never hurt the Daughters of Avalon."

Kerdik traced a line across my aunt's cheek, looking at her red face and taking in her spewed threats with only a passing interest. "It's been so long since I've seen the

Daughters of Avalon. Morgan is the most persistent, summoning me daily, but she hasn't seen my face in decades. Now you finally see me, and the first thing you do is yell like a child and strike my face? Perhaps I should've left you to the storm. You're fortunate I have an affinity for my handiwork. Must know how it all turns out."

He moved away from Aunt Avril, leaving her to struggle with her hand in the rock as he stalked toward me. "Let me see my crowning achievement, gentlemen," he said to Madigan and Bastien with mild annoyance.

Madigan reluctantly stepped aside, reasoning, as Bastien had earlier, that Kerdik did what he liked, and there was no use trying to stop him. My heart pounded wildly in my chest, introverting me with every step Kerdik took to close the distance. My horses pawed at the ground and snorted their unhappiness at Kerdik being so close to me, but no one moved to stop him. Roland moved to stand with Aunt Avril, watching our exchange carefully.

Bastien dropped his arm from around my back and gave me a whole foot of space between our bodies, but refused to drop my hand. That simple touch helped me to stand up straighter and face whatever rock-wielding magic was about to come flying at me.

Kerdik clicked his fingers in the dim cave, and a blue flame danced in his palm to shed light on us. Kerdik's eyes were light green, contrasting with the short sky-blue hair that stuck out of his Newsies cap. My intake of breath was paired with wide eyes as I studied the coolest genetic setup

I'd ever seen. I'd never met anyone with skin and hair as awesome as his. While the hair on his head was blue, his eyebrows and lashes were dark brown, outlining his expressions with a painter's grace. Kerdik's green epidermis didn't appear scaly, but was smooth, like an adolescent's before the sun and just plain life cracked and aged him. He had a narrow nose, high and sharp cheekbones, and an angular jawline that made his smile appear that much more face-splitting when he grinned.

Kerdik studied me with the same fascination, as if I was the dude with green skin. He showed me his hand without the flame, and reached forward to touch my face. I jerked back on instinct, and Bastien inhaled sharply, like he was afraid my reaction might set Kerdik off. I wasn't used to strangers touching my face.

Kerdik clucked his tongue to scold me, and reached out a second time, his thumb landing on my temple. His touch was gentle, his skin like silk. "This looks painful. How did you acquire such an injury with two protectors such as these in your collection?" His eyes glinted at Bastien and Madigan. "You think I don't recognize Untouchables when I see them? Which of you failed to keep my *Fleur* safe?"

Bastien dropped my hand and stepped forward, his arms banding behind his back like a soldier. He looked straight ahead, and though I knew he was scared, he didn't show it. "I did, your majesty. I failed to keep her safe."

Kerdik nodded, respecting the blunt honesty. "Very well. Then you shall be punished."

My expression twisted in a grimace. "What? Not a chance. It's not Bastien's fault I fell."

"He's your *Guardien*, no?" Kerdik glanced from me to Bastien curiously. "Or is it this one?" He looked at Madigan, whose expression darkened.

"Jeez, you're like the millionth person who's asked us that. No, Bastien's a free agent. He's helping me through Avalon, since I'm new here. He's not responsible for me. It's not his fault if I break a nail on the trip. And I barely know Madigan. He's just helping Bastien out."

"'Break a nail?' Is that what you want to tell me happened to you? I gave Morgan a perfect child, trusting she'd care for the gift. When she couldn't be trusted with you, little Elaine was given the chance. Are you telling me it's Lane's fault you've come back to me damaged?"

My eyebrows furrowed. I could practically feel Roland's anxiety peaking that I might rat him out. "I split off from Lane to come get the gems that were left in the Forgotten Forest. She doesn't even know where I'm at right now. Look, I don't totally understand what's going on, but hurting Bastien doesn't exactly help anything. We can move on from that nonsense when you're ready to tell me what you really want. Why'd you help us if you're bent on constantly getting into fights with everyone?"

The rain poured heavily half a mile away from our cave, nearing like an ominous spider. The thunder spooked the horses, who shuffled toward the back. Kerdik studied my features, still rubbing my temple with his thumb as if I had an ink spot that wouldn't go away. My lashes fluttered shut at the gentle touch that soothed my nerves. "My spitfire is alive and well? Lane is in Avalon again?"

I nodded and opened my eyes, unsure if I was supposed to be giving up this information. I wasn't used to men this gorgeous giving me such focused attention. "She's fine. Why'd you help us?" I repeated, and then realized I was staring at his lips with too much intention. "Okay, knock it off, dude. We don't know each other well enough for you to do that." I batted at his hand, mildly flustered at the intimate touch that made my stomach flutter.

Bastien whispered for me to calm down, his tension making me slightly off-balanced.

Kerdik caught my wrist in his long fingers, jerking the blue light in his palm up to illuminate every inch of my face. "Not quite the demeanor of a princess, but you're definitely a Daughter of Avalon. Morgan did well to breed with Urien. He was a dear friend of mine, of the highest quality."

I leaned back, blanching. "Dude, gross. Don't say 'breed'. It makes the whole thing sound like I'm a dog show competitor." I glanced at our skin, his hand on my wrist showing the contrast of the green on peach. I was temporarily stunned by the beautiful colors together. I finally wrenched my arm out of his grip, trying to hold my ground. "And if you were my dad's friend, then friggin' act like it. Be nice. Stop playing games and threatening people."

Kerdik smiled at my scolding. "Urien would've made a fine father, had he been given the chance." He examined my features too carefully, scrutinizing every detail of my face. "With your pretty countenance and that fire in your eyes? It's a good thing you grew up away from me. I would have destroyed any man who came near you."

Bastien's whole body was a ball of tension, and I didn't want anyone exploding in such close quarters.

I exhaled steadily and motioned for him to come out of the cave with me, away from the others. Kerdik followed my slow limp curiously, while Bastien, Madigan and Aunt Avril shot me looks of fear that were laced with a silent warning. I felt like my coaches, taking a problem player aside for a knock-it-off chat.

When we were exposed to the wind with enough distance from the others for a conversation, I shoved my hands in my pockets and cut to the chase. "Look, I appreciate you giving us a place to wait out the storm, but things are tense as it is in our group. You've got to be cool if we're going to be in such tight quarters. They're all afraid of you, so you know, stop putting people's hands through walls." I shot him a withering look. "I feel like I shouldn't even have to say that."

Kerdik reared back, amused and confused. "You're scolding me? You don't fear me?"

I quirked my eyebrow at him. "Do you want me to be

afraid of you? You made us this cool cave just so you could watch us cower? Somehow I don't think that's you, and I hope you know by now that the cowering act isn't for me."

"You're not going to ask me to fix your injuries?" He motioned to my face.

I held up my chin defiantly. "I'm not injured. I told you, I broke a nail, is all. So, unless you're secretly a stellar manicurist, you're off the hook." I motioned to the cave behind him. "Don't go scaring everyone in there just because you can. Not cool."

He shook his head. "I can't look at your face like that anymore. I haven't seen you since you were a baby, and I want the true picture of you. Hold still, and I'll fix it."

"Huh? Fix what?"

"Your face. It's all banged up. Be still. It's hideous like this."

I scowled at the sting of such cruel words coming from such a stunning man. "Dude, that's super mean. Is that what you want to teach me about yourself? That you call women 'hideous' on a bad hair day?" I shook my head, my eyes showing him that he'd cut me. "Maybe I don't look as cool as you, but I don't need you putting me down about it."

Kerdik reared back, as if confused about every single word I'd just said. "First off, the wound is hideous, not you. Second, you think I look cool?"

I lowered my chin to give him a decent glower. "You insulted me, I complimented you, and now you're fishing for another? Nice try. You know you look awesome with your skin and hair and all that. I haven't had a shower or a decent meal or a bed to sleep on in way too long. I don't care that I look like this, and neither should you."

Kerdik gaped at me, his eyebrows furrowed, utterly perplexed. "I don't know what to say to that."

"Good. You seem like you're prone to putting your foot in your mouth." I didn't want to be the Humpback Whale here, or have people look at my face as if it was a chore to do so. I looked up at the sky, and then started talking with my hands. "You know, so what if I'm hideous? The job was to collect the gems and bring them back to Lane. I get bonus points for bringing back my Aunt Avril, too, but no one seems to care about that. Because I have a uterus, all anyone cares about is how I look when I'm doing the job. Nonsense." I frowned at him, a note of hurt surfacing. "You're just like everyone else. You only care what I look like, not who I am."

"Then tell me who you are." He looked up at the storm as the wind shifted and started blowing errant warnings of rain onto us like well-aimed spit. Kerdik turned and popped out his elbow to me. "If you don't want me to heal you, can I at least escort you back into safety of my shelter? If you catch cold, I'm afraid I won't be able to resist fixing you, just so you can lecture me some more."

I debated my pride versus hurting my ankle more. "Okay. Hey, thanks." I blew out a gust of nerves. "Sorry if I'm being short. It's been a long one, and people fighting puts me on edge. I keep hoping Avalon will be this happy-skippy utopia, but it's like a breeding ground for tension." I looped my hand through his proffered arm, hobbling pathetically over the uneven ground next to his erect and gentlemanly posture.

"Oh, this is tedious. How can you stand it?" Kerdik paused to frown at my bum ankle.

"You're criticizing my wicked dance moves? This is how I dance, and it's awesome." I tried to force the pain away. Humor was good in situations like these. I did a sliding move with my free arm, letting it catch the tune of the rap song that bopped in my head. "You're just jealous of my mad dancing skills."

Kerdik narrowed one eye at my stubborn streak. "Oh, my mistake. I thought this was you barely being able to stand. Clearly you're dancing."

I dropped his arm, turned to face him, and slowly moved my shoulders to a bounce that was only in my head as we stood ten feet from the cave. If he'd known "Baby Got Back" then he could've appreciated how spot on my rhythm was, but his wide eyes only blinked at me as if *I* was the oddball with the super cool green skin. At least I made myself smile. Despite everything, I needed a solid grin. The wind was whistling and howling loud enough to set my teeth on edge, but I had Sir Mix-a-Lot, who could turn any situation into a dance party.

"This is what passes for dancing these days?"

"It does up in Common. Give it a try, Kerdik. Loosen up your shoulders a little bit."

He squinted at me like I was a weird bug. "You're being ridiculous."

"So what? After all I've been through to get here, I think I'm entitled to dance if I want to. And right now, I'm dancing circles around you, old man." I did a few taunting dance moves with plenty of attitude-laced head swivels just to make him laugh. "No, no. There's no laughing in dancing. Take this seriously!"

His hand covered his smile as he chuckled at my antics. "I can't take you seriously like that. You're going to hurt your leg even more just to... Well, I admit, I don't know what you're trying to do."

"Then it's working. I was trying to get you to chill out. You can't hang with us and be Kerdik the Destroyer. You have to be Kerdik the Dancing King. I'm telling you, our little group reached a boiling point long before you came into the picture. We can't handle more tension."

"Kerdik the Dancing King? That's preposterous." His words sounded pretentious, but I could tell by his churlish grin that he enjoyed being jabbed at.

"Well, you could always be Kerdik the Dancing Queen, if that suits you better."

Thunder cracked overhead, making me jump. Kerdik's smile vanished as he glanced up at the clouds. "You can dance all you like in my cave, *Fleur*. My hold on the earth is stable, but controlling the weather has never been my strong suit." Then he scooped me up like a bride and carried me to the others, who'd been watching us with mouths wide open. My heart stuttered at being literally swept off my feet by someone so attractive.

"Your foolishness almost got us caught in the rain," Kerdik lectured me while everyone else stood back, stone silent as he lowered my legs so I could stand.

"You're welcome. You needed that laugh."

His eyes narrowed, and as brave as I wanted to be, I was reminded in his cold look that he was the one with the control in this situation. "Indeed, I did. Now you'll hold still and let me be good to you. This ankle isn't fit for dancing, so don't fight me on fixing it this time. As we've established, I'm the Dancing King, so I know best." Kerdik waited until my scowl died into a glum nod of mild submission, and then surprised me by blowing me a kiss. The air that came from his mouth had actual weight to it, and felt like dust settling over my face. There was an odd tingling that started at my nose and filtered through my lungs, the oxygen invading my body and spreading the prickly sensation from my head all the way down to my toes. The whole thing felt deliciously ticklish from the inside out.

He held out his palm, and I gasped when green herbs started sprouting from the center. "Whoa! How are you doing that?"

His curious smirk was positively adorable. He crinkled the herbs in his hand, and combined them with a grayish mud he choked out from his fingers. "Now, now. If I gave up all my secrets, how would I impress you?"

I shrugged. "With your dance moves, obviously."

Kerdik chuckled, and each time a genuine smile crossed his lips, he seemed surprised by the crime of levity being tolerated on his features. It seemed he was more given to evil grins than actual levity. "Hold still, Dancing Queen. This will speed along your healing." He reached out and spread the gray herb-flecked mud on the scraped and sore side of my face. "Easy," he warned when he saw my nervous twitches at having someone touch my face. I wanted to jerk back, but the steadiness in Kerdik's gaze told me he really was trying to help me out. "I won't hurt you, *Fleur*."

I gulped and stayed still, letting the stranger rub mud on me. Once he'd covered the wound from my temple to the bottom of my cheek, he pressed his palm to the mud. Instantly it grew cold, hardening and cracking in the span of a minute, making my face tingle. When his hand grew wet, I stepped away, confused. "Whoa. What are you doing now?"

"I'm washing your face. Do you prefer the mud?"

"I guess not. But how are you doing that?"

"Elemental magic," he explained. "I can produce water on command." With his free hand, he held back the stray strands of hair while his other hand washed my face off. His fingers were gentle and smooth as he traced my features, lingering on my cheekbones to trace the crest.

"Much, much better. Now I can see you as you are." He brushed over my face again, drying me off.

I turned to Bastien, since I didn't have a mirror. "Does it look any better?"

Madigan stiffened and Bastien let out a whispered swear at the sight of my face when the tingling subsided. I raised my hand to traced the abrasions I'd felt before, but the skin was smooth now. "It's like the scrapes are a week old. I can barely see them," Bastien marveled.

Kerdik nodded in approval. "You're my gift to Avalon, and I'll look at you as I like. Now you're good as new. A prize if ever I saw one."

I tested out my ankle, and was surprised to find it perfectly healed. "Oh, wow. Um, thanks. That actually is really helpful. I guess that was slightly more than a broken nail. Sorry about the uterus comment from earlier, I guess. How'd you do that?"

"You truly know nothing about Avalon, do you."

"Only that you really shouldn't have fixed my ankle if you wanted any chance at smoking me in a dance contest. Now you don't have a prayer."

Kerdik laughed, popping his elbow to me like a gentleman once again. "Come, *Fleur*. Watch the storm with me. There's nothing like a front-row seat to an Avalon *tonnerre*. This is no doubt your first as an adult?"

"Yeah. Pretty crazy. There's nothing like this in Common. Truth? I'm a little nervous about the hairy mind-warping leeches."

"As you should be, though you've nothing to fear while I'm around." His voice turned sharp when he addressed the others. "Stay toward the back, or I'll send you out when the hail falls. I'd like privacy with my princess."

I cast him a withering look. "That's like, the exact opposite of what I told you I wanted. No more Kerdik the Destroyer. Maybe the next time you bark at people, add a little shoulder shimmy to it." I demonstrated for him just to make him smile.

"If only it were that simple." Kerdik glanced over his shoulder at the others in warning. Then he pressed his hand to the middle of my spine to secure my place at his side.

30

OLD BLESSINGS AND NEW FRIENDS

astien and Madigan were utterly silent as they moved to stand next to Aunt Avril at the back of the cave. Though it wasn't actually private, Kerdik treated our conversation as if it was, trusting the heavy rain to drown us out as it reached our cave. The two of us stood at the edge of the abode, with the others hugging the back wall. "I've been looking forward to meeting you, *Fleur*. Word spread that the *Voix* was in Avalon, so I tracked you down here."

"That's some stellar timing you've got. Not for nothing, but I didn't have a plan for how to get us out of this storm. Thanks for showing up when you did. And really, thank you for fixing my injuries. Totally annoying to be the weakest link. I already know nothing about this world, but to be limping on top of it? I appreciate it. I owe you like, seven chocolate milkshakes."

He smirked at me. "Seven, eh?"

"Sure. Eight would make you puke."

Kerdik secured me to his side at the mouth of the cave, and turned us so we were facing the storm. My hip was glued to his, and for the sudden intimacy of the whole thing, I didn't mind having him so near. It was nice to have someone to watch the storm next to.

Before I could stop myself from blurting out my confusion, my mouth ran away with me with no polish added into my words. "I don't know much about this place."

Kerdik was unruffled by my admission. "Well, I invented Avalon, so you can ask me your questions, *Fleur*."

"Um, well, how old is Avalon?"

"Old. Older than you."

I shot him a look that was filled with sass. "You stink at this."

The corner of Kerdik's mouth twitched upward. "Avalon is just over a century old."

I scratched my elbow and leaned into him. "I thought I knew my life, but now the most basic things seem like they need to be vetted. The Daughters of Avalon – Lane, my mom and the rest – are they..." I felt silly for asking. "Are they immortal or something?"

"Most of them are dead now, so no. They possess a bit more magic than most, but nothing so grand as immortality."

"That makes sense. Sorry. I feel like I'm a million miles

behind five-year-olds, who probably know all of this stuff." *Story of my life.*

"Anything else?"

"Are you related to the Daughters of Avalon or something? I mean, you gave them the Jewels of Good Fortune. That seems like something you'd only trust family with."

"I have no children," Kerdik said quietly, looking out at the rain contemplatively. Then he scoffed, coming back to himself. "Could you imagine me with a child? I get impatient if plants prove obstinate."

"You, impatient? I don't believe it. You're such a kitten."

His chest vibrated at my tease, and he nestled me a little closer in his half-embrace. It was cozy with Kerdik, comfortable without effort.

The water was so heavy that the wheat stalks were bending under the punishment nature doled out. I shivered, and Kerdik snapped his fingers to the others without looking behind him. "I shouldn't have to tell you that my flower needs a cloak. She's clearly cold. If you wait until she shivers, you've already failed. Anticipate her needs."

I cast up a dramatic eyeroll to Kerdik. "No one here is my servant. If I wanted to warm up, I'd go get a second shirt myself. I told you to be nice. I think you missed that part. Your spontaneous deafness is mildly annoying."

Despite my protest, Bastien's dirty spare flannel found its way over my shoulders. "Your majesty," he said with no hint of personality to him. I could tell he was still waiting for Kerdik's judgment.

"You didn't have to do that. Thanks."

Kerdik ignored my frown. "That's better. When you settle down in Avalon, be sure your servants are better trained than that one. Untouchables are fantastic protectors, but it's the submitting part they fall short on. Best train this one with a firmer hand."

"Oh, jeez. Look, I don't want to talk about that, since clearly you have no idea what kind of a person I am, or what kind of guy Bastien is. I've got other questions, and I'm guessing you're the only one who'll have an actual answer." I jerked my head to the far side of the opening and plopped myself down on the damp earth so I could lean against the wall.

Kerdik looked down at me with amusement. "I admit, I don't do much sitting on the ground."

"Well, that's the way we play today, chief. I'm beat. Time to take a break from being Kerdik the Destroyer, and just be normal for a few." I patted the ground next to me, eyeing his fitted, pressed trousers and dark gray vest that buttoned over his crisp white shirt. He didn't look like the type to get dirty while playing with the mud.

After much consideration, he sat next to me, leaning back on his hands. His right arm was slightly behind me, and if I leaned just a couple inches backward, I'd be resting against him. I made for sure to keep my spine rigid as I hugged my knees to my chest. I couldn't picture myself getting super cuddly with someone of his hotness caliber.

"How well do you know Lane, Avril, Morgan and all of them?"

"Well enough to know that no matter what gift I'd given them, they would find a way to turn it into a curse. Some have that ability, I'm afraid. Not all the sisters, but the more vocal ones were like that. I admit, I felt sad for Tyronoe and Gliten when I heard they had died."

"People seem to think that it was your responsibility to step in, to take the gems from Morgan and right all the wrongs. How much truth is there to that?"

"My, you're a direct one. Not bred for politics, that's for certain."

"You want to play games instead? I thought you'd be the kind of guy who appreciated not having to figure out people's motives."

"I do. It's just unexpected. The sisters are quite adept at burying their true intentions. I found it tiresome after a while. I anticipated you being much the same. Perhaps there's more of your father to you than your mother. Fortunate, that." He cleared his throat as we looked out onto the unending golden field that was hazy through the curtain of thick rain that darkened the night. "They came to me with constant complaints that their lands weren't producing enough, and the people were suffering across the board. They begged me for a solution, so I gave it to them. Imagine my dismay when my blessing turned sour in their hands after they started fighting over the gems. I can fix the land, sure, but I cannot fix greed. That's a poison which runs deep, I'm afraid."

"And Morgan? My mother is greedy?"

Kerdik raised an eyebrow at me. "As greedy as they come. But surely you surmised as much. If Lane was your guide, she must have educated you on Morgan's ways. Lane always had a clear head about judging people's character."

I nodded, and then rested my chin on my knees. "I guess I just needed an impartial person to confirm it. I don't know why I was holding out hope for things to be different." I studied the rain that punished the earth, as if the two elements were at war. "At least I've got my wicked dance moves. If I can't have a great mom, then I've got popping and locking to console me. Total win," I said glumly.

"Your dancing is unlike any in Avalon." I couldn't tell if he meant that as a compliment or not. "Morgan is greedy, but to an extent, we all are. I want a great many things, and I'd throw morals, mortals and rules out the window to get at them. I'm sure the same can be said of you."

"I'm not about to destroy whole kingdoms for the sake of getting what I want."

"There's nothing you want?" he hinted quietly at something, but I didn't have a clue what he meant. "I know your shortcomings. I know the snares in your mind that hinder you."

I stiffened and glanced over my shoulder to ensure the others couldn't hear us. My mouth went dry and my palms started sweating. "Dude, my mind is fine. And shut up about my shortcomings." I didn't want Bastien to find out I couldn't read. I didn't want him to know I was dumb. I wanted to be "Daisy", not "Remedial Rosie" to him. "Remember when I told you to be cool back there? This is not being cool. How'd you even find out about that?"

Kerdik moved his shoulder to touch my back so I could lean on him. "I'm sure it's no secret by now, *Fleur*. It's the payment your mind made to take in my blessing."

"Huh?"

"Do you think blessings don't require payment? That's the same trap the Daughters of Avalon fell into. I blessed them with the stones, but not all of them gave the payment, which was to work together for Avalon's best interest. Thus, the blessings turned sour. Blessings always require payment."

"What a sad worldview you have. Blessings are supposed to be only good. I feel sorry for you, thinking like that." I tapped my forehead while Kerdik puzzled out the confusion that someone actually pitied him. "You did this to me? You're the reason I..." I couldn't say "can't read" out loud.

Kerdik's dark chocolate-colored eyebrows pulled together in the center of his forehead. "The payment for the blessing of being the *Voix* was that you had to be kind to the animals who trusted you enough to speak, other-wise they would have turned on you and made your life miserable. What shortcoming are you referring to? Sleeping? Is that it? Because there's nothing to be done about that. Immense amounts of magic are necessary to maintain a gift like yours. I'm afraid there's no getting around sleep, my darling."

I raised my eyebrow at the term of endearment, when he was pretty much a stranger to me. "Oh. Yeah, that's what I was talking about. Sleep." I shook my head, bummed that there was no magical reason I couldn't do things a second-grader could. "Lane told me that my mom only kept me around so I'd be her Compass and lead her to the Jewels of Good Fortune. Is that true?"

Kerdik was quiet as we watched the rain. "Morgan doesn't understand love, though she does a fair imitation of it." His voice quieted to a gentle prodding. "Take that into consideration when you're reunited with her someday."

My shoulders slumped. "Thanks for the heads-up." When loud thumps crashed into the earth, I jumped, accidentally brushing Kerdik's shoulder. "What was that?"

Kerdik's arm drew around me and pulled me into his nook, warming me with a ball of fire he conjured in his free hand. I gathered Bastien's flannel around me more securely, and then leaned into Kerdik, indulging us both in the snuggle that was oddly comforting. It felt easy, like palling around with him was the most natural thing in the world. "It's only the hail. You're safe. This structure can withstand anything."

"Oh. I thought it was a dinosaur trying to jump on a

trampoline. It's like the sky is trying to take its anger out on the ground."

Kerdik gaped at me, as if I'd hit some mythological nail on the head with a guess. He skated over it and went back to the absurd. "I'm afraid I don't understand. What's a dinosaur?"

I blinked up at him. "Like, you know, a reptilian monster." I held up my hands like a t-rex and roared. Kerdik looked at me like I was telling a weird joke. "Okay, if you ever come up to Common, I'll introduce you to a little something called *Jurassic Park*. It's only the greatest example of terrifying monsters, plus the beauty that is Jeff Goldblum. You'll love it. You think you've got magic? Wait until you see Jeff Goldblum's smile. Totally dreamy."

"You're not afraid of the terrifying monsters?"

"I'm sitting here next to you, aren't I? Aren't you supposed to be the big, bad villain?"

He narrowed his eyes at me, trying to judge if I was joking or not. "Yes, well. I suppose most blame the fall of the provinces on me."

"Is that what you want?"

"I don't care what the Fae think of me. I'm not interested in picking up after the mess they've made."

I smiled sagely, channeling my inner Lane. "Ah. It sounds like you think your adventure is over. I've got news for you, pal. The adventure you go on with yourself isn't even half done."

Kerdik quirked an eyebrow at me. "And how would you know anything about my journey?"

I motioned to the troublesome cloud in his stare. "You've got that unsettled look about you. People don't look like that at the end of a satisfying journey. You've only put yours on pause. I don't blame you for that. Sometimes the trek to the end hurts too much to make it through without a few stops to regroup. But you're not finished with your story. Your song isn't nearly sung to its full potential yet."

Kerdik was silent a few beats. "You talk like you know, but you can't possibly."

I shrugged. "Maybe I don't know you, but I understand unfulfilled dreams well enough to get that you're not done taking yourself on many more adventures." I met his gaze with compassion. "Your best days aren't behind you, Kerdik."

We were both a little confused by our close proximity, but neither of us pulled away. I could hear Cheval warning me to be careful, that Master Kerdik couldn't be trusted. The three horses were scared for me, but they stayed back, watching with trepidation.

I tried to take it all in stride and just chill for a minute. Everything had been so harrowing on the journey here. The two of us enjoyed the sounds of nature pelting the earth just outside our little stronghold. "Whoa! I didn't realized the hail stones would get to be that big." I pointed to a perfect circular-shaped hail stone that was the girth of a bowling ball. "That's crazy. Imagine that one rolling toward the pins, right?"

"'Rolling toward the pins?' I'm afraid I don't understand."

"Oh, sorry. You probably don't have bowling here. It's just a silly game where you roll a ball about that size down a lane and see if you can knock ten pins down. Whoever knocks the most down wins."

"Sounds like a sophisticated kind of game."

I chuckled that he'd made a joke. "I can teach you sometime. It's fun. Sometimes simple can be amazing."

Kerdik pondered my words. "I guess that's true." His green hand cupped my bicep to rub warmth into it when a chilled gust of air caressed us. "I've seen many a storm here, but this is by far my favorite – angry though she is."

"Now that I'm not afraid I'll get knocked off my horse by a chunk of ice falling from the sky? This is probably one of my favorites, too. Something about nature getting all its anger out in one go is kind of spectacular." Then it occurred to me that Kerdik hadn't been seen in ages by anyone other than animals. "Why do you hide? Aunt Avril mentioned that you haven't been seen in a while."

"Hiding implies that I fear the Daughters of Avalon. I merely grew tired of the complaining, the toils and the drama. I saw no reason to return to utter ruin. Besides, I'm immortal. A decade or two is a mere breath to me."

"Then why are you here now? Two-for-one sale on awesome hats?" I teased, tugging on the brim of his.

His arm tightened around me. "I'm here for you. I wanted to see what kind of a woman my prize turned into." He studied the hail, seeing but not seeing it as he squinted through his pondering. "I like to think my blessings don't ruin the world. Sentimental, I suppose. Seeing you? It gives me hope that my love doesn't break beautiful things. Maybe now that I have you as proof, I won't stay so far away this time."

"Oh, wow. That's... Thanks for having faith in me. That's a hefty compliment. True confessions?"

"Well, they're the best kind."

"I don't totally know what I'm doing. I'm just trying to help out however Lane needs me to. I don't really get all the politics going on. Lane wanted to give you back the gems after the provinces get a little time to heal, but Aunt Avril wants to return them to their regions to redeem the land and help the people. Is there a wrong choice in that? I don't really know how to do the right thing in this world."

"I can't tell you that. I can only say that I've not seen such measured and even thinking in a Daughter of Avalon in ages. I can see Lane's mark of excellence and intelligence on you."

My head snapped to stare at him. I blinked in stunned amazement, emotion rising up in my throat. "You think I'm intelligent?"

"I'm sure I can't be the first to tell you that. Lane raised you well."

I swallowed hard at the compliment only Lane and

Judah ever gave me. With my GPA, it wasn't a label I often received. I cleared my throat. "Lane doesn't really do failure, so I'll be sure to pass along the compliment."

"Perhaps I'll pay her a visit myself."

"That's cool, but none of this freezing people's hands in the wall nonsense around Lane. Seriously, dude."

Kerdik was unperturbed that Aunt Avril was still standing at the back of the cave with her hand frozen in the wall. "This is how I handle ungrateful pests."

"Cool ability, but you go after Lane like that, and you'll see a whole other side of me."

"Is that so?" His tone sounded torn between bemused and threatening me not to try my hand at intimidating him.

"Yeah. Mess with Lane, and I'll straight up cry."

"You'll cry?" he repeated, mocking my serious threat.

"Yup. Fights amuse you, but genuine emotion seems to confuse you. Mess with Lane, and I'll cry all over you. You'll be soaked in tears, and you'll be so uncomfortable, that you'll wish you were never ever mean to her just to get me to knock it off." I shot him half a smirk to let him know I was mostly joking.

Kerdik laughed, and it sounded good rolling off his full lips. "Now that you're back in Avalon, I don't think I'll stay away so much. You amuse me, *Fleur*."

"If you're like most of my guy friends, you're allergic to tears. So if you know what's good for you, you'll iron out your temper before you start making regular appearances.

Otherwise..." I gave him an ominous look of warning, and then threw my head back, fake crying so loud, I made Roland jump.

My theatrics gave birth to matching grins on Kerdik's face and mine. "I admit, I'm surprised to find I don't mind your company."

I don't know why, but this made me laugh all over again. "Man, you suck at compliments. Just say, 'Rosie, you're the coolest chic I know,' not 'I'm shocked I don't hate being around you.'"

"'Rosie'? You don't go by your given name?"

"Nah. My friends call me Rosie."

"And I'm your friend?"

I blinked at him, smiling. "Well, you could always be my puppy, but thanks to your blessing, I've got plenty of those. And you certainly haven't earned the title of 'Dancing King' yet. I think 'friend' is the label you should go by."

Kerdik moved his arm from around me so he could play with my fingers, examining the differences in the tones of our skin. He seemed starved for touch. I couldn't imagine spending so many years away from everybody, isolated and alone. His smile started in his chest from the warmth that had survived in his heart, and then blossomed out onto his face when he looked at me. "Friends, then. I rather like the sound of that, Rosie."

THE FUN IN NOT BEING CAREFUL

Kerdik clicked his fingers and sent out a fire that burned in a neat foot-thick row just outside the cave when I shivered again. The flames held, despite the torrential rain. The others were still in the back of the cave, but they weren't as rigid as before. Roland stood next to Aunt Avril, since she couldn't sit, and Bastien and Madigan reclined near the horses, who'd tucked themselves in the far corner from Kerdik. Kerdik and I sat in our huddle together for hours, watching the hail and commenting on the oddly-shaped balls that caught our eyes. There were whole handfuls of comfortable silence where we let the magic of nature lull us with its spell of solace.

When the hail finally stopped beating the earth, a slop and slush sound reached my ears over the rain. "What's that noise? It sounds like a ketchup bottle farting."

"What? The leeches are falling. They'll reach us soon enough." Kerdik motioned to his fire when I stiffened at the reminder that we weren't just shooting the breeze, that there was actual danger out there that was still coming. "Not to worry. They won't cross fire."

"Oh, that's a relief. Thanks for keeping us safe. Truly. We didn't have a solid plan." I listened to make sure the hail had stopped. "Do I have time to run out and grab a chunk of hail before the leeches come our way?"

"You do, but you won't." He snapped his fingers without looking at the men. "Bring her a ball of hail. The larger the better."

I stood, unwilling to let that kind of nonsense fly. I held up my hand to save Bastien's pride, so he didn't feel the need to go running when someone snapped their fingers. I couldn't even picture that, and didn't want to. "I got it. Anyone else want one?"

Aunt Avril shook her head. "Be careful, Rosalie." Her warning had many layers to it as she stared into my eyes across the way.

Kerdik stood beside me, frustrated that I wasn't living up to my queenly parentage. "You'll stay right here and let one of your protectors go fetch one for you. Perhaps your future *Guardien*."

"Bastien's my friend, not my servant, and I don't even know Madigan. Neither of them are my *Guardien*. My *lueur*'s tucked safe in my gut, where it belongs." I patted my abdomen. "I can take care of myself just fine."

Kerdik's frown of consternation was actually kind of precious. "I don't want you running out in the rain. You could slip and fall."

I chuckled at the sweetness. "But you just fixed my ankle for me. It's good as new." I sighed when he still looked hesitant. I didn't want him to get worked up and glue my feet to the earth or something. "If you're so worried, then come with me. Hurry, though. I don't want to get my brain sucked by the leeches." I unbuttoned Bastien's shirt and walked over to hand it to him so I didn't get it wet. His eyes were wide with shock at our exchange, but he said nothing more than warning me with his gaze to be careful.

Kerdik looked around at the massive display of nature and held out his hand to me. "Quickly, though. I won't have you losing your mind just to have a trinket to hold." With his palm outstretched toward the ground, he mimed for the fire to sit, as if it was a dog, eager to obey its master. A two-foot-wide space cleared for us, permitting us safe passage out into the storm.

"Let's go, then!" I all but dragged him out into the thick rain before he could overthink the fun. I was soaked to the skin in seconds. The water pelted us so hard, I swear I could feel the welts forming on my arms. I scoured the area for the perfect piece of hail, and finally found one that looked about right. "That one!" I pulled Kerdik over, laughing when I slipped in the mud and he caught me.

"Be careful, Rosie!" he admonished me.

"Why? Where's the fun in being careful? How am I supposed to teach you how to bowl without a bowling ball? That one's perfect." I scampered over to the ball of hail that was the right shape and size, and hefted it up with a loud "oof!" I hadn't been expecting it to be quite so heavy.

We stumbled back to the safety of the cave, laughing and shivering when I dropped the ball on the floor. "That's it? That's the one you wanted? I could've made you that," Kerdik pointed out, his grin wider than ever at our little adventure. The rain sparkled on his lashes, adding nuance and cuteness to everything he did.

"Huh? You can make bowling balls?"

He blew out a loud raspberry, his hands on his knees as we both bent over to catch our breath and admire our prize. "I'm an elemental warlock! I can form things out of ice easily. We didn't have to soak ourselves for your treasure."

I chucked his shoulder. "Sure, but now I know what you look like when you're having fun. I think you needed this bowling ball more than I did. Wasn't that fun?"

Kerdik's smile of surprise at my logic was positively adorable. "It was. You're right; I haven't laughed like that in ages." His smile stopped and his eyes grew earnest. He straightened and reached out with both hands to cup my shoulders. "In absolute *ages, Fleur.*"

"Your majesty, the leeches!" Roland cried out, pointing to the mouth of the cave with wide eyes.

"Of course." Kerdik didn't even look at the threat, but roared his fire higher, and spread it out in a line to cover the whole front of the cave.

I heard a sizzle and pop, followed by a miniscule cry that sounded like a deflating balloon. I grimaced. "Oh! Was that a leech?"

"Indeed. Sit with me, darling. Tell me more about your dinosaurs and bowling. Tell me everything, and make me feel as if I was there."

"You really shouldn't ask me to tell you about Jeff Goldblum movies. He's only the greatest actor in the universe. I think it's because he's so tall and dreamy, while also being a little awkward. Gives the rest of us weirdos hope that we too can fight our very own dinosaurs."

The next few hours were spent with the others whispering on their side of the cave while Kerdik asked all sorts of questions about my life with Lane. He wanted to know the basics, of course, but also the details of the things that made me smile. For the villain everyone painted him as, Kerdik was actually pretty great. We shot the breeze until my eyes started drooping, and a yawn caught me. It felt like it was nearing on three in the morning or so.

"Ah, you've used too much magic today."

The firelight illuminated the sky-blue notes of his hair that stuck out from his hat, warming us while the storm continued to rage just outside. "It's pretty normal for me. I'm not sleeping like I need to on these treks, though. I think it's all catching up with me."

"Would you like me to make a room where you can sleep more privately?"

I shrugged, impressed he had that kind of magic on tap. "Uh, is that something you can do?"

"Of course. I made this structure easily enough." He glanced over his shoulder and barked so his voice would carry over the wind, the rain, the screaming leeches and fire. "You, Brownie. Your charge requires rest. Where do you post yourself when she's vulnerable?"

Bastien stood, his arms behind his back and chest puffed like a true soldier. "Right next to her, your majesty. I won't leave while she rests."

"Very good. If something should happen upon her while she sleeps, whose head shall be removed and tossed around like one of her bowling balls?"

Bastien didn't even flinch. "Mine, your majesty."

I gave Kerdik a light shove. "Oh, knock it off. No need to threaten Bastien. I'm not his charge, I already told you. You should learn to get along with people, especially Bastien. He's a good guy. You'll like him, once you stop threatening to tear his head off. You two should spend some time together tomorrow."

Kerdik quirked his eyebrow at me. "Do you assume I'll still be here when you wake? Do you think I'll be around long enough to foster a fondness for your friends?"

My face fell, but I tried to recover enough of my "whatever" expression to disguise my disappointment. I liked hanging out with Kerdik when he wasn't being a bossy tyrant. He didn't seem to have as many of the "boys on this side, girls on the other side" hang-ups. Having had mostly dude friends my whole life, I missed the uncomplicated camaraderie. "Oh. I didn't realize you'd be gone when I woke up. I can stay awake a little longer. Let's keep talking."

Something tender and precious swept across Kerdik's chartreuse features. "You wish me to stay? You want me to be here when you wake?"

I shrugged. "I mean, you don't have to. I'm sure you've got more important things to do. I was being selfish. Go do your thing."

Kerdik wrapped his arms around me in a hug I could tell he wasn't well-versed in. It took a few seconds, but eventually I sunk into his chest, leaning my head to his shoulder while our curled-up legs knocked together. He kissed the top of my hair, and then lifted my palm to press his lips into the center. "If it's me you want to see when you wake, then it's me you shall have, my dear."

A sweet smile lifted the corner of my mouth at the grand nature of his affection. "It's nice being friends with you."

"It's nice being around a woman who doesn't ask me for use of my magic."

"But you've used a ton of your magic on us already." I winced. "Sorry if that makes you feel used. I really don't want that."

"Nonsense, my girl. I gave you shelter and kept the

leeches away because I wanted to keep you safe. You didn't actually ask me for any of that. You'll see that I give grand gifts that don't turn sour at all – that is, when people are grateful." He shot a glare over his shoulder at Aunt Avril, who scowled against the back wall.

"Oh, well hopefully our next adventure is less harrowing, and more bowling and watching movies about dinosaurs." I stood, brushed my jeans off, and offered my hand to him to yank him up.

He seemed perplexed by the simple gesture, but finally took my hand, rising up to stand before me, taking in my features with confusion he didn't bother hiding. "I would love nothing more." He kissed the back of my hand like a gentleman, drawing out a blush at making me feel like a lady. He chuckled at my shyness. "Oh, now. Don't do that. You're far too lovely. Adding a blush to your cheeks? It's unfair."

My neck shrank, my chin dipping down as I touched the back of my hand to my cheek to cool it. "Okay, okay. Enough with the gentleman stuff. It totally throws me."

"Sleep well, *Fleur*. I'll be here when you wake, and I'll watch over our fortress while you sleep."

"Thank you. And hey, don't threaten anyone while I'm sleeping. Be the guy I like, not the scary one they pee their pants in front of. Dancing King, not Destroyer."

"I shall do my utmost, darling." His eyes shifted to Bastien in a silent threat. "Stand back against that far wall away from the others next to *Fleur*. I need to make a room for her so she has privacy. A princess shouldn't display vulnerability out in the open."

"Yes, your majesty." Bastien and I obeyed, moving away from everyone and pressing our backs to the stone, looking across the cave at the members of our little group. Though I knew it was coming, I still squeaked when a sheet of solid rock shot up out of the earth. It cut us off from the others by forming our own little room, separating us from the rest of the group.

The fire stretched in front of our narrow doorway that looked out onto the wheat field. The flicker danced on Bastien's expression, which finally gave way to the terror he'd been choking on since Kerdik came into our lives. "We're leaving at first sign of the storm letting up, so fall asleep quick, Rosie," he whispered firmly.

"Yes, boss." I closed my eyes and started snoring, pretending to fall asleep upright. I peeked at him to see if he'd cracked a smile yet, but he was too worried to joke around. I waited for him to sit down in the narrow space before I laid on the ground, shifting until I found a comfortable spot. My body ached anew when it finally was given hope of turning off for a few hours. "You alright, chief?"

"No. Nothing about this is alright." He lowered his voice further, but I couldn't hear him over the storm.

"Huh?"

When he repeated himself too many times, he grew frustrated and climbed over my legs, shifting my body so he could lie next to me. He rolled me on my side and spooned me, his lips tickling the shell of my ear. "Kerdik is the most dangerous creature in Avalon, but you treat him like he's a girlfriend coming over for tea."

"Would you rather I cowered?"

"No. But it's messing me up to see you so close to him. I mean, we all still have our heads, so at least there's that. Tread lightly, Rosie. Kerdik is feared for a reason."

"I know. I get it. I'll be more afraid in the morning, okay? I'll put it in my day planner."

Bastien leaned down and kissed my cheek. "Glad to hear you're taking me seriously." He exhaled, dosing me in a heavy gust of his Christmasy-cinnamon scent. "I'm sorry about Roland."

"Not for nothing, but I wouldn't let Judah talk about you the way you let Roland run me down. That sucked, Bastien. You should've had my back from the beginning. I'm only on this journey because of you. Roland wouldn't have tried to hurt me if you'd laid down the law earlier on."

"You're right. No excuses. I think I was just so thrown by it all, and I didn't handle it right. I'm sorry. I'll be firmer with him in the morning, and I won't leave your side. You're doing us the favor with the jewels and whatnot. You shouldn't have to be afraid you'll be attacked." He cleared his throat. "I mean, I can't be with you the way I want to in public." He ran his hand over my arm, squeezing my bicep. "If I wasn't promised to Rachelle, I would be yours without a blink. I keep trying to push you away by turning mean, but it kills me a little bit every time. If you hated me, that would be easier."

I didn't know what to say to all of it. "Stop being a jerk to me. Your drama is your own. I don't deserve to be hurt by Roland, or by you."

Bastien swallowed. "Agreed. I'm sorry. I suppose it's too much to ask for a fresh start in the morning."

I snuggled into him, too tired to stick to my indignation. "Why don't you start now. Be sexy and cuddly, okay? I'm tired, and I need to sleep."

Bastien snorted, and then shook his head as his own thoughts took prevalence. "Kerdik was right; I didn't watch out for you like I should. I keep forgetting you're the Lost Princess. You make it easy to forget that you're just as untouchable as I am. And I keep forgetting that you're not from here, and you need to be guarded from attacks."

"Untouchable? This sounds like a long conversation I'm going to have to be awake for. Can we save the important talks for another day? I was pretty clear a second ago that your job description is to be sexy and cuddly. Everything else can wait until later."

Bastien finally seemed to snap out of his funk and rolled me over, his body facing me in the dark. We were lit only by the fire in the doorway, but it was just enough to catch his dreamier features. "Is this better? Is this what you ordered, Daisy?"

"You're just missing one thing." I ran my fingers over his stubble and leaned in for the kiss I'd been longing for.

Bastien inched backward, a look of warning in his eyes. "Not while Master Kerdik's here," he whispered. "I can practically feel him watching us through this wall. I'm serious, Rosie. It's bad enough Mad suspects us, and I'm pretty sure Roland already knows. But your aunt? If she found out you're kissing an engaged man, things could go south real fast. By the books on this one, sweetheart."

"Oh, fine. You owe me like, a really amazing kiss, though."

"First chance I get where Avalon's most terrifying warlock isn't right next door." He looked down at me and brushed his nose across mine. He glanced over his shoulder to the entrance warily. "Just one kiss," he whispered to the night, promising himself more than warning me. I hadn't pushed him further, and the fact that he wanted to kiss me despite the danger made me swoon for him.

"Whatever you need to tell yourself, chief. If you can stop at just one, you've got better self-control than I do."

Bastien looked deep into my eyes. "I'm not sure I'll ever be able to stop wanting to be near you." When Bastien's lips brushed mine, my whole body bent to accommodate his. My back arched, my leg looped around his, and my lips molded to his soft and insistent ones over and over again. The rain pounded on our stone roof, adding to the we're-in-the-middle-of-nowhere feeling I could take a bath in, reveling in the luxury that it was. "So much for one kiss," Bastien murmured as he went in for more, and still more, and yet somehow, never enough.

32

PRIVATE AND PUBLIC

Waking in Bastien's arms was the breath of fresh air my soul desperately needed. I'd finally slept deeply, and for hours in his burly embrace. "You awake?" he whispered, his nose nudging my cheek.

I didn't bother to open my eyes. "If I say no, will you keep holding me?"

"Always." His lips buried themselves in the crook of my neck and kissed a line along my jaw. "I've been waiting to kiss you all night. This little room is messing with my mind. Makes me feel like we're all alone."

"We are," I teased. I stretched and then shifted us, pulling a fast one so he was on his back, and I was straddling him. I felt powerful, deviant and finally like I had a say in something. "It's our own desert island." I leaned down and sucked on his lower lip, taking no prisoners and foregoing any pretense that our passion could be tamed. I knew we would have to be good and socially polite soon, so I took my ground where I could get it.

Bastien wasn't in the mood to pretend he wanted to keep his distance. His hands found their way to my backside and squeezed the swell, making my back arch and my toes curl. I loved the taste of Bastien, and couldn't get enough. His flannel unbuttoned beneath my frenzied fingertips, eager to get closer to his warmth. His t-shirt was tugged over his head and cast aside so I could trace the scope of his broad chest.

He broke the kiss and looked down at his scarred body, panting through his desire for more, which conflicted with his nerves at being so exposed. "I didn't always look like this. These scars, I…"

I captured his lips before he could tell me how much he hated his body. "I love the look of you." I devoured his lips, pressing my pelvis to his while I straddled his lap. "I love the feel of you."

His hunger for me multiplied at my declaration. Bastien lifted me and tipped me backwards, pressing my shoulders to the dirt so he could cover me with his toned physique. He hitched my leg over his hip and traced the slope of my thigh through my jeans, while his lips made a perfect mess of my control.

I didn't choke on the *lueur* at all, and reveled in the kiss we could finally have without holding ourselves back. I needed just one uninhibited moment to feel like I still had a choice in any part of my life.

I wasn't expecting the wall next to us to rapidly suck itself into the ground, leaving us on display for the others, who gasped at the scandal. I swore and moved to cover myself, though I wasn't the one without a shirt. It was Bastien's kiss that made me feel gloriously naked, and that was a very private thing.

Bastien sat up and quickly threw on his shirt, tugging it downward. He faced away from the others to hide his scars from them. His back wasn't that much better, though. "Apologies," he offered to Aunt Avril, his head bowed and eyes averted. Her hand was still stuck in the rock wall, her forlorn expression replaced with one of scandal and a mild dose of shame at my brazen behavior.

I sat up and dusted myself off. My cheeks were burning, but we hadn't done anything too racy. I mean, we were kissing, not making babies mere feet away from my new family. I forgot that in Avalon, kissing means a whole lot more than it does up in Common, implying long-term intentions and whatnot.

Kerdik watched us carefully, studying my small movements and Bastien's hand that reached down to lift me up after he stood. He still couldn't look at the group, but addressed them all with a brave voice. "So, I'm sure you all gathered as much, but Rosie's mine." His hand stayed locked onto my fingers, unwilling to cast me aside for social propriety this time. I didn't know what to make of his declaration, other than that finally we were moving forward, not having to hide anything. But to call me his before we'd even had a conversation about it felt... off. I began to appreciate the ocean of difference between our two cultures.

Roland spat on the ground at Bastien's feet, livid. "You're engaged to Reyn's sister! How could you do that to Rachelle?"

Most unsettling was Kerdik's careful study of us. It was like he was building a plan in his mind, but for what, I couldn't tell you.

Bastien cleared his throat. "I claimed Rachelle's hand because Captain Burke raped her, got her pregnant, and then left her for dead. I did it to save her reputation. You know that, Roland."

Roland's fists were clenched at his sides. "Reyn would murder you if he saw you carrying on with the witch. If women could be Gancanagh, I would swear on my life that she was one of them, charming you to follow her wishes."

"Reyn knows all about us," Bastien replied, since apparently I'd gone mute. "Lane knows, too."

Aunt Avril shook her head in dismay. "I can't believe Captain Burke got away with devastating the Judge's daughter."

"He paid for it with his life. Spilled his blood on my knife in Rachelle's name." Bastien lifted his eyes to meet Aunt Avril's, which were now filled with concern and compassion, and not the condemnation he'd been expecting. "She's in a coma, and doesn't know she's engaged to me. Rosie and I have been together for a while now, and we're keeping it quiet out of respect for Rachelle."

"And what happens when we get back, Bastien?" Roland's shout came out in accusation, the hot head. His temper conflicted terribly with the early morning sunshine that was supposed to brighten the day and lighten moods. "What happens to Rachelle's reputation then? What happens when she wakes up one day? The witch won't let you go!"

Madigan had heard enough. His beefy arm coiled around Roland's throat from behind and squeezed a gasp out of him. Though Roland was an average-sized dude, anyone looked small when compared with Mad's height and strength. "Tha's enough out of ye. Bastien's an Untouchable. Don't forget what tha means, or I'll remind ye the fun way."

Kerdik didn't bother looking at the fly that bothered him, but merely held up his fingers and snapped them. In the next breath, Roland's lips were sealed shut with some kind of gummy mud. He struggled against the impromptu gag, and started freaking out even after Madigan dropped his grip on the duke. "I've heard enough from you."

Madigan frowned at his conquest. "Well, tha feels like cheating. I had him."

Kerdik narrowed his eyes at Roland. "You'll not call my prize a witch. I would know if she was, and she isn't. A vixen, perhaps, but not a witch." Kerdik's eyes fell on

Bastien, who bowed his head respectfully. "What is your plan for when Rachelle wakes? What of Rosie then?"

"I don't know," Bastien whispered, rubbing the nape of his neck in anguish. I hated that our connection was causing him pain. "I didn't plan to fall for her, and I tried to push her away as often as I could. It's getting... It's too hard to stay away anymore. If I wasn't engaged, I'd take her *lueur* and vow to be her *Guardien* this very second, but that's not my life. I don't have those options."

Madigan's intake of breath was the one I paid attention to. He was the one who seemed to know Bastien best and have his back without question.

"You would?" I didn't mean to speak, but the words flew out before I could censor them.

Bastien turned to me slowly, looking at me as if I was the only one in the cave – as if I was the only woman in the world. "I would. If you would have me as your *Guardien*, I would serve and protect only you until my last breath. I'm pretty much there as it is. Even without your *lueur*, I'm afraid I can't stay away from you." And he did look actually fearful of the commitment he verbalized.

My eyes widened, and my heart rose to choke my throat. "Bastien, I don't know what to say. That's... thank you."

Bastien squeezed my hand and turned back to the others. "That's how serious this is, and how much I would give her if it was mine to give." His morose eyes met mine in silent apology. "But it's not mine. I belong to Rachelle, even though she doesn't know it. Even if she wakes up one day and curses me for trying to save her name this way."

I dropped his hand. Not out of shock or anger, but because it wasn't mine to hold. I shoved my hands into my pockets and hung my head, trying not to get worked up. It was the grand declaration, followed by the reminder of the separation to come. The kiss, followed by the crash – that's the way it always seemed to be with us.

"What of this Rachelle's baby?" Kerdik inquired.

"Died months before it ever saw the light of day. I didn't count on falling for Rosie. I didn't count on any of this. I was a bounty hunter and a hermit before I met her. And I've never kissed Rachelle, or had any kind of relationship with her. I did it because her brother is one of my best friends, and that's what you do when a brother needs help. I couldn't sit back and watch his family go down like that."

Kerdik nodded, as if he was done and understood the scope of it. "You want to be with this man, *Fleur*?"

"I do. But not like this. Not sneaking and hiding it. I don't want to make a joke out of Reyn's sister. So please, guys. Don't say anything about us. We're dealing with it as best we can." I tried to be brave and mature about it all, raising my chin. "When we get back to civilization, I'll put some distance between us. Bastien will go back to his life in Province 1, and I'll go with Lane to her region until we have a better plan for what to do with the gems."

Bastien leaned against the cave wall, his thick arms

crossed over his chest. "Don't talk like that, Rosie. We'll find a way. Just give me some time to figure this out. We can be together. We'll find moments that can be ours."

I shook my head, wishing for a little privacy to get through this too-adult conversation. "We'll find moments for me to be the other woman? We'll find moments that could ruin Rachelle's reputation and embarrass her family if people found out?"

"But my engagement's not real! I would never cheat on a woman I was actually with."

"Her friends don't know you're not really together. You can't save her reputation and break it." I felt on the verge of being too vulnerable in public, so I knew I had to make a fast escape. "I'm going for a stroll. Be back in a few." I walked out into the sunshine, shocked that most of the wheat was completely bent and broken from the tumultuous weather.

"Rosie, wait!"

I heard Kerdik's firm voice that held no question that he was in charge. "You stay here. I'll see to her."

33

KERDIK'S HAT, HIS RING, AND HIS DARK DEED

Kerdik wasn't dressed for a run, but I was. My walk shifted to the jog I needed when I heard his footsteps gaining on me, and then it shifted to a run. I bolted through the field, wishing for a soccer ball and a goal to take out some of my frustration. Running would have to suffice for now. The cool morning air stung my skin as my arms pumped and my tears threatened to choke me.

Then suddenly, Kerdik was a few meters in front of me, materialized out of nowhere. I guess he hadn't needed to dress for a run after all. Kerdik held out his arms for me, and darn it, if I didn't trust him through the obvious menace. I cleared the distance and crashed into his embrace, knocking him back a few feet, but not bowling him completely over. "There, there," he shushed me, holding me to his chest as if I belonged in his arms.

"Is this what you want? You want Bastien for your *Guardien*?"

My forehead wrinkled in confusion. "I don't even really know all that's entailed in being something like that. Do I actually need one?"

"Someone to guard you and your household? Most certainly. You have an undeniable sweetness about you, which can be a deadly liability in Avalon."

The thought of chaining myself to someone I didn't know made me panic, so I tried to wrap my mind around the whole thing as gracefully as possible. "I guess if I have to have one, I'd want it to be Bastien. I don't want to trust myself to a stranger. I've never felt..." I shrugged out of his hug, embarrassed at how I'd carried on over a guy. "It doesn't matter. It'll end when we get back. How it's supposed to be. I've got to focus on this gem crap anyways. Help Lane get Avalon back on track. This place isn't my home to begin with. Best Bastien and I don't attach too deep. I'll be going back up to Common once Avalon's settled."

Kerdik looked on my red face with compassion no one would believe unless they could see it. He was painted as such a villain, but I got to bask in the kindness he seemed to have on tap only for me. "If Bastien is what you want, then it's him you should have."

I offered up a wan impression of a smile. "If only life was that simple. Sorry for the whole scene back there. I'm not used to having a love life, much less having other people watch all the drama go down. I just miss Lane, is all." I shook my head at myself, banding my arms around my stomach to hold my guts safely inside. "I'm such a mama's girl."

"You see Lane as your mother, then?"

"Of course I do. She's my best friend, and I'm not used to being cut off from her like this for so long."

Kerdik wrapped his arm around my shoulder and led me back in the direction of the cave. "Come, now. Everything is fixable. You'll see." He paused a ways before we reached the cave, and took my hand in his. "It's not normal for an eligible maiden to take a *Guardien* who does not become her husband."

"Oh, jeez. We've barely had a handful of kisses, and there's already an ocean of problems. I can't even think in the realm of marriage, K."

"K?"

I shrugged. "You need a nickname. 'Dick' doesn't seem like the frontrunner in that arena."

Kerdik chuckled, and then played with my knuckles, eyeing the ring finger on my left hand with a calculating gaze. "I want you to wear something for me."

"Is it your hat? Because I'm kind of dying to see what your hair looks like under that thing."

Kerdik grinned, took off his Newsies cap, and then placed it on my head. His light blue hair was short along the sides, and combed neatly on top. The part just to the left of the middle was done in a perfect zig-zag, running from front to back. It made him look put together, yet still a touch unbalanced. Despite having worn a hat the entire time I'd been around him, not a single hair was flat or out of place. The blue against his kelly-green skin was a sharp, beautiful contrast I couldn't help but gawk at. Pair that with the white dress shirt, nice slacks, gray vest and those dark lashes? Kerdik looked... dapper. A fancy brand of casual.

"Cool. Can I touch it? I've never seen hair like yours. Do you dye it, or does it look like this naturally? It's super way beautiful."

"I've looked like this for a very long time – longer than you could fathom." Kerdik dipped his head so I could feel the soft blue. I tried to muss it, but it kept returning to its original Ken doll shape, as if Kerdik traveled with an invisible comb.

"Why are you wearing a hat, then? If I had cool hair like this, I'd show it off all the time."

"I admit, I've never thought of my hair as something to show off. It marks me from afar, as does my skin. People mistrust me on first glance because I look so very alien. I don't know why I think the hat will make some sort of difference." When I went to remove the hat from my head and return it to him, he shook his head. "Keep it. Perhaps I shouldn't hide who I am."

I smiled up at him, my gaze connecting with his uncertain eyes. "I think you look great. Dashing in that dangerous smooth talker kind of way."

He tucked a few errant curls behind my ears that had come loose from my messy bun, like I was his doll. "I want you to keep my hat, but I also want you to wear my ring."

I swallowed hard, confused at the strange request. "Why do you want me to wear a ring? Rings are kind of a serious thing where I'm from."

"They are here, as well. My ring will place a protection on you. Should you need me, you can hold it to your heart, and I'll answer your call. I haven't made myself accessible to the Daughters of Avalon in years, but I think I'll make an exception for you, oh Queen of Dancing. The Daughters only wanted my company to ask for more favors, and more. They wanted to use me for my magic. Something tells me you'll be different." His eyes narrowed in threat. "Don't let me be wrong about that."

I mulled over the gift that sounded nice, but had a tinge of a warning to it. "Okay. Thanks. But I mean, you've already done me favors. You got us out of the storm, and you healed my injuries. I don't want you to look back on this time together and think I was making you do those things. I don't want you to resent me the way you do my aunts and my moms."

"I don't mind helping you; I mind being used. I can spot the difference well enough. Will you wear my ring?"

My eyebrows pulled together. "You realize I didn't ask you to protect me, though, right? You're only doing this because you want to be nice?"

"I'm sure you're the only person who's ever accused me

of being nice, but yes." He nodded, holding my hand between us, as if he was asking me to be his Valentine. "Will you wear it?"

My eyes softened when I took in the note of insecurity that snuck through his cool demeanor. "Hey, sure. Of course I will. Thank you. That's really cool of you to go to such great lengths to make sure I'm alright. You know, you can always just come with us. Pal around on the journey."

Kerdik smiled at me as if I'd just told him he was beautiful (which, let's face it, he totally was). "Thank you. See? I knew you were a good choice to give this ring to. You're already a far better person than the Daughters of Avalon ever were to me."

I didn't know what to make of this; I couldn't picture Lane being mean or entitled to anyone. "I've never owned a ring before," I admitted.

Kerdik quirked his eyebrow at me. "But you're a princess. Surely you can't be telling the truth."

I tilted my head to the side. "How about you and I don't lie to each other. No, I've never had a ring before. Lane and I weren't exactly living the princess life up in Common." I motioned to my jeans and my whole non-royalty demeanor. "I don't know if you could tell. I seem to have left my crown in my other pair of beaten up old jeans."

"I know a princess when I see one, disguised as you are." Kerdik raised my hand to his mouth, keeping his eyes fixed on mine when his lips parted to reveal a ring between his teeth. His eyebrows jumped upward twice to reveal the playful nature in him that had lain dormant for far too long.

"Oh! Whoa. That's freaky. How'd you do that?"

Kerdik chuckled, still staring unblinkingly at me when he inserted the ring finger of my right hand into his mouth, threading it through the white gold and sliding my digit across his slippery tongue. I tried to suppress the guilty shivers the intimate act gave me.

When he pulled my finger back out, he kissed my knuckle, smirking through my blush as I wiped my damp hand on my jeans. "Dude, ring or not, you can't suck on my fingers. Friends don't do that."

Kerdik took my scolding with grace, bowing his head slightly to me. "Of course, *Fleur*. Just make sure to keep my ring on your finger. Promise me you'll never take it off."

I blinked at him, confused at the sudden seriousness. "Not even to wash my hands?"

"Never. This is a grand gift, and the only responsibility you have in accepting it is that you can't let it leave your finger."

I frowned, but then shrugged. "I guess I can promise that."

"Very good. Press it to your heart and call my name three times when you need me. Then I'll come to you."

I looked down to examine the beauty that took my breath away. It wasn't just a white gold band, which would've been the nicest piece of jewelry I'd ever owned, but the strands of gold twisted to look like vines twining around my finger. It bore a large square-shaped aquamarine gemstone, with three smaller diamonds clustered into triangles on either side. I let my gasp fly free, amazed at how grown-up my hand looked with his ring on my finger. Suddenly my nails seemed short and uncared for, and the small imperfections on my skin stood out anew. I began to understand why Jill was always getting manicures; she had a lot of nice rings. "Kerdik, I can't wear this."

His expression darkened like a passing storm. "Why not?"

"Because it's too nice. People are going to think I stole it or something. I've never seen anything so incredible. It sparkles. I mean, I'm casting a shadow on it, and it still shines like it's got its own personal sun behind the stones. It almost looks like it's glowing. How did you do that?"

Kerdik chuckled that this was my reasoning for trying to return the ring. "I'm pleased you like it. Wear it always."

"My right hook is going to be lethal with this thing." I bit down on my lower lip, trying to fish around for the right thing to say about this very adult gift. "It's the most beautiful thing I never knew I could touch. You really made this for me?"

"My prize should have a grand treasure befitting her inner sunshine. I should like to make certain you're taken care of. This will help ease my mind when we're apart."

I couldn't take my eyes off it. "What about you? What if you want to get ahold of me? You guys don't exactly have cell phones here."

"What do you mean?"

"I mean, I can get ahold of you now, but what if you want to go bowling or something? What if you're in trouble, and you need help? How do you call me? I don't know how to pull a magic ring out of my mouth."

For some reason, this seemed to bring out real emotion in Kerdik. His eyebrows tented as he drank in my features with new appreciation. When he spoke, his voice came out choked. "I chose well, giving you my ring. You wish to be near me only to play? Not to ask for favor upon favor? You wish to help me if I'm in danger?"

I tore my gaze from the shimmering beauty on my finger to quirk my eyebrow at him. "Why the crap would I ask you for a favor? I only just met you. Makes me a little sad that you think that's all friendship is for." I shook my head and tsked him. "Bowling. That's what I need you for. Talking about stupid stuff and seeing who can eat the most tacos in one go. Spoiler alert: I can eat like, a million tacos."

Kerdik looked down at my upturned face as if I hadn't been sleeping in the dirt for too many nights in a row. He looked at me as if I was lovely, and in that moment, I actually felt it. When he extended his arms to me, I didn't hesitate to grant him the hard hug he desired. I wrapped my arms tight around his toned body and squeezed to be sure he knew I appreciated him – with or without the present. He didn't let go, but used his chin to move my head to his chest, pressing my temple to his collarbone. "Your heart is a thing of true beauty. I admit, I thought all loveliness gone from Avalon."

I rubbed his back while we held each other. "Dude, if you get this choked up about bowling, wait until I teach you soccer."

"I look forward to our many adventures, my darling. Now go off on your mission. I have things to attend to."

"You're not coming with us?"

He pulled back and shook his head. "I'm afraid not." Then he tapped his finger under my chin until my head was angled up toward him. His eyes grew serious in warning. "Do not take that ring off, *Fleur*. Not for any reason whatsoever. Promise me."

I frowned, and then examined the beautiful treasure with curiosity. "If it means that much to you, of course I won't take it off. That's fine, K."

He snapped his fingers, and I heard Aunt Avril cry out in relief. I'm guessing that was her hand coming loose from the rock wall. "Come, Avril. Take your niece on a walk for some fresh air before it's time for you all to go. Perhaps her goodness will rub off on you."

Aunt Avril's movements were stiff, and I could tell she was furious with Kerdik, but said nothing. She jerked my elbow to turn me around and marched me away from the cave as fast as she could until we were out of earshot. "Listen to me, Rosalie. Master Kerdik is not to be trusted. It's his gifts that turned Avalon to ruin. It's his games that are dangerous to get caught up in. That you're on his map now can only mean terrible things for you. Give me the ring. His ring doesn't belong on your finger." She hissed at the stunning piece of jewelry as if it was a monstrosity.

I stiffened and jerked my arm from her grip. I could only allow her to pull me around for so long. I stopped in my tracks and lifted my chin. "I know I'm not real royalty, like you all are, but this is my ring. It's the only real ring I've ever had, so don't try to ruin this for me. You've got three rings on. Why would you try and take mine from me?"

"Because you're wearing a curse as if it's something to brag about," she hissed, her composed face turning toward menace. Her even tone dropped to reveal something darker, filled to the brim with a territorial demand she didn't seem a stranger to. "Any gift from Master Kerdik is a curse. Give it to me, and we'll drop it in the field for the birds to find."

I was about to open my mouth to let loose the full range of my don't-boss-me attitude, but a loud cry cracked across the field, setting the hairs on the back of my neck on edge. I didn't wait out the fight with Avril, but bolted back toward the cave where Bastien was flat on his back, shouting and tugging on his chest like something was about to birth from it.

"No! Bastien, what's wrong? Madigan, help him!" I cried as I sprinted. Kerdik was standing over Bastien, murmuring something I couldn't understand, his palms outstretched over Bastien's writhing body.

I dodged Roland and lunged for the man in agony, but Madigan caught me around the middle with one arm. "Quiet, Princess. Ye don't want to interrupt, or the warlock might have to start all over again."

"Bastien's in pain!" I shouted, thrashing against Madigan's too-agile muscles. "Let me go!"

"He's rebuilding parts of Bastien to make him better at protecting ye. Shut your gob and let the warlock fix all tha's broken."

Bastien rolled over and clawed at the ground, taking fistfuls of earth into his calloused hands as his eyes bulged. He bellowed out agony I knew I could never unhear. I eventually stopped fighting Madigan and clung to his bicep instead, willing it to hold me in place until the madness stopped.

Bastien's howls seemed to stretch on forever, tearing at my insides. When they finally died down after what felt like a million agonized minutes, and his body slumped in the dirt, Madigan released me, coming along beside me as I ran to Bastien. With tears in my eyes, I shoved Kerdik angrily and fell to my knees by Bastien's side. "What did you do to him?" I screeched as I fumbled with the canteen of water Cheval nudged toward me. I unscrewed the top and dumped a little over Bastien's face to wash the dirt and sweat from it.

Kerdik took my anger in stride, though it was clear from Madigan's arm that made to block me from Kerdik, that everyone thought I was going to be shot onsite for offending the great warlock. Kerdik straightened, his tone clipped. "I healed things that were long broken in his body. If he's to escort you through Avalon, I won't have your guard be subpar. I did him a kindness. He's good as new now."

"It sure as a crack in the head didn't sound like a kindness! He was in pain!"

"Yes, well, I told him that he would be punished for allowing my prize to be injured. I didn't mute the agony that comes with reparations of this magnitude. Some of his bones that healed incorrectly long ago had to be re-fused into their proper alignment. That should serve as a reminder for him not to take his post lightly in the future."

"Dude, you and I are going to have words about this. Is he okay? Did you permanently damage him?" My trembling hand flitted over his heaving chest as I nudged my knees to his hip. "Bastien, how can I help?"

Bastien reached out and gripped my hand with barely any strength, his palm slick. "Go take the horses into the field and wait for me there."

"What? No! Let me help you."

Bastien shook his head, his eyes pained. "I don't want you to see me like this. Mad can help me." When I opened my mouth to protest, he bellowed, "Please, Rosie!"

Kerdik helped me up, snapping his fingers at the horses, and leading me dumbfounded into the field. "How could you hurt him like that? I've never heard a man yell so terribly. You were out of line, K. It's like you waited for me to be away from him so you could break his body."

"Rebreak, actually. And of course I did." Kerdik dismissed the nearby Aunt Avril and Roland with a wave of his hand. They scattered from the gesture, as if an axe swung from his palm to chop off their heads. Roland's muddy gag disintegrated, but he said nothing, lest the gag come back in a more permanent fashion. Kerdik grabbed my shoulders and leveled his gaze at me. "I rebuilt him so he'd be better suited for his post. I'll not gamble your safety on a *Guardien* who's not up for the task. That you chose an Untouchable was wise, but broken as he was, you needed me to fix him for you."

"You shouldn't have hurt someone on the off-chance it might help me. I don't want to get ahead like that. That's not who I am."

He squeezed my shoulders, willing my eyes to stop shooting him daggers. "I waited for you to be further away because I knew you'd be too unselfish to think of the long game, and I was right. This is a necessary bump if you want to survive the Daughters of Avalon. Some of them were ruthless and manipulative. Morgan's army shows no mercy."

"You hurt Bastien! You hurt him on purpose."

Kerdik stiffened. "I'll not explain my motives to you again. When you've calmed, you'll see that I was thinking of your wellbeing, even though you seem unconcerned with your own survival. You wanted me to be your friend? This is what that looks like."

I didn't know what to make of the whole situation. "You shouldn't have made him suffer, K. That's sick, and you know it. It's not Bastien's fault I broke a nail."

"Stop telling me you broke a nail! Your lovely face was bruised and scraped, and you could barely walk! What I did will ensure that doesn't happen again."

I don't know why I let Kerdik pull me into his embrace, or why I stayed there as long as I did. I felt so turned around, confused by everyone and everything in a world I couldn't make heads or tails of. "You need to apologize to Bastien," I ruled, my words muffled in Kerdik's white button-down. My hand moved to rest over his charcoal vest, alighting on his leonine chest without hesitation.

"I'm certain I didn't hear you correctly. Warlocks do not apologize."

"Friends do. I don't care what kind of magical unicorn you are. You hurt Bastien on purpose. I can make my peace with the rebuilding thing because I see you were trying to help, but you purposefully made it painful when it didn't have to be? Apologize to him."

Kerdik stiffened. "You cannot be serious."

"You hurt the man I..." I shook my head when the right words escaped me. "I can't have my guy and one of my few friends here picking fights with each other. Be my friend and make nice with my guy. That's how this works." When Judah and Jill started up, I made sure to get on her good side. Hung out with her so many times to make sure she was cool with me being around Judah, that I'm sure she was probably pretty sick of me by the end.

Kerdik exhaled. "I keep forgetting how little you know about our world. Precious as your ideals are, warlocks don't apologize. Bastien needed that lesson, and he'll carry it with him for a good long time. Should he forget to take his post seriously, I'll be back to remind him of the high premium I place on your life."

"That sounded nothing like, 'My bad, Ro. I'll totally set things straight with your guy. I took it too far, and I'm super way sorry.'"

He tucked a lock of hair behind my ear and stroked his fingertips down the slope of my unmarked cheek. "I am sorry I upset you."

My nose scrunched. "Is this your first apology? That was weak."

"As a matter of fact, it was my first apology in at least three decades, and it's the most either of you will get from me."

"Weak, K."

Kerdik pressed his lips to my forehead, warming me as he rubbed my back. "I'll visit again soon when I have the time. Now tell me how grateful you are that I saved you from the storm."

"I am grateful for that, but it doesn't give you an excuse to be mean to Bastien."

He picked up my hand and kissed the ring he'd placed

on my finger. "Tell me you won't take off my ring, and that you'll call when you need me."

"Of course, but I..."

Kerdik tugged on the brim of the Newsies cap that he'd secured on my head. "Tell me it was nice to meet me."

I sighed, guessing that I wasn't going to get what I wanted out of this exchange. "It was nice to meet you, Kerdik."

"I'll come see you again when I've got more time. Until then, travel safely, *Fleur*."

With a sweet brush of his nose across mine and a heady inhale to take in my scent, Kerdik vanished.

34

AUNT GOLLUM

The ride toward the woods where we'd left Draper, Lane and the rest of our party at was long and slow. Bastien was in too much pain for his horse to gallop, so we cantered the whole way. Just being touched caused him to hiss, so he requested Madigan take me on his horse.

Ever since Bastien declared that I was his, Madigan was slightly different around me. He was more helpful, though not more chatty. He didn't look at me like I was some threatening bug anymore, but rather like I was someone he was resigned to never be rid of. He didn't leave my side, taking Bastien's furtive glances at Roland as a warning that I couldn't be left alone. Bastien wasn't up for guard duty just yet, so Madigan was my constant shadow. I don't think either of us were all that thrilled about it.

When hour number seven-hundred-thousand-million

stretched on before us, I tried my hand at conversation, turning my head so I could see part of his scowling face. "So how'd you end up in the Forgotten Forest?"

"Ye ask too many questions."

I guffawed. "Hello. I've been totally silent most of the day." My spine was completely erect, so I didn't accidentally lean back on his chest. Madigan didn't exactly give off a cuddly vibe.

"I don't ask questions about the worst day of your life."

"Fair point. Sorry if that was rude. I just know nothing about you, and I'm bored."

"Ye don't need to know about me. I'm to watch ye until Bastien's on his feet again."

"You two go way back?"

"Aye. Far enough back that he trusts me to watch his lady."

"I'm not his..." I sighed, exasperated. "I guess maybe I am. Avalon is weird. This is not how this kind of thing happens in my world."

"Well, you're wearing the warlock's hat and his ring. I didn't assume you'd live after shoving Kerdik to get to Bastien like ye did, but here ye are. Whatever magic ye hold, it's stronger than any I've seen."

I turned back around to face the front. "It's called being nice. That's my superpower. Feel free to try your hand at it. Not quite as impressive as leaping tall buildings in a single bound, but I find it suits most situations."

When he didn't answer, I let the silence sit there for a few minutes.

"Where are you from? Your accent's different than the others'." When he didn't answer this, I turned to give him the stink eye and repeated myself.

"Ye ask too many questions."

"Is it like, a secret or something?"

Madigan sighed irritably. "I'm from Éireland. It's a country in Faîte that's an ocean away from here."

I turned to face the front again. "Do you have family there?"

Madigan offered no attempt at a response, so I knew the answer couldn't be a good one. His hands remained tangled in our horse's mane, since we didn't have reins. His arms caged me in, but his body was stiff behind mine, like he was wary of human contact, but had been forced to endure it until Bastien was better. I prayed that would be any second.

I tried a few more break-the-ice questions before giving up on making friends with Madigan. It seemed he would only answer the questions I asked to his face. Either he was hard of hearing, or he was a grumpy jag. I was leaning toward the latter of my two working theories. I decided to focus on the horse instead.

Our horse, Harry, was enamored of me, simply because I was the *Voix*. He started spilling his whole life to me, which was pretty fascinating. "How many horses like you are there?" I asked, giving his mane a stroke.

"Seven. We weren't born, but we were made by Carman and Kerdik."

I glanced to my left to take in the tall trees we passed by. "Who's Carman?"

Madigan stiffened. "You'll not mention tha name, Princess. We've already got Kerdik who might show up at any moment. I'll not risk our necks by bringing talk of Carman into the mix. I don't care how charming Kerdik thinks ye are, never say her name again. Tell the horse to change the subject before my temper's tested."

"Sheesh. What a drama queen you're turning out to be. Fine. Harry, tell me about something that won't piss off Madigan."

"Mad," he corrected me. "Ye belong to Bastien now. The Brotherhood calls me 'Mad'."

"Oh, okay. Do you prefer being called 'Mad'?"

"I prefer people know their place. The lads in the Brotherhood call me Mad because they'd die for me. I don't bother with people outside the circle. Nothing but trouble."

"Hello, I was outside the circle just this morning."

"Aye, and so far you've brought me nothing but trouble. Bastien's barely upright because ye made friends with a monster."

I hung my head as the guilt washed over me. "I'm sorry. I didn't know Kerdik would hurt him." When Mad didn't respond, I wondered if there might be something to my guess at his deafness. I turned my chin so he could see my lips move. "I tried to get Kerdik to apologize, but he wouldn't even consider it."

"Aye. Tha's the thing about monsters."

I gave up on talking to Madigan and switched back to Harry, who was way less intense. As the day stretched into evening, and the sun disappeared so the blue moon could loom over us in the sky, I couldn't stifle the yawns as my eyelids began to droop.

"We're stopping for the night," Bastien spoke up. He pulled Cheval toward a smattering of trees and dismounted with care. "You're yawning, Rosie."

I was shocked he'd been paying attention to the small cues. "I can probably go another half hour, if you need."

"No. We can't drive you this hard. Master Kerdik was right; I wasn't watching out for you like I should've been."

I blinked at him, confused at the humble confession. "It's cool. Sure, we can stop now. Thanks, Bastien. I am pretty tired."

Madigan got off the horse and helped me down. "I'll go hunt up something for supper while the princess sleeps."

"No." Bastien's hand found its way around my back, and both of us exhaled at the contact we'd been missing. "I'm still on the mend, and I can't trust Roland." He didn't bother lowering his voice to spare Roland's feelings, but called him out on the fact that we'd traveled all this way to rescue him from oblivion, and he'd broken Bastien's trust. "I need you to watch out for her while she's sleeping and while I'm laying down. Everything's still pretty jacked, Mad. Not gonna lie; that was rough."

Madigan nodded once and barked over his shoulder at Roland, who was helping Aunt Avril down off her horse. "Roland, go hunt us up something heartier than apples. I'm starved, and I don't do hungry well."

Roland nodded and went off without a protest, no doubt glad to be away from me. Aunt Avril walked with grace into the smattering of green-trunked trees and brushed away a few errant branches and leaves. "There. That should make a decent bed until we return to civilization, and get you a real mattress." She held out her hand expectantly. "Let me take your things. They'll only burden you in sleep."

"Thanks." I still didn't know what to make of her sudden bossiness that morning, but handed over my backpack to her without arguing.

"Your hat and your ring," she prodded, her hand outstretched. "You won't be comfortable sleeping with them."

I didn't have a huge attachment to the hat, other than sentimental value, but I didn't fork it over when my gut reared back in warning. "That's alright. They won't bother me. Thanks, though."

"Rosalie, take off that ring." All pretense of airiness was gone, and her palm was still open between us. "Give it here. You have no idea what to do with something like that."

I chewed on my lower lip. "Kerdik told me not to take it off."

"You're listening to a warlock over your own flesh and blood?"

"I... But... I mean, I promised Kerdik I wouldn't take it off. You really want me to break a promise I just made this morning? That's not me."

"Give me the ring, Rosalie."

Bastien unbuttoned his flannel, letting me handle this while he untucked his white undershirt from his jeans. I made a loose fist with the hand that had the ring on it, looking down at the shimmering beauty as I weighed my options. "It doesn't feel right to take it off. And not to piss you off, but it's too soon to play the blood relations card. We know nothing about each other. I don't know much about you, and you don't know even the basics about me. Thanks for the offer, but no. The ring stays on my finger until I take it off."

"Master Kerdik's gifts are a curse," she warned. "I'm only trying to save you. Give it here, and we'll send it off with one of the horses."

When Cheval didn't chime in with a hearty "screw her," I lost a little of my certainty. "No, thank you. I'm tired, Aunt Avril. I'm going to sleep now, okay? Please don't push me around like this. I'm twenty-two. I'm allowed to have a piece of jewelry. You've got three rings. I should be allowed one."

Her eyes softened, and my hackles rose when I smelled

the foul stench of a manipulation in full swing. "If that's all, then I'll be happy to give you one of my rings. Two, even. I'll trade you. This one's from my father, King Lucien." She twisted a yellow gem that was perched on a matching gold band from the pointer finger on her right hand. "It's from your grandfather. I'd be happy to give it to you. I don't have any daughters of my own. It would give me nothing but joy to see an heirloom like this on your finger."

My mouth fell open that she was using the memory of her own father – my late grandfather whom I'd never met – to get the jewel off my finger. I was about to answer as diplomatically as possible, when Bastien spoke up behind me. "I bowed to you earlier to set the tone of respect when I saw you in the Forgotten Forest. Don't make me lose all my patience for you duchesses now. Rosie said no. You'll listen to her."

"She's carrying a direct link to Master Kerdik, Bastien. Don't tell me that's not dangerous. The monster broke you down."

Madigan didn't pull any punches. "Shut your gob, ye greedy wench. I never thought I'd see the war of the Jewels of Good Fortune in action, but ye Daughters of Avalon don't let up. The ring belongs to Rosie. If I catch ye asking her for it again, I'll fit ye with a gag just to be rid of your scheming chatter. Morgan's sister, if I ever saw one."

Aunt Avril's cheeks turned red. "That's not what this is. This is me trying to save her from his serpentine hands."

"The only snake I see right now is wearing a dress, Duchess." Madigan turned his back on her to face me, and pulled out his dagger. "I didn't care about the ring much before this, but if I see it off your finger, I'll track it down and draw blood, Rosie. I'll not see Bastien's lady jerked around like this." He muttered under his breath as he stomped off. "Playing the grandfather card. Pathetic."

Aunt Avril opened her mouth, but I held up my hand to stop her. "I'm going to sleep. I'm not pissed, but I wouldn't test Mad, if I were you."

Aunt Avril straightened her dress and brushed her hair back. "I think I'll go water the horses. Excuse me."

I looked down at my ring, my heart aching that so much fuss was being caused over such a small thing. It was such a nice gift, but now it felt selfish to hold tight to something that was material and superficial.

Bastien draped his flannel shirt over my shoulders. Though everyone knew about us, he still glanced around before he kissed my temple. He kept his lips there and breathed in the scent of my skin. "I see you kicking yourself. Don't. Mad was right. She's a Daughter of Avalon. They'll fight for Master Kerdik's jewels to the death. I've seen it happen over and over. I guess I always assumed it was only Morgan who couldn't control herself, but man, to use your dead grandfather like that? Don't take it off your finger, Daisy. I mean it."

I nodded, solemn as I slipped my hand into his. "I never had any real jewelry before. That my first grownup ring causes a fight in my family the very first day I get it? Something about that takes a little of the shine out of the whole thing."

He kissed my temple again, and then gave me a look of pure compassion, viewing my struggle clearly. "Let me see what all the fuss is about." Bastien lifted our entwined hands up to examine the jewels, putting on a show to cheer me up. He let out a low whistle. "Wow. That really is something. It'll make your right hook that much more lethal."

I snorted. "That's exactly what I said! You're funny." I looked at the shine under the moon. The dim light from the moon filtering through the trees made the aquamarine that much bluer. "I think it's pretty."

"It is, honey." He led me over to the space that had been cleared for us. Bastien slowly lowered himself to the ground, making several "oof" noises, and sounding like an old man trying to lay on the forest floor.

"You're in pain still? Where does it hurt?"

"Only everywhere." He waved off my concern. "I'm alright. Just whining. Hoping to get a little sympathy from a beautiful woman." He held out his arms to me, smiling when I sank down into his body space – half on my side next to him, and half leaning my front to his as my body curled around him. He didn't waste time with teasing, but went straight for my lips, kissing me until my eyelashes fluttered shut and my limbs started tangling through his. It had been too long since we'd kissed, and I'd missed the flavor of Bastien.

We finally came up for air when he winced. He didn't want to admit he was still hurting, so I didn't call him out on it. I slowed our kiss until we were lightly nipping at each other's lips, like taking small puffs from a cigar we were both heavily addicted to.

Bastien rubbed his nose to mine. "I don't like you on anyone's horse but ours. When you wake up, I'll be better and ready to ride with you. I trust Mad, of course, but I missed you." He squeezed my hips. "Holding onto you, feeling your body against mine. I miss everything about everything you are."

"I was only a few feet away, you know."

"Too far," he smirked, going in for another kiss, and another, and still more, and somehow still never enough.

TOGETHER, BUT NOT

The next day brought a bittersweet joy that finally Bastien and I could be together without hiding, but it would only last for the duration of this trip, which was almost over. We kept our morning makeout private on the floor of the forest until I started choking on my *lueur*. Bastien didn't freak out, but handed me a canteen and rubbed my back until my eyes stopped watering and my choking subsided. "You stayed with me," I said with a note of wonder coloring my voice. "Thank you."

Bastien sighed. "I shouldn't have split on you that first time. I want to take your *lueur* and be your *Guardien*, but I have Rachelle to consider."

I nodded, trying to keep a bland smile on my face. "I get it. It's fine. I don't really know enough about the whole thing to give my *lueur* away without Lane there to put her stamp on the whole thing. You won't get any pressure about that whole thing from me."

Bastien rubbed the nape of his neck. "That's the other thing. I... Lane... I don't think she'll approve, and I know that's kind of a deal breaker for you."

"Why wouldn't she approve?"

"Because I'm me. I'm a hermit who lives alone in the woods. Lots of blood on my hands. Engaged. Not exactly who you picture your daughter settling down with." He hefted me up, his fingers twined through mine as we made our way to the horses, who had grown restless after an entire night of doing nothing. The holding hands in public was a new thing to me, and for some reason made me a little more introverted than I wished I was. My voice grew quieter, and I kept my eyes to myself after the obligatory morning greetings.

Madigan motioned to a flat rock that had a mangled two-headed dog on it. "Roland hunted us a dog to eat. Have your fill, and let's be off." The skin had been ripped off and fileted, and the was meat cooked over a fire they'd made while I'd been asleep.

I wasn't an overly emotional vegetarian. Judah and Jill ate meat all the time in the apartment, and I didn't say one word about it. There was something about seeing the kill split open, with bone and sinew spilling out of its carcass, that turned my stomach and pricked my heart anew. I opted for yet another apple and munched on it while Bastien had his fill of dog meat.

"Ye should eat," Madigan scolded me, the space between his eyebrows wrinkling as he frowned.

"I am eating. Apples are food, you know."

"Aye, but it's not often we take the time to hunt. Won't know when we'll get meat next, so best take advantage."

I kept my voice quiet and pulled him away from the others to privately explain my conundrum about being able to hear the animals, and not feeling right eating someone I'd had a conversation with. "It's not the same for you. To me it feels like eating a friend's body. Apples will work until we get somewhere that there's more food for me." I shook my head at myself. "I'm really not trying to be picky. I promise I'm not trying to be difficult. I'm not complaining or anything."

Madigan's mouth fell open after my reasoning came to light. "I didn't think about tha. I guess it would be a wee bit uncomfortable eating someone you'd spoken to. Ye can't live on apples, though."

I shrugged. "I can't live with myself if I eat a friend. I'll be fine. It's just another day, right?"

"Aye." He pointed his dagger toward Roland, who was eating with Bastien and actually smiling. I hadn't seen my cousin smile yet, and the expression looked odd when I was so accustomed to his scowl of blatant hatred. "Tha one didn't come near ye all night, but I still want ye to stay away from him. The duchess, too. She's got greed in her eyes, so no matter what, don't take the ring off. I mean it. Not just because Master Kerdik says so, and not because ye want to wear it, but because if I see it on her finger, I won't hesitate to cut it off her. I'm starting to think the Daughters of Avalon might be blaming Morgan for everything, when Morgan was the only one smart enough to pull off what they all wanted to do."

I rubbed my temples. "Okay. I wasn't planning on taking it off, anyway. Thanks for the heads up, though. The whole thing felt really strange."

"Master Kerdik's not to be trusted, but neither is your aunt. I'm watching," he assured me, though I couldn't tell if he meant that as a threat or a kindness.

When the others finished their meal, I hefted myself up onto Cheval, with Bastien riding behind me. He was in better health and spirits today, making sure we took the lead on our gallop, so he could tuck his hand under my shirt and stroke my navel. The hours passed while he teased my skin, the wind whipping at us while nature grew greener and lusher. "You're driving me crazy," I admitted.

"Good. Consider this payback for all the times you made me insane wanting to be near you." His head was next to mine, my temple resting against his chin while we rode. I'd safely tucked my new hat inside my backpack before I'd fallen asleep the night before. Though I loved the feel of it on my head, I didn't want it to go flying off me when we rode faster than usual. Our bodies moved together easily, and I wished we could always be in sync like this. He kissed my hair and said low in my ear, "Is it wrong that I don't like to see another man's ring on your finger?"

I shot him an eye roll as I twirled the gem on my knuckle. "You know it's not like that."

"I know, but still. Can't fault a guy for being a little jealous."

I didn't know what to do with that information. I mean, it was so weird. I'd never had a guy be jealous of my attention before. "Huh. I never pictured you as the jealous type."

"Me neither. Guess you bring out the beast in me."

"Good thing I can communicate with animals."

Bastien growled and then bit down lightly on my neck. Goosebumps stood out on my skin when he started sucking on the juncture between my neck and my shoulder. I couldn't hold back the gratuitous moan, my embarrassment peaking quicker than I could shake off his animalistic advance. "I love the taste of your skin," Bastien breathed into my ear.

I inched my shoulder away from his mouth. "You're going to make me fall off this horse. You might be used to being a lot more open in public, but I'm not. I don't want Mad to hear me groan like that. Totally embarrassing."

"Apologies, Princess." He frowned as he straightened, though his hand remained on my stomach under my shirt. "But you should probably call him Madigan. He only likes the Brotherhood to call him Mad. Gets touchy about stuff like that."

"Oh, he asked me to call him Mad last night. Something about me being your lady makes me an unofficial member of your boys' club, apparently."

Bastien stilled, like an animal caught in headlights. "Oh. I guess that makes sense. To Mad, yes, you're one of us. That's good. But if we come across any other Untouchables, Rachelle's my lady, so best not confuse them yet. I need to figure all of this out."

I kept my chin up while my spirits sunk to the dirt. "You've got all day to puzzle it out, dude. But maybe we should stop kissing until you do sort it all out. I know I brought it upon myself, but now it's making me feel about twenty kinds of cheap and eight kinds of slutty. Maybe I shouldn't be kissing a guy who's got a fiancée that's so engrained in his life. She's probably a really nice girl, and I'm throwing myself at her fiancé. Not cool." I held up my hand to his protest. "I know, I know. I get the ins and outs of the situation. I'm just saying you should take some actual time to make sense of it all. You can't very well do that with your tongue down my throat. I should've been more careful. I let it go too far. It's my fault, not yours. I had all the facts, and I kissed you anyway."

Bastien slowly took his hand from under my shirt and banded both arms around my midsection, hugging me tight to hold my heartbreak in. "I'm sorry I'm putting you through this."

"I'm putting myself through it at this point, and it's time I stopped being selfish. I'm sorry I'm making you feel torn.

I get it. If you have to be off the market, I totally understand. I'll be sad, but I know you want to do right by Reyn's family, and I don't want to make you less honorable." I hung my head. "But that's exactly what I've been asking you to do. If Lane wants me to get a *Guardien*, I'll find someone else. That way you won't have to hurt Rachelle."

Bastien tightened his grip around me. "You're breaking it off? Just like that? We finally get on the same page, and you're jumping ship?"

"I'm trying to make things easier on you."

"Life without you isn't easier. You living with another man would kill me. Absolutely kill me." He rested his forehead to the back of my head. "Just give me time to talk to Reyn and his father. We'll figure this out, Daisy."

I didn't respond because my mind was already made up. I'd indulged enough and done the wrong thing too many times with Bastien. I needed to get my head screwed on straight and focus on the mission. Delivering the gems to Lane was job one. After that, I wasn't sure how I was going to pry the rest of the jewels from Morgan's hand.

My mother's hand.

The mission needed to be top priority. Then, if Bastien was still around, maybe I could investigate the uneven thumping of my heart that pattered clumsily whenever he was near.

36

ACCUSATIONS THAT BREAK US

When we finally reached the forest we'd left the search party at, I breathed a sigh of relief that I could hear Remy's voice calling to me. I wasn't sure how long they were willing to wait for us in the exact same spot. Cell phones were the one thing missing from Avalon. And cars. And tacos. And indoor plumbing. And tacos.

Tacos, tacos, tacos...

I pointed Cheval over to Remy, who came out of the woods with alarm on his face as he flagged us down. *"Princess! We were worried you'd never be returned to us. Three Cheval Mallets? How is that possible?"* Remy gaped at the identical horses.

"Hey, Remy. Guys, this is my friend, Remy. He's a healer. Remy, this is Duchess Avril, Duke Roland and Madigan the Formidable. Where's everyone else?"

Remy was distraught, and helped me down with eager hands. The second I flung my arms around his neck, he crushed me to his chest. I chuckled at the sweetness. *"I was so afraid the Forgotten Forest would swallow you whole, and we'd never have you again. Are you safe? Are you well? What happened? Why did it take so long?"*

"We're alright. The Forgotten Forest is like, a long way away. Came back as fast as we could. Where is everyone?"

Remy shook his head while I ignored the others. I let Bastien explain to them that Remy and I could talk to each other. *"They're gone, Princess. The Queen's Army found us, and they took Reyn to her palace. Duchess Elaine rode with them, and Damond, Draper, Rousseau and Duke Lot are all trying to make their case to Morgan so she'll release Reyn."*

I relayed the news to the others. Bastien was already getting back on Cheval, a cold look of determination washing the playfulness from his features. "I'm going to the palace, then. It's me Morgan wants to punish. I killed Captain Burke, and she's trying to pin it on Reyn because she can't punish an Untouchable."

I nodded and moved to put my foot back in the stirrup. "Okay, then let's go."

"You're not coming," Bastien scoffed. "Morgan doesn't need to know you're in Avalon."

I blinked up at him, confused. "Reyn's my friend, too, and he's important to Lane. I don't think it'll exactly be a secret I'm in Avalon if Lane storms the castle. I mean, everyone knows she took off with me." I put both feet on the grass.

"No, honey. Morgan's manipulative, and you're sweet. I don't want you within a thousand feet of her. Mad, I won't ask you to come with me, since Reyn's not in the Brotherhood, but can you take Rosie with you and hide her somewhere until I bring Reyn home?"

"Aye. Come along, Princess."

I crossed my arms over my chest and glared up at Bastien. "Isn't the plan for me to try and take Morgan's jewels from her? How am I supposed to do that without meeting her and actually getting into her castle? Seems like now's a good a time as any to go meet my mom. Maybe she'll let Reyn go if I ask."

Bastien's teeth ground together as he fished for a hole in my plan. "Morgan's evil, Rosie! You have no idea what we're dealing with, here."

"Tell me a better plan to get the jewels back. That's why I'm here, isn't it? I'm supposed to find the gems and give them back to the Daughters of Avalon. I've got Lane's now, Roland can have Heloise's gem back, and I can send Gliten's with Lane to give back to Province 3, where it came from. Aunt Avril's got hers, Lot's got his, Morgan can have the one she was originally given, but the other three need to be found."

Roland's head perked up. "You're going to send my mother's gemstone to my province?"

I threw my arms up in the air. "Of course I am! What do you think we've been doing all this time?"

"I thought you were trying to steal the gems for Morgan le Fae," he admitted, perplexed. For the first time, he was looking at me like I was a person, and not something evil and disgusting. I barely recognized him.

"Oh, I really can't stand you, and I don't say that about many people." I smacked the back of my hand into my palm and spoke slowly. "I. Live. In. Common. What the crap would I want with your gems?"

"Surely jewels have value in your world."

"Not as much as a whole kingdom's survival. Do you really think I'm that petty?"

"You're a Daughter of Avalon. I know you are."

My fists clenched and my nostrils flared. "That's it, man! You and me are taking this outside." I glanced around at nature, cringing that my challenge made little sense, since we were already outdoors. I motioned for him to dismount and held my fists up. "Come and get it, you jag. I'm through looking over my shoulder to keep an eye on you."

Mad and Bastien got off their horses and stood between us, though Roland didn't look like he was ready to tear my head off (for once). My cousin held up his hands in surrender. "If you're going to turn over the gems, then I was wrong about you."

"Not good enough! I could've died because of you." I don't know why his compliance made me angrier than his attacks had, but my temper flared dangerously. Judah called this the Rosie Danger Zone. "Do you know how excited I was to get a cousin? I wanted to meet you so badly, I crossed into the land of no return to find you! Then you turn out to be this? Having a family sucks!"

Aunt Avril was digging in Bastien's pack for the last of our apples, paying us no mind. Mad was silent, but placed himself between us like a brick wall facing Roland, should he decide to strike.

"Would you like me to apologize?" Roland offered, his mouth in a tight line.

"I'd like you to jump off a cliff, you jackweed. I don't want your apology, and I don't want a cousin. Take Heloise's gem and go home."

"Reyn is one of my closest friends. I'll not leave him to Morgan le Fae. Bastien, if you'll have me, I'll ride with you to throw in what power I still have to save Reyn."

"How are we going to explain that you're back? Everyone knows you went into the Forgotten Forest."

I glowered at the men. "Um, how about with the truth? I'm coming with you. There's no way to keep me secret from Morgan and still find the jewels she stole. Two birds with one stone this way."

Bastien held up his hands to the both of us. "Wait! Just let me figure this out. There's got to be a way to keep Rosie from Morgan and still get the gems back."

I was through listening. I stalked over to Cheval and

gave him a pat. "Cheval and I are going. Not sure you should come, Bastien."

Bastien reared back, his face twisting in defiance. "I'd like to know when you thought you were calling the shots. I'm your *Guardien*, and you don't go riding headfirst into danger without me."

I narrowed my eyes at him. "First off, you're not my *Guardien*, so don't play the babysitter card with me. Second, I don't think you should come because Morgan clearly hates you. Might not want to go strolling up to her castle, since she's got it out for good old Bastien the Bold. I'm not being mean; I'm thinking practically. I'm trying to keep you safe."

Aunt Avril slowly mounted her horse. "I'm returning to my home. Morgan stopped listening to me long ago, so I won't be of any use to you today. Safe travels, Rosalie. Give your people my regards when you lead them back to your homeland, Roland. I'm going to take my gemstone back to Province 8, and see if I can redeem my land somehow."

She didn't even bother offering up a hug, but turned on her horse and charged off before I could tell her goodbye. My chin lowered and my shoulders slumped as the fight fled from my fists completely. I stepped back and stood next to Remy, whose arm draped around my back to pull me protectively to his side.

Bastien seemed to see the shift in me and softened. "Look, it's not safe for either of us to go to Morgan's castle, but I have to try. I can't let her kill Reyn for something I did."

"Fine. Then we'll go together."

Bastien closed his eyes. "I don't like this."

I shrugged as Remy tucked my forehead under his cheek. "I don't much care. It has to be done."

Bastien pinched the bridge of his nose. "Roland, go ahead and take Heloise's gem home to your province. I know Province 4 was absorbed by Morgan, but if you have your own jewel again, maybe you can split your people off from her and reclaim them."

"I'm coming to help with Reyn," Roland protested, his chest puffed.

"We don't need Morgan to know Rosie can get in and out of the Forgotten Forest right now. Morgan shouldn't know that Rosie has her Compass ability at all, or she'll put her to use tracking down the Jewels of Good Fortune for her province. Plus, we can't go taking the only jewels we have straight into Morgan's palace." He held Roland's gaze with a command that made me understand just how valuable he would've been to the army before he left. "Save your land while you can. Go home a hero and redeem Province 4."

Roland shook his head. "I can't abandon Reyn like that."

Bastien's voice rose to a shout. "I can't be looking over my shoulder the entire way to make sure you don't take another swing at Rosie. You haven't earned the right to take this trip with us. I've got enough on my plate, dealing with Morgan and watching Rosie. I can't add you to the mix. I love you, brother, but I can't trust you. My word should've been enough from the very start, but it wasn't."

Roland's mouth fell open. "Tell me you wouldn't have thought the same thing in my position."

"I risked my life going into the Forgotten Forest for you! I deserve *all* the benefit of *all* your doubts. You belong in your province, so go back there. I'll come for you when Rosie's squared away."

Roland hesitated, but then nodded, his dimpled jaw clenched tight. "If that's what you want, then I'll fall in line." He moved toward Bastien's pack that was lying open on the ground and knelt down to fish out his mother's gem. He frowned, and then dumped the contents out on the grass. "Where is it?" His hands moved frantically over the clothes and the few pieces of fruit that were left. "Where is it?!" I took a step closer, but jumped back to Remy's side when Roland barked at me. "What did you do with the gemstones?"

My eyes widened, and I stepped back in shock. "What are you talking about? They're right in the bag. I didn't touch them. I haven't gone near the pack."

Bastien dove for the bag and shook it to make sure, sorting out everything until he came up just as empty as Roland had. "No! Where are they?"

"Could they have fallen out?" I hoped aloud.

As suspected, Roland cast aside his newfound apology

and stood, seething in my direction with his fists clenched. "Boy, did you have me fooled. I can't believe I let my guard down! We have to search her."

I turned the pockets of my jeans inside out. "Clearly I don't have the gems."

Bastien stood slowly and narrowed his gaze at me. "Where are they, Daisy?"

His question slashed a mark across my heart. "They were supposed to be in *your* bag! I haven't gone near it this entire time." Cheval and the other two horses chimed in on my behalf, but if you can believe it, no one listened to them.

Bastien picked up my hat from Kerdik, and bunched in his fist. "Then how did this get in there?"

My blood ran cold and my mouth went dry. "I d-don't know. I mean, it was dark last night when I took my hat off to go to sleep. Maybe I put it in the wrong bag. But that doesn't mean I stole the gems. Search my bag, Bastien. You really think I'd do that?"

"I don't know what to think anymore. Mad, search her pack."

We waited, and I hoped with everything in me that somehow the gemstones were in plain sight somewhere. Madigan turned up nothing, his face unsympathetic to my nervous squirm. "It's not here, Bastien. Do ye want me to search her?"

When Bastien hesitated, Roland prodded him over the cliff with a childish jeer. "If you were truly impartial, you wouldn't hesitate to search her. This proves she most certainly is a witch, and her hold on you is deadly!"

Bastien leveled his stony gaze at me. "No. I'll do it. Everyone wait here. If it's not on her, then we'll have to retrace our steps. It's possible it fell out." He grabbed my bicep with a firm command to his grip, and led me deeper into the woods, ignoring Remy's silent protests that this wasn't right.

"Bastien, where are we going? Would you let go of me? You don't have to jerk me around."

When we finally got so far into the woods that we couldn't see the others, Bastien released his harsh hold on me and crossed his arms over his chest. "Strip."

I guffawed. "Pass. Is that seriously the best pickup line you've got?"

"I'm serious, Rosie. If you don't want me to search you, I get it. I'll send Mad in to do it. But I can't leave you alone with Roland, and Remy would lie to cover for you in a heartbeat. Trust me, I'm your best option here."

"Are you kidding me with this? Bastien, I didn't steal the jewels!"

"Then you should have no problem letting me verify that."

"Um, except that you're asking me to take my clothes off. That's a problem for me."

He sighed, looking older than usual with the tiresome weight of life in Avalon. "Fine. If I don't find anything on you, I'll take off my clothes, too. That should level the playing field as far as humiliation goes."

"Is this your first time talking to a woman? I don't want to see you naked after this. I can barely stand to look at your face! This is how little you trust me after everything? This is what you want me to do?"

"It's what needs to happen to clear your name. I won't be constantly looking over my shoulder, worried Roland's going to come after you. This should calm him down, and put everyone's fears to rest."

Indignation mutated to rage that began to boil under my skin. "You care more about Roland's irrational fear than about my whole body? I can't believe I fell for you!"

Bastien's jaw clenched. "Let's get this over with, Daisy."

"Don't you *dare* call me that. I'm not your Daisy. I'm nothing to you." He'd started calling me that because he said I didn't have scary enough thorns to be a Rose. He was the one who'd inked his arms and torso with swirls and thorns to cover over his scars. I should've known he'd be the thing that cut me.

He held up his hands, his jaw tight. "I'm sorry. Rosie."

I should've made him rip the clothes from my body, but I knew I'd never recover from that violation. I tore my shirt over my head and threw it at him with all my rage. "There! Are you happy now?" I'd barely gotten the hang of my new body, and now I was showing him my torso, clad only in a nude-colored bra.

"Everything, Rosie. Look, this isn't my best day either, okay? Let's just get this over with and hope for the best."

"'Hope for the best?' How exactly do you imagine we bounce back from this?" I kicked off my shoes and lobbed them at his face, then my socks. I tore off my dirty jeans and whipped them at him, angry tears welling in my eyes. "Boy, Rachelle's sure in for a treat! What a gentleman she's marrying."

Bastien exhaled, his arms still banded across his chest. "Everything, Rosie. I'm serious. I have to search you so we can clear your name."

My face was red as the tears trickled down my cheeks. "Just so we're clear, you and I are over after this." I unhooked my bra and threw it at him, resisting the urge to cover myself. His eyes instinctively climbed to the trees overhead, which for some reason made me laugh. Maybe I was a little unhinged. "You can't make sure I'm not my mother's daughter without looking, Bastien. This is what you wanted, wasn't it? Well, get a good look. First guy to see me naked. Boy, am I a lucky girl it all went down like this."

Bastien looked down at the grass, shaking his head. "Don't be like this, Rosie. You know this isn't how I wanted this moment to happen."

"Well, it's how you're making it happen. This is exactly how you chose to end things between us. You get to be the big man, and I get to be the girl left naked and crying in the forest. Captain Burke's right hand, if ever I saw one."

He kept his eyes on the grass, swallowing hard. When he spoke again, his voice came out in a whisper. "Everything, Rosie."

I let out a hollow sob as I slid off my underwear and left them in the dirt. I didn't say a word as his eyes slowly climbed up my body. His slight intake of breath and wide, guilty eyes didn't even register as a compliment to me. "Turn," he instructed, his voice choked.

I obliged him, and slowly settled into a calm place in my mind where I felt nothing. The shame, anger, fear and utter devastation all combined and short-circuited into white noise that muted the world. "Happy?"

"You're clear." He picked up my clothes and handed them to me, and for a second, I thought I saw his eyes moisten. "I'm sorry, honey. Believe me, I didn't want it to go down like this."

"Go away." I pulled on my underwear, unwilling to work up a good tirade. My bra snapped into place, and I yanked my jeans up, unable to look at him. I'd barely seen my new body in the mirror more than a handful of times, yet he'd demanded a full viewing. What I'd thought was finally, finally, finally beautiful about my body now felt ugly and tarnished. I wished for my boobs to shrink back to their nonintrusive A-cups, and for my hump to curve my back so I could hide in plain sight again. No one had ever ordered me to take off my clothes back then.

"I can't leave you alone in the woods. I'm your *Guardien*."

I jerked the rest of my clothes from his hands and shoved my shirt over my head, feeling one-tenth more myself. "You're nothing to me. Go."

"I can't," he repeated, his eyes filled with self-loathing. "It's my job to keep you safe."

I don't know why this was the tipping point, but my fist shook with a will of its own. Without warning, I swung out and smashed my fist to Bastien's face, unapologetic as Kerdik's ring cut a line across his cheek. Blood bloomed from the slice, and he had the nerve to look shocked when his eyes met mine.

I had no compassion for the position he was caught in. There was no excuse for what he'd just done. I leveled my finger at him, my voice taut with rage. "You're so concerned with getting to the bottom of who I am and who Roland is that you've completely forgotten who you are. Are you the man you're supposed to be?"

Bastien lowered his chin in shame. "No, ma'am."

Thunder shook through my veins as Lane's words boomed out of my mouth. "I know who I am, and you aren't going to be the man who takes that away from me!" Before I decked him again, I closed my eyes and did my best to rein myself in. "I never want to see your face again."

Bastien nodded once, his hand over his torn cheek. "I'm sorry, Rosie."

"I don't care. Go back to Roland. Enjoy being sorry, but do it far, far away from me. Your journey to figure out who you are has a long way to go still, and I don't want to spend my life watching you stumble through the mess to get there. I've got my own adventures to see to. My adventure isn't you, Bastien." I watched as he moved out of the forest, his head down and his shoulders weighted with the utter devastation of the beautiful thing we almost had. I sat down on the grass and tugged on my dirty socks and shoes, taking my rare moment of finally being alone to break down and let my tears fall as freely as they wished. I was embarrassed that this was the first time I'd ever taken my clothes off for a man.

I needed Lane to make it all better. I wanted Judah by my side to restore my faith in the male species. As weird as it sounded, I missed Draper, though I barely knew him. He'd trusted and accepted me implicitly, so much that he let me take him straight to the Gévaudan without blinking an eye. He would never, never have asked me to take my clothes off.

I hugged my knees to my chest and squinched my eyes shut, hating Avalon and everything in it.

37

GOODBYE, BASTIEN. HELLO, MOTHER.

I led the way to Morgan's castle after it was decided that Aunt Avril had most likely made off with the jewels. Roland took one of the horses and rode in the direction of her Province to chase her down and snatch back his mother's gem, Gliten's and Lane's. Not even so much as a friggin' apology from him. Class act.

I rode on Cheval with Remy, leaving Bastien to saddle up on Remy's horse. Bastien rode behind us, as per my request that I not have to look at his face ever again. Madigan didn't say a word the entire ride, which wasn't entirely unusual for him. Remy caged me in with his arms, and though he tried to keep his thoughts to himself, the occasional worry broke through. *"I never doubted you for a second,"* and *"I'm so sorry, my princess."*

I didn't respond, and didn't want to talk about it. We

rode in silence until we reached civilization. The lush greenery seemed to explode from every square inch of nature as we crossed over into Province 1. There were flowers as big as my head, blooming just because they friggin' could. The air smelled like a blast of green and freshly-cut pine. The warmth of the sun kissed my skin, and the wind died down to a gentle hum, but none of it renewed my spirits. I didn't need directions, but let my gut pull me toward the castle that began to be visible over the horizon.

Mad spoke up for us to take a break and refuel before we got there, but I didn't want to talk. I knew the plan, and so did they. It was me who'd be traded for Reyn, and that's how I'd play it to my mother when I met her. Reyn was a good man who had never once questioned me or my intentions. He would go with Lane and make sure she had someone to hold her hair back when she got the flu. He would twine his fingers through hers and go on long walks, smiling at the neighbors because he understood what a true prize she would always be. Reyn would love Lane, and she deserved someone who would always be good to her. That was worth trading myself for. Lane was worth it all.

I was about to meet my birth mother. I hadn't bathed in days. I was tear-stained and wearing filthy clothes, but I was about to meet my mother.

"Go faster, Cheval," I urged him. I wanted to get this over with. I wanted to get away from Bastien and the whole mess. Though I had a magical horse, he couldn't ride fast enough to outrun all the garbage I was desperate to leave behind – but we could sure try.

Cheval kept up a steady stream of "I'm here for you, kiddo" kind of talk, but I didn't have it in me to thank him. I simply patted his mane and kept my mouth shut, lest I open it and a horrible sob escape my lips.

When we reached the towering gray stone castle, my heart thudded in my chest that this was the place I'd been born. It was enormous, stretching too high into the sky. I couldn't even picture myself crossing the bridge, but somehow I'd lived here, once upon a time. The sun was just starting to set over the parapets, but I could still pick out the details that made my mouth drop open. I couldn't count how many stories tall the whole thing was – at least fifteen. It was wide and had a moat around it with fish that leapt above the surface and splashed back down. There was ivy climbing up the stones all the way to the fourth floor, and the stained-glass windows had ivy designs in reds and yellows. The land surrounding the castle was blooming with life, but the castle itself looked cold and angry, the gray stone unmovable in its sneer. It was a grimace smack in the middle of utopia.

Cheval took a nervous step back in agreement of my assessment of the aura of the castle. He made it crystal clear that he wanted to ride me in the opposite direction. I dismounted ungracefully and kissed his cheek. "You should go on back to your life, now. Thanks for everything, Cheval. We wouldn't have made it without you."

Cheval looped his head over my shoulder and let me wrap my arms around his thick neck. *"I wish I could stay with you, Princess."*

Tears pricked my eyes at having to say goodbye to a solid friend. I hated this part. No matter how many animals I said goodbye to through the years, it never got any easier. "I wish I could stay with you. Your Forgotten Forest sounds mighty tempting right about now," I whispered.

Cheval stiffened, his tone coming back sharp. *"None of us will ever take you there if it's your intention to stay. You were meant for great things, not escaping into nothingness."*

"Tell me it gets better. Tell me that someday it won't hurt this much."

"For you? It only gets better."

"Tell me my mother will like me. That she'll smile when she sees me, and we'll have buckets of time to braid each other's hair and play catch together. Tell me she'll be happy to see me, without my birth blessings."

Cheval's hesitance was telling. *"I wish I could tell you that. Instead I'll say that no matter how Morgan is, you should always be you. You're the best you I've met in ages."*

I kissed him again and nodded. "Thanks. You're a good friend. Those are hard to come by."

I hugged Harry, letting him give me the same kind of farewell while Madigan dismounted. "I thought I told ye to stop back there. We don't have a plan."

"We don't need a plan. You did your part. You helped

get the gemstones out of hiding. You can go live your life now. Take Bastien and go do whatever it is you boys do."

"Princess, I'll not leave your side." Remy was adamant, but I could feel his nerves. This was the woman who'd ordered his tongue to be cut out.

"No. I could never make you do that. Morgan's responsible for taking away your words. I wouldn't let you come in with me just so I don't have to go it alone. It'll be fine. Lane's inside, right?"

"Should be. I don't feel right about leaving you."

"I don't feel right about leaving ye," Madigan said right after Remy. "I've nothing to return to, neither. I'll watch out for ye in there. I'm an Untouchable. Ye need one of us, or she'll eat ye alive. We're one of the few Morgan doesn't cross."

I shook my head. "No. I didn't bust you out of the Forgotten Forest just so you'd have no chance at a normal life. Go off with your buddies in the Brotherhood. Do your thing. I'm fine. Once I find the gems, I'll grab a horse and run them to Lane in her province. Then I'll go back to my life up in Common. Avalon will be good."

When Bastien stepped forward, he couldn't meet my eyes, but kept his gaze on my kneecaps instead. "Morgan will send soldiers to Common to snatch at you, just like before. She's not going to just let you go, Rosie."

I glared at him, my teeth grinding together as my toes curled inside my shoes. "I'll figure all that out when it comes. It's not your problem. My job was to find Roland and return the gems to the Daughters of Avalon. Enjoy a lifetime of putting up with Roland. Job one is done, and I'm working on job two. After that, I get my life back. I can lay low." I fished around in my pack for Kerdik's hat to cover over my windswept hair and attempt to make myself look more presentable. Despite everyone telling me what an evil person my mom was, part of me wanted to look nice for her. I wanted her to like me, even if she wasn't all that likeable herself.

Bastien shook his head. "It's not that simple. Morgan's ruthless. You have no idea how dangerous all of this is."

"I survived Roland and you, didn't I? I'm practically bulletproof at this point. You don't get a vote on what is or isn't best for me. You're out. You're fired. You're dismissed. Whatever you need me to say to get you away from me permanently."

Bastien's voice was pained, his eyes climbing up to meet mine, pleading with me to forgive what couldn't be glossed over. "How can I make it right? Tell me what to do."

I wasn't willing to have this conversation again. "Madigan, it was nice to meet you. But seeing as I'm not Bastien's lady anymore, you don't need to stick around to make sure I live. Have a good one, Lucky Charms. Peace out, guys." I chucked his shoulder, hefted my pack onto my back, kissed Remy's cheek and tried to keep my face stern while I stomped toward the double-wide bridge, where two guards stood sentry.

My heart thudded in my breast, my mouth so dry that my tongue stuck to the roof. Stalking off into the castle and waving my flag high didn't seem like the best move in the world, but it was the only one in my arsenal, and had to be done. I checked in with my gut to make sure the remaining four jewels were somewhere on the property, and felt the ping of confirmation. There was no way out of Avalon, but to go further into the heart of the problem.

"Run along, little peasant," one of the guards greeted me. He had rust-colored hair and a smattering of freckles across his forehead. They each wore black clothes with a red and gold button-up official-looking jacket overtop, with a variety of medals and whatnot to announce which rank they were. "It's been a long day, girl. I won't hesitate to put you in the stocks if you test me."

The soldier next to him leered in my direction. "Put her in the stocks, Earl. Let us have a go at her. Look at that face. I bet she's got plenty of fight in that pretty little body."

I lifted my chin, trying to look composed and regal in my filthy clothes and unwashed skin. "You can tell my mother, Queen Morgan le Fae, that her daughter's come home." I lifted my hat so they could see me more clearly, pausing just long enough to take in their gasps of alarm. "Now let me through, or I'll have you all thrown in the stocks for being total tools. See how long your fight lasts."

I don't know why the rage boiled over on this poor fool, when most of it was directed at Bastien. My fist saw no justice, only injustice and fury. I didn't hold back, but socked the crass dude hard across the cheek, slicing the skin enough to draw blood and give him a bruise by morning. I wanted to feel repentant that I'd gotten in a fight when Lane had expressly told me I couldn't do that anymore, but I didn't have regret in me anymore – Bastien had used up my last drop of the stuff.

Both men dropped to their knees, apologetic and awash in fear.

I reached down and snatched at the ear of the stunned soldier who'd leered at me. He looked like he might pee himself at any second. "You're coming with me. See how my mother takes to you making sex jokes about her daughter."

I bent him forward as the rusty-haired soldier fell away and formed a line for me to walk past over the bridge. I gripped the nape of his neck, leading him to the closed wooden front doors of the castle that stretched taller than a two-story house. I could feel his panic and humiliation welling as he begged me for forgiveness.

With my free hand I pounded on the door. "Morgan le Fae!" I called, my heart banging in my chest. My palms were sweaty, and I had too many conflicting emotions warring inside of me. I wanted her to like me, and I wanted to run away from her. For better or worse, I was ready to meet the woman who'd given birth to me.

I summoned all of my courage and belted out, "Mom, I'm home!"

Love the book? Leave a review.
If you don't leave a review,
I'm totally sending the Gévaudan after you.

ALAN L. MONEA

38

RICH GIRL

Continue the series with *Rich Girl*,
book three in the Faîte Falling series.

My fingers twitched as they tugged and pulled on each other in my lap. Despite the gentle light from the oil lamps hanging in the four corners of the long, hollow throne room, I felt as if there must be a spotlight on me. In hindsight, barging into my mother's castle after having punched one of her soldiers may not have been the most princess-like move on my part.

I hadn't seen her since I was a year old, but there she was – me, with a few alterations. Our matching brown, wavy hair, heart-shaped face, slender button noses, and hourglass figures were spot on for a genetics test, but I had a few freckles on my right cheek, and her skin was creamy and spotless. Her curvy frame was far more exaggerated than mine – her waist smaller and her hips wider – but the blueprints were there. While my eyes were blue and hers green, they were the same shape. Her hair was pulled back into one long braid that ended at her waist, and her hands were smooth and unused.

I was more built for the soccer field, and had the thick thighs to prove it, but my mother was made for the very throne she sat on as she stared at me. She took in my humble demeanor with a scrutinizing eye that seemed laced with a hint of longing. I knew the look well, as it was most likely mirrored on my own face. I'd been taken away from her so young; it was strange to think that, were she not wearing a gold crown and all the queenly trappings, I might not know I belonged to her.

Well, really I belonged to her youngest sister, Lane, who took me from the castle when my mother started getting power-hungry. Lane raised me as her own.

Morgan's voice was composed and even, lower in tone than mine. I wondered if she'd ever considered becoming a jazz singer. "Duchess Elaine of Province 9 confirmed that you are the child she stole. Have you anything to say to that?"

I worried that when I opened my mouth, a frog might pop out. There were a dozen soldiers lining the walls of the throne room, plus one official-looking dude to the side near the base of the throne, and his page boy, all staring at me with wide eyes. Why wouldn't they be here? Totally normal to be well-guarded when meeting your daughter for the first time in twenty-one years. "Um, yeah. Lane raised me up in Common. I only just found out about you and Avalon and all of it, so here I am. Thought we should meet each other. Maybe you could stop sending people to try and abduct me."

I didn't see much of a point in pulling punches. She hadn't welcomed me with opened arms, and the sting of her first words to me were still fresh. "Get that filthy peasant out of my castle," was hard to bounce back from. But what mother-daughter relationship didn't suffer a little turbulence from time to time?

Morgan watched me with narrowed eyes, her red painted pointy fingernail touching her lips. I felt like she was studying every square inch of me. I wished we could get to know each other a little less formally. I mean, there were a dozen guards lining the walls, for crying out loud. She was in a red gown on a golden throne, and I was in jeans and hadn't bathed or had a proper meal for days. She looked mildly amused by my blatant "let's deal with this" attitude. "I had every right to try and rescue you. Elaine was foolish to think I would forgive and forget after all this time. You are *my* rightful daughter, not hers."

"My dad sent me with her. She didn't steal me." I really hoped Lane hadn't stolen me. I wanted to believe that my life with her had been the right kind of good, and not a twenty-one-year joy ride. I'd been permitted to see Lane for a total of one minute when the exchange was made upon my arrival to the castle – Reyn for me. Lane begged me to come to Province 9 with her, but I refused, giving her a look that told her we were sticking to the plan, and she would accept it. "It's time I got to know my birth mother," I told her, acting as coolly as I could. "You should go to your province and do your thing. I'll keep in touch."

Lane knew how to read my eyes – always did. It's the rite of motherhood or something. When I would lie and say "I'm fine," she knew to start popping popcorn and gear up for a long venting session after I'd had time to process whatever it was that got me down.

When I kept my distance and gave her no more than a cool handshake, we both studied each other's trembling chins and nodded. "I'll look forward to a weekly letter from you. If I don't receive one, I'll pop by for a friendly chat, so you, me and my dear oldest sister can catch up."

"I think that's a great idea." Then I whispered quickly, "Aunt Avril has your gem. Roland is trying to capture it back. Find Bastien. He can help you get your gem back from her."

And that was that. I didn't get to hug her, to fall in her arms and tell her all that I'd been through. I didn't get to blubber away all my problems and lay them on her capable shoulders. I simply waved goodbye, watching as she left with Reyn, and left me with my birth mother.

Morgan's mouth was in a firm line. "If you hadn't been

taken from me, you would know that when you're in court in front of the queen, you don't fidget. You stand up straight and conduct yourself as if you've been raised with some sense of decorum."

I tried to obey all her commands, keeping my chin high to show her I wanted to make this work. Oh, how badly I'd wanted this to work. "I'm sorry, Mom. I can do better. You might have to be patient with me. I was only a year old when I left the castle. You can take my lack of decorum up with my dad."

"Would that I could. Your father fell ill just after you were taken. Province 2 invaded our kingdom on the eve you went missing. Elaine took you to evade capture on his orders, but she should have returned with you the second I rid Avalon of my late sister Tyronoe's greed. Urien's grief was so great over losing his only daughter that he never recovered." Then her voice sharpened, jerking me from false sweetness to the edge of the ever-ready knife of her threatening tone. "And do not call me 'Mom'. You may call me 'her majesty most high', since that's who I am. You are too old to call me 'Mom', and I am too young to be seen as one."

My face pulled at the gut-punch I hadn't realized she could do in the span of a few sentences. "Okay, your majesty most high. Sorry about that." I bit my lip and didn't argue about the very different version I was being spun of my escape from Avalon. Lane had told me Urien was worried Morgan was trying to slowly kill him, so he instructed Lane to take me and run. My gut pulled me in the opposite direction of Morgan's words. As much as I wanted to believe the best in my mother, my gut had never once lied to me. "Oh. Lane was waiting until she was sure all the sisters who were a threat to me were gone. Then she brought me back to you." I cleared my throat through the lie. "I'd like to meet my dad, when he's feeling up to it."

She looked at me like I was a bug with a convenient excuse she couldn't shoot Lane for. "He won't even know you're there, but I see no problem with you spending time with a useless stump."

I reared back, but kept my mouth shut so I didn't voice a contrary opinion so early on in the game. She knew as well as I that we were locked into a long con. She assumed the goal would be to get me to work for her to find the last four gems, but my end game was to steal the gems she'd hoarded from her sisters and return them to the fallen provinces. That way all of Avalon could flourish, and not just Province 1, where Morgan le Fae held far too much power. I'd already found three of the jewels, and they were most likely tucked in Province 8, where my Aunt Avril was returning with her own Jewel of Good Fortune. She'd stolen the jewels from us, so either they were there, or my mistrustful cousin Roland had managed to take his late mother Heloise's gem back to his home in Province 4. Better he hunt her down than keep trying to prove that I was manipulative and prone to jewel thievery.

Well, I mean, I *was going* to have to manipulate Morgan

to try and steal her jewels, but it really was for the greater good. Honest.

When the silence between us was too thick for me to attempt busting through it, Morgan stood, a fake smile plastered on her face out of nowhere. I'd known the woman all of half an hour, and I could tell plain as day that the smile was fabricated. There was too much saccharine in the corners, too much planning in her eyes to really seem joyful. She clasped her hands together and took the stairs down from her throne's elevated platform so she could stand five feet in front of me. "My daughter, home again. Avalon shall have a celebration like it never has before. Rigby, see to the details. The fledgling provinces shall be invited to see the Lost Princess, returned to me at last." She clicked her fingers to the official-looking man who was standing at the base of the throne. Dude had perfect posture, and was dressed in beige fitted trousers, a white dress shirt, and a red suit jacket. The crimson with gold threading matched Morgan's long robes and the guards' stiff uniform tunics.

"Right away, your majesty most high." Rigby gave a slight bow to his head and snapped his fingers to a page boy who kept tight to his heels. "Summon the heads of staff to await instruction in the galley," he told the boy, who ran off after bowing to Morgan, and then shockingly, to me.

Morgan was apparently just getting started with her to-do list. "A grand celebration for the entire kingdom in two weeks' time, so Rosalie can meet her suitors. That should be enough time to get word to the provinces and give them the opportunity to travel to us. Then in a month, we shall have a royal ball where Rosalie will pick her husband. But only invite the heads of the provinces and notable guests to the ball. No need to pretend the peasants own gowns well enough for a dance. No, no. They can stay at home for that. Give them something to long after, aspire to. Do you think two weeks is enough time to groom her?" She asked of Rigby, ignoring my dropped jaw. "If you need more, take it, but let's not stretch it out too long. The people will want to see her settled in our province as soon as possible. I can't imagine how many people have seen her like this already. It'll be an uphill battle to groom all of this out of her." She motioned to my entire being, and my heart sank.

"Yes, your majesty. I'm certain two weeks won't be a problem." Rigby had a long nose, dark wavy brown hair that curled at his neck like a forty-year-old Disney prince, and closed off eyes that didn't give anything away. My gut didn't so much know what to do with him. He scrutinized me from head to toe, no doubt assessing what sort of major damage control he'd need to pull to get me to look like a princess.

I held up my finger to pause the nonsense train that was already leaving the station. "Um, let me stop you right there. I'm not exactly ready to pick a husband. I appreciate the party and all. I mean, that sounds awesome. The Avalon-wide celebration will no doubt be a blast. I've never been to a royal ball, obviously, so I'll be glad to go to whatever you like. But I'm not even dating anyone, so getting married inside a month is where I draw the line." I shrugged a simple, silent apology.

Morgan blinked at me, and up close I noticed her eyelashes were unnaturally long. Not like when Jill wore fake eyelash extensions, but like, a whole knuckle long of mascaraed, curly lashes. They jutted out from her eyes like dark spiders trying to crawl their way out of her eyeballs. I blame the dim lanterns' light for not picking it out before. Her words came out slow and measured, as if responding to someone who was stupid. "A husband is necessary for you. You're of age, and it will look poor on my household if I have a daughter no one wishes to marry."

I raised my eyebrow at her. "Because I don't get married in a month, it means I'm an old hag no one wants? I hardly think it's that dramatic. I'm new to Avalon. Blame it on me settling in. Blame it on be being an old hag at twenty-two, I guess. I don't much care. Point is, I'm not marrying a stranger just because people will think it's weird I'm single. I don't care if people think I'm odd." I offered up another shrug as if to say, *This is who I am. Deal with it.*

She brushed off my protest with a wave of her bejeweled hand. "You won't be married off to a stranger. Suitors from all over will make their offers for marriage when you're announced at the celebration feast for Avalon in two weeks. They'll offer their hand to you in marriage, and you can pick the one who offends you the least. We'll announce your choice at the ball."

I tried to fight back my grimace, but I'm pretty sure I lost that battle. "Look, I'm out of my element here, so I'll defer to you in most things about your culture and what-not, but marriage? That gets to be my call."

Morgan's eyes skewered me with laser-like focus. "I see you've spent far too much time with my sister. Willful and foolish. Though, you're still young. There's hope for you."

I brushed off the slam on Lane, who I loved like a mother. I could tell any protest I made to Morgan would fall on deaf ears. "Is Lane alright? You two worked things out?"

"She's returned to the barren wreckage of Province 9 to resume her post, though none of her people will follow, I assure you. I don't see her in twenty-one years, and all of a sudden she's on my castle steps, demanding I give her the judge's son from Province 2. She was never a fool for a man's love, but I saw the desperation in her eyes." Morgan pfft'd, as if the notion was ridiculous. "I guess some people can change. I expect her to marry him soon, with the way she pled for his life. He will suit her well, since Reyn is of noble quality, young though he is."

The castle, while spacious and vast, started to feel like it was closing in on me. I didn't think I could wait the one-week mark to communicate with Lane. Call me a baby, but in that moment, I needed my mommy. I didn't want to get married to someone I didn't know. I didn't want to get married at all just yet. "Can I borrow a horse and a guide to take me to Province 2? Just to make sure she's alright."

Morgan frowned. "Surely you don't need a guide. You're the Compass. If you want to find her, there's no doubt you can."

My plan wasn't totally well thought out, but I went with it all the same. "Yeah, I didn't even know about that ability until we came to Avalon." Okay, that part was true, but a lie bubbled on my tongue. "I'm about as useful with finding lost things as the next girl." I didn't want Morgan to know I could be her ticket to finding the additional Jewels of Good Fortune. I wanted her to like me for me, not for what I could do for her. "Maybe it was a gift that went away or something. I don't really know how all your magic works. But yeah, I'm not a gleaming GPS to finding lost keys or wallets or whatever. Got turned around four times on my way here." I shrugged in a *what can you do?* kind of way.

Morgan's nostrils flared, and I began to debate the awesomeness of telling her my gift was a dead-in-the-water duck with no hope of resurrection. "Master Kerdik, that snake. I'll try summoning him, though I'm not sure what good that'll do. He never comes when I call anymore." She cleared the distance between us, and brave as I wanted to be, the reappearance of her fake, coiled smile made me jerk back before I remembered myself.

This was my mother. I was supposed to want to be near her. What the crap was wrong with me?

She gripped my shoulders with fingernails that were

far sharper than they looked. "Beauty, don't you worry. Your queen will fix what's broken in you. Master Kerdik will put you back together, and your Compass will be good as new. It was your birth blessing; I highly doubt it simply vanished. Perhaps you just need to be taught how to use it. I can certainly help with that."

I nodded, unsure what else I was supposed to do. "Sure. Some mother-daughter bonding time sounds nice."

Morgan glanced down at my dirty clothes and retracted her hands from me, as if I was covered in feces. She snapped her fingers at Rigby without looking at him. Rigby was ready with a handkerchief he placed in her expectant palm. She all but snarled at me as if I was a disgusting bug she needed to wipe her hands clean of. "Straighten her up, Rigby. See to it the seamstress gets her a properly fitting wardrobe. Something grand for the celebration, and a few gowns in the colors of my crown for the courtly meetings when potential suitors come to call." When I opened my mouth to shut down the noise about suitors, Morgan reached out and snatched my lips, holding them shut. In a command that was quiet but firm, she instructed me with two words that made me recoil. "Be beautiful. That's what's required of you. Do not disappoint me."

Lane had never done something so disrespectful to me. I knocked Morgan's hand out of the way, not even pretending to play nice. "Dude, don't put your hands on me, and don't shut me up like that. It's friggin' rude."

It was as if all the soldiers stopped breathing as one. Rigby was motionless, watching the exchange with widened green eyes that were suddenly expressive with a silent warning for me to behave. I kept my chin up, and tried not to look defiant, but instead to appear calm and rational. I tried to look like Lane – a woman who didn't need to prove herself, or fight to get her point across.

I didn't understand the assault that was coming when she pulled her hand back and let her palm smack across my face. My cheek stung with betrayal, anger and a deeply slicing wound that might never heal. Morgan's words came out cold, sifted through lips that barely moved through her flaring anger. "Rigby, see to it my daughter is educated on our ways."

"Yes, your majesty most high."

"Remove her from my sight before I strike her again and leave a mark on her petulant face. It would utterly ruin the celebration." She raised her finger to me in a threat. "But don't think I won't take a switch to your back-side, little *bête*."

I didn't know what that word meant, but I'm guessing it wasn't "daughter" by the disgusted way she said it. I felt the pressure of moisture building behind my eyes, but I refused to let them fall.

"Yes, your majesty most high. Come with me, your grace," Rigby said to me with a slight bow of his head in my direction. He gave Morgan a deeper bow before extending his elbow to me.

I took the gentlemanly offer and moved with Rigby out of the throne room and out into my new home in the cold, stone castle.

Continue the series with *Rich Girl*, book three in the Faîte Falling series.

ABOUT THE AUTHOR

USA Today bestselling author Mary E. Twomey lives in Michigan with her three adorable children. She enjoys reading, writing, vegetarian cooking, and telling her children fantastic stories about wombats.

While she loves writing fantasy, dystopian, and paranormal tales for her readers, Mary also writes romance under the name Tuesday Embers, and cozy mysteries under the name Molly Maple.

Visit her online at www.maryetwomey.com, and sign up for her newsletter, so you never miss a new release.